Katherine Saunders

The High Mills

Katherine Saunders

The High Mills

ISBN/EAN: 9783744777292

Printed in Europe, USA, Canada, Australia, Japan

Cover: Foto ©Andreas Hilbeck / pixelio.de

More available books at **www.hansebooks.com**

BY
KATHERINE SAUNDERS,
AUTHOR OF "GIDEON'S ROCK," Etc.

WITH NUMEROUS ILLUSTRATIONS.

PHILADELPHIA
J. B. LIPPINCOTT & CO.
1872.

THE HIGH MILLS.

CHAPTER I

HERE is a turn in the road from Bulver's Bay to Lamberhurst from which the High Mills are first to be seen, looking like two pinned insects writhing on the hill.

It was at this turn of the road that M i c h a e l Swift first saw them at noon on the third day of his journey. He stood still, his bundle on his stick, his face raised towards them, with the look of a man seeing at last in substance and reality what had been his chief vision awake or asleep, for years past.

It was such a look as Jacob might have cast upon the fields of Laban, Christian on the shining palaces of the Beautiful City, or Columbus towards the shores of the New World.

When he withdrew his eyes from the mills, Michael turned to look at the road by which he had come; and, dropping his bundle, took his stick and drew a little line across the road, saying to himself with a smile as full of sorrow as tears can sometimes be of joy, "Here my life is cut in two."

On one side of the line lay Michael's thirty-two years of peaceful, honest life, all darkened now by the great sorrow which had driven him forth; on the other remained only the High Mills and the hope which was too wild and daring to be told to any living creature, but for the sake of which he had left all he cared for in the world.

Michael had changed his travelling clothes at the last village that he passed, and was going into Lamberhurst in his white miller's dress. He was of middle height and broad-shouldered, and possessed all the vigour and careless grace of well-used muscles and per-fect health. His face, too, was broad, and always pale; and this and his dark beard and eyes gave him a slightly Eastern look, which, however, was forgotten at the first sound of his hearty English voice.

Everything he saw was as fresh to him as if he had indeed entered upon a new world, a new life. He had never before been more than twelve miles from London; and this old village in Southdownshire, where life was still much the same as it had been a century ago, was full of wonder for him.

He laughed at the fat-legged children running into the cottages at his approach. He marvelled at the little Norman church, at its rich black old door, guarded with rustic white gates, which would have been thought too humble for the lowest cottage in *his* village. He went on a few steps into the churchyard, which was treeless and breezy, and where there was about one gravestone to twenty little mounds without. "Are folks here content to be buried, name and all?" Michael wondered; and he thought that if he grew old and died before his hope was realised, it would be better that he too should have his name go down into the grave with him.

As he was thinking of this his eyes fell on a stone bearing many repetitions of the name "Ambray;" and Michael no sooner saw it than his face became disturbed; a deep reverence came over it, and he took his cap slowly and with trembling hands from his head.

The first tracing of the name was fast following the bones of its owner to decay, but Michael could just read underneath it "of Lamberhurst Hall." There was next a John Ambray, of Lamberhurst Hall, then some names which Michael passed quickly over till he came to that of a captain who had distinguished himself at Waterloo, and from this to the soldier's eldest son, George Ambray, of Buckholt Farm.

As he read this name, Michael bowed his head lower, and turned quickly away, treading gently in the grass, on which his eyes were fixed with a gravity as profound as if each green blade marked some dust dear to him.

The smell of wood fires came stronger on the fresh March breeze, and soon Michael reached the little inn by the sign of the Team, where he entered and asked for some ale.

The lad to whom he had spoken pointed into the little bar-parlour, where Michael had

5

already seen four or five smock-frocks round a table, and a tanglement of drab-gaitered legs underneath it.

It was market-day, and the heads of several of the neighbouring farms having gone to the town, the company in which Michael found himself was, he soon understood, composed mostly of old men who had been left at home in charge; and who had taken this opportunity of a quiet meeting and discussion of their several grievances, in the presence of the sympathising landlord of the Team.

Michael had never seen anything like these men in his life before. They all stopped talking as he sat down at the window, and stared at him, exchanged looks with each other, then stared at him again with as little regard for what he thought of it as if he had been a stray animal wandering at large in the village.

Michael returned their gaze with more than the surprise natural to a townsman meeting farm-labourers of a remote country place for the first time. An innocent prisoner, seeing impotent age or idiotcy on his judge's face, might have had such a look of foreboding—almost terror—as came into Michael's eyes at the contemplation of these creatures of his new world.

Turning away from them to the window, he saw a boy running past, then heard heavy shoes in the passage, and in an instant a little smock stood in the doorway, and a small voice, full of excitement, was shouting—

"Ma'r S'one! The mill's agoing!"

At this every one looked at a little old man at a corner of the table.

Michael looking also, saw that Ma'r S'one (which he afterwards heard was a Southdownshire abbreviation of Master Stone) was quite different from the rest of the company, who had impressed him so unfavourably.

Ma'r S'one was very small and gentle-looking, and seemed to be almost visibly diminishing in size, under the influence of age and toil. His tanned hand shook on his knee like a dry leaf in autumn longing to flutter down and be at rest. His little eyes were bright, and ever ready to fill with childish surprise, or dismay, or pleasure—indeed, Ma'r S'one was very like a withered child looking gently on life as on a hard school, from which he waited patiently to be sent home. Afterwards, when Michael had much opportunity of watching him, he noticed that he never seemed quite at his ease, but appeared constantly haunted by the fear that he was not doing all that he could to please people, and might get into trouble. No one could ever

persuade Ma'r S'one that any portion of his time belonged to himself. His presence now at the Team was quite a piece of self-sacrifice, for Ma'r S'one drank nothing but water, and hated to leave his work, but he had been much too frightened at giving offence to refuse to go with those who had demanded his company. "All things to all men" was Ma'r S'one—but most innocently, and for nothing but peace.

When the boy called out that the mill was going, and every one looked at Ma'r S'one, his little eyes filled with astonishment, and gazed about helplessly. At last he fixed them on the boy, and asked—

"Be ye sure, Tum?"

"Ye'es," answered Tom, jerking his head back to look through the outer door—"goin' a good'n! Come and look 'eself, Ma'r S'one."

So Ma'r S'one got up, and, leaning on his long-handled thud (for without some such aid he could not walk), and jerking his shoulder-blades as if he found it difficult to realise that they were not burthened with a bundle of sticks or hay, he went to the door and stood beside the boy, looking out up at the mills.

Michael watched him as he looked up with bright wondering eyes, which presently grew full of childish awe.

He came back shaking his head, and said in a trembling voice as he sat down—

"Poor old Ambray! I thart missis 'ud wuk 'im up to it—I thart she woard."

Michael, who sat holding his mug of ale without heeding it, and looking on the floor as he listened intently, heard several grunts of sympathy; and some one asked—

"Ah she's been at it agen, then, eh, Ma'r S'one?"

"Ye'es," said Ma'r S'one; "I fetched her a sheert o' paper yest'y, and she writ to him un she must and woard let the mill, as he couldn't wuk it 'e'self nor pay a grinder. And then she carled me in, and I see her a lickin' it to make it steeik, and a thumpin' it, and she scraaled the name on it and says to me, 'Take this 'ere up to t' High Mills, Ma'r S'one, and look shearp.' I wur most afeard to go, I wur."

"The old flint might tark her 'ead arf afore she'd got me to gone," asserted a voice at the table.

Ma'r S'one looked at the speaker with the humble admiration with which a weak little boy looks at a school-fellow of superior size, and repeated meekly—

"I wur most afeard to go; and when I heerd old Ambray's cough, I thart I shud a tarned and gone down t' hill agen ; but if I had, she'd comed 'e'self. So I gived it in, and they telled me bide a minute, and I heerd him fell off his cheer a coughin' and a chokin', and the wife wur on her knees holdin' up his 'ead and cryin', and says to me, ' Go, Ma'r S'one, there's no good to wait. Tell the missus John Ambray is old and helpless, but he has a son, and we have sent for him.' "

Michael had turned his back, and was looking up at the mills with wild eyes and white lips.

" It's beh oped you telled her that, Ma'r S'one," said the landlord of the Team.

" Ye'es," answered Ma'r S'one; " she wur jest arf in the caart—she and Ann Ditch— with th' butter under 'em, and she on'y larfed when I telled her, and says, ''Arl very fine, Ma'r S'one, but la's la', and right's right.' "

" But it beant all la' that's right, naythur," said an old man sitting next to Ma'r S'one.

Michael did not stay to hear the slow and complicated dispute which followed this bold assertion, but paid for his ale, and nodding gently to Ma'r S'one as the representative of the company, wished him good morning, and went out.

Though it was but one by the Dutch clock as Michael left the Team, Lamberhurst had sunk deep into its afternoon stupor.

Time dragged such a rusty and reluctant scythe over these downs of which Michael's new world consisted, that it is no wonder the inhabitants found it necessary to take him by the forelock to get on at all. So at three or four in the morning, the working day began ; and who then could wait later than eleven for the noon, or seven or eight for night ? Time, however, kept a strict reckoning with those who tried to beguile him in this way, and got what was due to him by stretching out the weary lives a score or so of years beyond the usual length. Sitting in the door-ways, or crawling with sticks and crutches along the little passages, or peering from the windows, Michael saw several of these aged debtors whom the tyrant would not suffer to depart till they had paid what they owed him to the uttermost farthing.

At the smithy, by the steep lane leading up to the High Mills, the horse that was being shod, the smith who was beating the red-hot shoe, the two men looking on, and the fire itself, with the March sunshine on it, all seemed to Michael to be more than half asleep.

The ducks about the pond apparently thought there was at this hour nothing in water requiring the attention of more than one eye, or on earth that made it worth standing on with more than one leg. The calves brought down to drink had fallen into a trance with their mouths full of water, which dribbled back into the pond, while the shadows of the overhanging catkins fell lightly on their sleek sides.

Michael Swift, as he strode through the village in his miller's clothes, every muscle and nerve of his body strung to action, and his face worn by sorrow and full of fervour, looked not unlike some white-robed messenger of fate coming with hands full of good and evil to waken this lethargic little world.

CHAPTER II.

ALTHOUGH that lane to the High Mills was to become to Michael's feet as familiar a way as they had ever trodden, he remembered noticing nothing about it then but that it was steep and chalky, and seemed to end in a sharp line against the sky.

He had not gone far up before the wind which had lulled a few moments rose high, and suddenly he heard the grinding of the millstone and the rushing of the sails.

He had been expecting this sound ever since he set foot in the lane, listening for it, yet it came upon him with a tumult that bewildered and staggered him. He listened to it as one piloting a ship through perilous ways listens to the breaking of the waves upon a reef, his lips hard set, his eyes contracted, to prevent either breath or glance betraying the fear that is in him.

Michael could not keep his feet steady ; his steps wavered from side to side of the narrow road. The higher he got, the more overwhelming to him became the voice of the little mill, which as yet he could not see. It was eloquent of things he dared not think of at this time. It filled the stark black hedges with visions of a face from which his own turned shudderingly away. It was in vain that his will strove against his imagination, which clutched at everything the mill's voice offered it—the vision of a little child laughing and clapping its hands at the sails turning merrily in the spring breeze—a lad's face at a mill window looking out upon the morning, flushed like itself with the hectic beauty of false promise—these, and many others such as these, Michael's fancy seized upon as the sound of the mill filled his ears.

At last something white came flashing up over the hill-line and against the vivid March sky.

The tips of the mill-sails were in sight, sweeping slowly round, for the wind had sunk.

Now that Michael was so near to what he had been journeying towards for three days, the energy died out of his limbs, so that he could scarcely drag them along; the whole journey began to appear to him a foolish and desperate thing.

He could see all the top of the mill now—the little sails opposite the great ones, and a tiny window.

A few steps more, and the whole scene he had so often pictured was before him—not as he had pictured it, but all strange—so strange, that old thoughts, which had grown half-lovingly, half-fearfully round Michael's picture, fled; and, before new ones had time to grow and fit themselves, there was nothing in his mind but dreariness, confusion, and a desire that was really a sharp pain after the home left—a bitter sense that the smallest thing *there*, in the place hidden from him by a three days' journey, was nearer and clearer to his perception at this moment than all which lay close before him.

He had thought of the two mills in a pleasant country field—the white one trim and orderly, and the old black mill beyond it, useless and falling to decay; but little had he imagined what kind of world they stood in—what valley crowned with a shining little circlet of sea lay stretched before them—green, plenteous, and so lovely as to be strange and foreign to eyes which had seen no farther than poor Michael Swift's. So as he looked on it his eyes grew heavy and sick; like a poor soldier's which, filled with the loved face he has left behind him, are compelled to look upon the smiles and gestures of some dancing peasant girl.

But this was no time to pause and give way to the bitterness of being a stranger in the land. The wind came up from the sea, and the voice of the mill aroused him. He looked up at it. How gaunt it was and weather-worn! How impossible he found it to look at the little windows without seeing the same face at each—the fresh boyish face with eyes blue and careless—that *would* meet his and kindle with tragic prophecy as they gazed at him.

Suddenly a real face appeared at the little square window of the grinding-floor. Not the face that had been haunting Michael since the mill had been in hearing and in sight. This face was aged, long, white, and stern, and with no colour in it but the cold steel-grey eyes which looked out beyond where

Michael Swift was standing right on to where the road from Bulver's Bay curved low among the downs.

Michael understood well the meaning of the look, and moved aside, because he could not bear to stand even unseen between it and its guest.

In moving he went towards the mill, which was going now with a velocity that reminded him how unfit perhaps to regulate its speed were the hands trying so feverishly to save and keep it from passing away from them.

At this thought Michael lifted his head and pressed on towards the mill door, with a tender pity in his face like one who hastens to the assistance of a child in distress or danger.

He went straight and opened the door, but when he stood inside among the sacks of flour, with the name of Ambray on them, and saw some feet coming down the little ladder from the dressing-floor, his confusion and dizziness came back, and he scarcely knew how he should face the tall white figure that was coming slowly down to him.

He was holding his hand to his side and coughing as he came, though Michael saw this rather than heard it because of the din of the grindstone, which drowned every other sound.

His grey eyes were fixed on Michael, whom he had seen approaching, and had come down to meet. He was very tall, and still upright in spite of his illness, which had left him white as the deal shaft he held by as he stood still at the foot of the steps. Michael could not tell if his hair was really white, for it was covered with flour, as were his eyebrows and lashes.

Michael could not speak; he moistened his lips and moved them, but no sound came through the noise of the grindstone.

The long ghostly figure holding by the shaft and coughing his painful and, as it seemed, silent cough, began to wonder at him, and the grey eyes to gather some impatient fire.

"The—the master?" Michael said at last, with a voice which he felt might ruin him, but which the miller thought strong and pleasant enough.

He nodded sharply, and Michael's hand went to his cap. Then the old man shouted above the din—

"And servant too." And at this Michael took his cap right off and held it in his hand.

The miller stared at him, but not so sternly; for respect is sweet to those who have had it, and lost or think that they have lost it.

The wind was gentler now, and Michael

had no trouble in hearing his own voice and making it heard when he said—

" I heard you were without a grinder, and I have come to offer myself."

The old miller looked at him in a way that made Michael's heart beat high with hope. This was not because he saw in that look the least intention on the miller's part of engaging a grinder, he knew well nothing was further from him than any such purpose ; but Michael could see that his proposal had disturbed the old man with what he himself felt to be a vain desire for that which he must refuse. Michael knew that as he looked at him he was considering his strength, and hopelessly longing that it might have been in his power to use it for the saving of the mill ; he knew that he was thinking of the services he offered, and coveting them with all his soul and with all his poor weary body that longed to give up struggling against its chains of pain, and lie down to lessen their weight.

Reading all this with those simple clearseeing eyes of his, Michael did not despair when the miller said—

" I am not in need of a grinder. Who told you I was ? I do not employ one. I manage the stone and everything myself."

" So I heard," answered Michael, avoiding the haggard eye, and fixing his own on the name on a flour sack against the great scales. " But I heard, too, that there was like to be some change in your arrangements just now."

Ambray coughed painfully. The thought of what the change might be—the giving up of the mill—had made him tremble as he stood.

" No," he answered shortly. " No change that will make me engage a grinder."

" This person that was talking to me about it," said Michael, " was thinking you were likely to be making a fresh start altogether to put a stop to some change that was talked of about the mill. I don't know the rights of it exactly ; but this friend of mine was saying that he was sure you would see that it would be the best thing you could do now to hire a grinder at once."

The miller gave Michael a bewildered and an astonished look, then bent his white brows in thought—painful and puzzled.

" No," he said at last, looking up with decision ; " I don't think of doing any such thing."

Michael took his cap from under his arm, but instead of putting it on, as Ambray expected to see him do, turned it about in his hands thoughtfully.

" You'll excuse me," he began, looking up suddenly at the tall old miller, " if I take the liberty of mentioning that I know you couldn't—I mean that it would make no difference to me putting off the matter of wages for a few weeks or so."

Old Ambray did not answer, but stood looking at him through and through.

" Now," thought Michael, " he thinks I have got into some scrape, and want to earn a character at his expense." He put his hand into his pocket, and taking out a little old leather case, drew from that a paper which he gave to Ambray.

This was the written character Michael Swift had received from the manager of some mills he had worked at for five years.

" What is this ? " asked Ambray, opening it as he spoke.

" I should like you to look at it," answered Michael, " in case you change your mind."

The miller read it through and returned the paper to Michael, repressing a sigh as he did so.

" Yes," he said, looking at him with more interest. " These are good lines—very good lines. You ought to get a good thing from these. These are famous mills too—I have heard of them. My son—I have a son in London—wrote to me about them."

Michael never afterwards understood what impelled him to look up at that instant, and meet the miller's eye, and give that little answering nod as the old man said, " I have a son in London." He has often felt it since to be one of the greatest sins he ever committed.

While Michael was hanging his head and suffering over this little involuntary act, Ambray was regarding him with a certain wistfulness in his wan eyes, and asking himself, " What does he mean—this well-to-do-looking fellow, with his good lines, coming to *my* mill when he might go anywhere ? I take it he is not quite sharp."

Then he thought, " Perhaps he has come to Southdownshire to see after some important place that will take some weeks to settle about, and only wants to fill up the time." And here Michael saw that he again began thinking how well it would be for him if he could by any possibility agree to his proposal.

" Why have you come down here, so far from where you worked before ? " inquired Ambray suddenly.

If Michael was for a moment at a loss for a reply, the miller did not perceive it, for his cough came on through his having spoken more quickly than Michael had yet heard him speak ; and by the time the fit was over Ambray was conscious of having received a simple and satisfying reason for Michael's presence at Lamberhurst. It was something about his having half arranged to engage himself at a steam mill near Bulver's Day, but that finding there would be more night-work than he cared to undertake, he had given up the idea altogether.

The fit of coughing had so exhausted and depressed Ambray, that sinking on the sack of bran Michael had pushed near to him, he fell into a fit of gloomy thought, and appeared to forget Michael's presence, and to remember nothing but his weakness and the many troubles that lay so heavily upon him.

The sunshine streamed in under the door and through the little window all clogged with flour as with an indoor snow, and to make the mimicry of winter more complete, a robin came and clung to the window-frame, pressing its scarlet breast against it in its efforts to peck at a flake of bran sticking to the inside of the window. The old black mill-dog got up from the corner, where he had been eyeing Michael ever since he entered, and came and licked his hand with a glance of stolid and decided friendliness.

As Michael patted him, the feeling that he should stay took hold of him very strongly.

At this moment a little bell high up in the mill began to ring with a weak tinkling sound that was scarcely heard above the other noise. It was the bell that was struck by the machinery when there was no more corn in the shoot over the grindstone.

Michael, having been used to the same arrangement in the mills where he worked, was half-way up the steps before he remembered where he was.

He paused and looked back hesitatingly.

"Where are you going?" asked Ambray gruffly.

"There's the child crying, as we call it in our mills," answered Michael with a smile; "shan't I go and feed it?"

"Let it cry," Ambray said, beginning to cough ; "leave it alone."

Michael paused on the ladder with brows lifted in surprise.

"Isn't that a pity?" he remonstrated ; "the wind's getting steady now. I shall find some corn on the shooting-floor, shan't I? I'm a good nurse, master ; I can't bear to hear the child cry and not go and feed it. I shall find my way."

"Let it cry, I tell you!" shouted Ambray, "and come down with you." As Michael obeyed, the old man, touched perhaps by the gentleness of his steps and look, added bitterly—

"Let it cry. Let it be hungry. Let it starve. I have no more to feed it with. No ; there's no corn on the shooting-floor, there is no corn in the mill. Be off, my man. I like you, but you've come to the wrong shop. Go your ways with your good lines, and luck attend you."

CHAPTER III.

In his heart the old miller did not take it ill that Michael, instead of obeying him, remained standing by the ladder ; looking as if all the shame of the confession lay with him for having been the means of bringing it out.

"I won't deceive you, master," he said at last ; "I guessed something of this before."

"Then why the—then, what do you mean by wanting to be my grinder?"

"Why not?" said Michael. "For one thing, I don't take all I pick up here and there for gospel truth, 'specially in the country, where folk must have something to keep them from stagnating. And then, too, the thought came to me, that perhaps if this lady that owns the mill and sells you the corn, if she heard you'd a good, strong, steady-going sort of grinder, she might be willing to leave things as they are a little longer, to give us a trial."

The miller mused over this profoundly, and studied Michael from head to foot.

"I thought that was her reason for wishing to put the mill in other hands, your keeping no man, and—and not having good health yourself?" Michael ventured to add, after a silence of some moments.

"Reason—her reason !" said Ambray, with a wrathful light gathering in his eyes. "It's no use going into that. The truth is, the woman wants to get the thing out of my hands altogether, if she can—if she can. But while I keep the mill in use, I have a sort of right to it : but that's nothing to do with you. As for what you say, I don't know but what there's something in it—in fact, I do see something in it."

He sat thinking, pressing the fingers of either hand to his temples, which Michael could see were still throbbing with the agitation of his last coughing fit.

"Well," he said, rising up to his full height, and taking hold of the shaft, "there can be no harm done by trying what you have proposed—it's not a bad proposal—not at all. I can't see the woman to-day ; she's never home till late on market-days, and if she were," he added to himself reflectively, "it's a chance if she'd be sober. No; we'll go in the morning,—that's if you really think you care to waste your time over the experiment."

"Why, what can I do better?" answered Michael, trying to speak only cheerfully, and to conceal his deep thankfulness.

"I can give you a good bed," said Ambray, with the faded light of a bygone hospitality in his eyes. "And, though there's no corn in the mill, there's bread in the house. Come—come home and see my wife."

Michael's eyes fell with a reluctant look. Then, as if a thought had suddenly come to his assistance, he glanced round the little room and shrugged his shoulders.

"It seems to me, master, the mistress would do right to send me back with a box on the ear if I leave such a place as this," he protested. "Look how that window is choked up—the brush must go to work here at once, or we shan't be able to see one pollard from another soon, or bran from sharps."

"Nonsense," grumbled Ambray, who did not like being opposed, and whose cough was aggravated by Michael's brush filling the air with white dust. "I'm going home to tea. You'd better come too."

Michael made a grimace.

"Tea, master?" he remonstrated, "before three o'clock! Come now, you must have a little patience with me. I shall get used to your country hours all in good time, and turn the day upside down as well as any of you. I've no doubt in a week or two you'll find me quite ready to spring up like a lark—no, I mean like a nightingale when the sun sets, and go to bed when the lark gets up. But who can be reformed all at once?"

"Have your own way, then," answered the miller, a smile playing for an instant on his thin white lips as Michael held open the door for him.

CHAPTER IV.

LIKE some churchyard ghost, Michael thought, that had gone wandering abroad at midnight and been overtaken by the sunshine before it had found its way back to the grave, the figure of the miller, tall and white, passed slowly across the corner of the sunny field.

He stood with the door in his hands for some moments looking after him with a gaze that had in it the tenderness of a child, the awe of a slave.

Then he shut the door gently, as gently and reluctantly as if some bright form, soft,

odour-breathing, and lovely, had just floated out, and he feared that the edges of a silken train might still be lingering on the threshold.

With his thumb upon the latch, he turned and looked around him, and up the little steps, and slowly realised that he was alone in the mill.

He realised that he was alone, and yet his eyes began immediately to look and turn slowly or quickly as eyes that are riveted on the movements of some person or thing whose presence causes restlessness and fear. The invisible object of Michael's gaze was felt by him to be anything but ghostly. The face and form that he felt living and moving about the mill were full of vigour and youth, and indeed it was the richness and fulness of life in his spectre that made it the more terrible to him. Many times he had the sense of hearing a clear strong whistle, or a snatch of song in a rich, young voice that seemed now in the room where he was, now above in the upper floors, and now upon the steps. When at last Michael's gay and busy ghost seemed to him to have passed up these steps, and to be moving about the dressing floor over his head, he could not keep himself from following.

Ascending the steps slowly, he reached this place, and gazed through the dusty glass door into the tiny closet that served as an office.

There was a little white coat which Michael knew could never have belonged to old Ambray hanging up here, and nailed against the wall he saw a tiny common looking-glass which he was sure was never hung there by the grim old miller.

Turning from the office, he was passing along by the great flour-bin in the middle of the room, when he saw on it in a patch of sunshine a confused mass of sketches and scribbling. The sketches were mostly of windmills, and all seemed to have been done by the same hand, which had evidently been possessed by a restless ambition to improve upon its first childish sketch of a windmill. In the top sketch it seemed to have fulfilled its desires, for a fantastic frame was pencilled round it, and just inside the frame was written, in a hand bold and flowing, "George Ambray."

The scribbling among the windmills consisted only of repetitions of the same name and a few dates and obscure records; but a little on one side two names were carved on the wood with a penknife, and a date, the 1st of March, two years back was cut beside them. Michael's eye was caught by this date instantly, and he drew in his breath as he saw it, and then stood gazing on it and on the names, "George " and " Nora," till the light and life seemed first to die out of his eyes, then to flash back strong and moist as he looked with an almost passionate sympathy at the spot where the cutting of the names and the parting which he knew by the date had followed it took place. So absorbed was he in this scene of two years ago that he behaved exactly as he might have done had it been taking place before his eyes. He watched the remembered, or the imagined, "George" and " Nora " across the room, and even went to look down the steps after them, and hurried to the window to see them go across the field. While standing there he heard the door opened below, and the old miller's voice calling him.

Michael started, then hurried to the ladder, but before descending it he stood still, and passed his hand across his face, and drew two or three deep breaths.

He came down at last whistling carelessly, so that Ambray should think he had not heard himself called.

" You're soon back, then, master," he cried, with pretended surprise.

" Yes," answered Ambray, sitting down on the sack of bran again and sighing heavily. " I've been speaking to my wife about this, and she thinks a deal of it. I only hope she won't think too much of it," he added in a lower voice. " But she thinks we ought to see the woman to-night about it, if that's anyway possible."

" Is that wise," asked Michael with a comical look of fright and awe, " if, as I think you did say, the lady sometimes gets a little—a little over-excited on market-days?"

" Hold your tongue with your lady," cried Ambray; " a pretty lady !"

" Is she now?" said Michael, with affected simplicity.

" You'll see for yourself," answered the miller, half savagely, half amused.

As Michael stood waiting further orders, Ambray startled him by saying suddenly—

" Didn't you know then that my brother George Ambray married a hop-picker ?"

" Me !   I know nothing," stammered Michael confusedly.   " I am quite a stranger here."

" Yes," growled the old miller, fixing on him eyes chilled and hardened by a life-long disappointment, " he did, sure enough, and was killed at five-and-twenty out a-hunting.   He was a gentleman, was George Ambray.   Ah, you wouldn't take me for his brother

if you'd seen him.   Yes, he was taken when he little expected it, and then everything was hers ; and she kept everything, the High Mills and all, though she had a paper that only wanted his name, making them over to me.   Years ago she'd have liked to turn me out, but she daren't, for the whole countryside would have been upon her.   Besides, the mill did well ; she couldn't have had it better filled, she knew that.   But she's trying it on now.   Yes, and the Lord knows where she'll stop ! "

" She's a rich woman too, I hear," said Michael.

" Rich !   Why, my brother when he married her had Buckholt Farm down there where she lives now and scrapes her gains together and plays the miser, and clacks her tongue from morn till night.   He had the farm and mills—the old black one went too then—and half the church tithes, and some hop-gardens over at Tidhurst besides ; then she married Grist, a retired chandler from Bulver's Bay—pretty comfortably off—in fact, there's no telling exactly what he did have."

" But I thought she was a widow," said Michael.

" So she is ; Grist isn't in your way if you think of making yourself agreeable to her to-morrow, or to-night.   He was taken off by dropsy twelve years ago."

" No," answered Michael, laughing and shaking his head ; " the mill wants Grist, but not the miller."

The smallest of jokes went a long way in Lamberhurst, and if there ever was a man who found a joke at the expense of the enemy of his life unpalatable, old Ambray was not that man.   It warmed his heart towards Michael even more than the good lines he had thought so much of.   He laughed till his old disease, as if enraged at seeing another power usurp its place in the poor old frame, drove off his mirth with a hard fit of coughing. But when this was over he looked at Michael with a large and hearty liking.

" Come," he said, " I feel like a man who has been giving his guest nothing but bad wine when he's still some of the right stuff in his cellar.   Things are not so bad as they seem at the High Mills, Michael Swift.   I shouldn't have borne what I have if I hadn't had good reasons for patience.   I have nothing to look to for myself, but I don't care for that—what's life to me now ?   The grain is ground, and the meal sorted, the flour taken away, and the bran left.   No, I am nothing to myself now, nothing but an ache and a burthen.   God knows what the world would be to me if I hadn't my boy to think of, and if I couldn't look forward to a better lot for him than mine's been. But it's something to hope and live for to see all that belonged to my father come back to my son doubled, ay, more than doubled. That's what I live for, Michael Swift; that's the wind my sails are set to."

He looked up at Michael to see if he was as much impressed as he intended him to be. He was satisfied, and it struck him vaguely at the same time that he was about ten years older than he had first thought him.

Michael was leaning on the bran bin, resting his elbow upon it, and holding his beard and lower lip crushed in his hand, while his eyes were fixed on Ambray. He felt that they were very haggard, but he dared not move them from the miller's face.

"*How* old did you say you were?" asked Ambray with a kindly interest.

Michael had not mentioned his age at all as yet, and in his confusion now it occurred to him he had better tell a falsehood about it. But it lay like a piece of lead on his tongue, and he could not get it out. He ended this little struggle by saying, "I am only thirty-two, master, but five years of millering——"

"Takes ten of life," Ambray finished for him. "I often think that Miller of the Dee they sing about—a water miller, of course—must have been blessed with uncommon good lungs to have worked and sung from morn till night, as they say he did. I know I've found the work enough for mine without the singing."

He was silent a moment or two, then began in a troubled voice:—

"I don't know whether I'm glad or sorry that my son gave it up. It seemed a sin to keep him at it when there was every prospect of his taking the upper hand at Buckholt Farm in a year or two; but since things have gone so contrary lately, I have doubted a good deal whether I did right in not keeping him to the mill. Well, I was telling you how the land lies between my sister-in-law and us. It's this way. I had a brother besides George, her husband, and he died and left his little girl with us quite unprovided for. George took her, and for a wonder his wife made as much of her as if she'd been their own, and when George was killed, and his wife married again, little Nora was sent to a good school at Bulver's Bay. When Grist died, the little thing was had home again, and her aunt soon let it be known she was to have everything. George, that's my boy (he was called

after my brother), well, he and Nora were always together—it didn't matter to them whose ground they were on. There was never a day without her being over at the mill, and he had the run of the farm, with his aunt's leave or without it. They were as headstrong a pair of children as ever lived, and when they were grown up and chose to say they were engaged, Grist couldn't help herself; *she* knew Nora, and so, not having to choose between taking the pair or losing 'em, she agreed to it. I often think she only did so because she thought that was the most likely way to make the girl change her mind, for she's a deep one, Jane Grist is. As for my George, she'd care little about breaking *his* heart, but Nora she *is* tender over; in fact she's the only creature she ever had a liking for in her life."

Michael now roused himself and began to put some sacks up together against the wall, but seeing that Ambray looked at him with a frown of impatience and annoyance on his pale face, he came back to the bin, and again leaned on it in an attitude of respectful attention. As a punishment for what he considered Michael's lack of proper interest in his affairs, Ambray remained silent.

"Does Miss Ambray live at the farm?" Michael at last ventured to ask very humbly.

"She does and she doesn't," the miller answered. "It's her real home, I suppose, but she's sought after so much, and she's away a great deal visiting here and there. She's been staying this six weeks—ah, more than that, pretty near all the winter—over at the Bay, at old General Milwood's, at Stone Crouch. He was an ensign of nineteen when he fought at Waterloo with her grandfather, who was over sixty then. The young people at Stone Crouch are mighty fond of Miss Nora. Money—money, what can't it do? Why, my wife was a head taller than her, and the prettiest girl in Lamberhurst, and nobody ever made *me* jealous. But, Nora—ah, what a fool that boy of mine is! Not but what *she* worships the very ground he's trodden on. Why, she never missed a day all this winter riding over to ask if we'd heard from him—till the last few weeks she's got tired, and no wonder! no wonder!"

Michael, with his brow on his hand and his elbow resting on the bin, held his breath at this silence, for he knew what would come after it—the burst of pain and anger that had been so long restrained.

It came, and Michael's form so shuddered under it that the old padlock hanging loosely to the bin shook and rattled.

"Ah, Michael Swift!" the miller cried, lifting up his head with a kind of proud abandonment to shame and grief; "my son is using us very badly—ungratefully! wickedly! Ah, what I have done for that boy! What I have gone through for his sake, the God I have made less of than him only knows! He fancied himself an artist, and nothing would do but he must go to London and study; and we two old fools, his mother and I, of course must set *his* opinion against all the world's, and get him his way by pinching and begging, and by hook and by crook. Two years he's been away now, and only troubled himself to come home once. Four letters I've written to tell him how Jane Grist is using us, and not a line have I had, except the answer to the first to say he couldn't come, and some hint about breaking off his engagement with Nora; but that was temper, and the girl shall never hear of it. He didn't want to hurry himself home, that's all, and showed his temper in that way. It was a sort of warning to us not to thwart him, I believe. Jane Grist is in high glee, the cat! and thinks Nora well rid of him, and tries to starve us out of the mill, out of the parish, out of the girl's sight; and I write to George and tell him all this, and he—he stays on, making game of us, no doubt, with his fine artist friends.

"But he can't last out long without money—that's my comfort. He'll be humble enough when he's in want again, though he *was* too proud to have his old father and mother go up to London to see him, as they offered to once when times were better. Ah, that was the first blow, that was. He was 'among friends,' he said. *Friends*, the young scamp, what friends had he such as us? He had 'no means of making us comfortable.' *Comfortable*, the young hypocrite! Ah, has he not done that?"

A long fit of coughing followed Ambray's bitter outburst. Michael remained bent over the bin motionless and mute.

The miller said nothing, but he could not help feeling surprise and disappointment at his silence. He thought he had secured a good-natured, sympathetic listener, who would be almost certain to defend his son, and in that manner give him the sweetest comfort that, in George Ambray's absence, the world could afford him.

He got up from his seat on the bran-sack in an ill-humour as soon as his cough was quieted, and told Michael to shut up the mill, and go round to Buckholt Farm to inquire what time Mrs. Grist was expected home.

Michael rose, and came and opened the door for him. Ambray pulled his coat-collar high up round his neck, and passed him without looking in his face. For this, when he was gone, Michael sighed with a great thankfulness and relief.

When he had shut himself in again, he leant his back against the door, and stood looking down with the expression of one contending in his mind against some unreasonable misery.

He stood so for some moments, then went to where the sun streamed through the little window, and looked up at it. Here a look of comfort and faint triumph came into his eyes, and he said softly—

"Ah, George, boy, if *you* could speak for me, you would!"

Afterwards he went about his work of shutting up very quietly, and with a calmer manner than he had yet had since he entered the mill.

He appeared to treat almost with reverence every little duty that came to his hand. The old dog followed him from floor to floor; the setting sun streamed warmly through and through the mill. Michael, though he dared not yet look back and wonder what they were all doing at home, began to feel less strange and chill at heart.

He did not care yet to look far out over the downs when he went to shut the doors leading on to the little terrace, for fear his thoughts should be driven by force of contrast to the dear old green at home. He only took one vague, sweeping glance over all—the stretches of light and shadow, the little line of sea, the mills on the far-away heights laying their sails like weary wings at rest against the sky—the white lane up from the smithy where a party of riders were waiting, their voices ascending in a pleasant murmur with the ring of the blacksmith's hammer and the tinkling of a sheep-bell in the mill-field.

Michael had locked both doors, and was going down the ladder to the next floor with his gentle, noiseless step, when all at once he stood still, and put up his hand to shade his eyes from the sun that streamed towards him. His other hand was still holding by the upper floor, and his eyes full of self-doubt and amazement were looking towards the great bin.

He knew that the mill must for him be incessantly haunted by forms and voices of the past, and for a moment or two he could scarcely feel sure whether he was looking at a phantom of his brain or a reality.

The object of his doubt was a girl in a riding habit, standing by the bin with her back towards Michael, and looking at George Ambray's sketches and the two names carved there.

Michael had barely time to say to himself, " I am not dreaming—it is a lady," before she bent her head and touched the names with her lips, then glided to the steps, and without Michael having seen her face, vanished down them as if her feet had been used to them from childhood.

And they had been used to them from childhood, Michael was sure, for he knew that this was Nora.

CHAPTER V.

MICHAEL had not to find his way to Buck-holt Farm that evening. He had only just come into the road out of the white lane when he saw a party of tipsy labourers on their way home from the Team, and Ma'r S'one was amongst them, himself perfectly sober and gentle, and looking the meekest and sweetest-tempered of victims.

On being drawn away and questioned by Michael, Ma'r S'one said he was sure his mistress would not be home till late, as he knew she was going to take tea with an aunt of her second husband's, who kept a draper's shop at the Bay.

So Michael wished Ma'r S'one good-night, and went back up the lane.

It was with a dreary feeling that he remembered he did not even know where the miller's house was, and should be obliged to ask his way to it. He had seen Ambray when he left the mill go down a slope at the corner of the field, and he went on in that direction till he came to some cottages, which he would have fancied only the poorest farm-labourers lived in, till at the garden gate of one he saw the miller standing, evidently looking out for him.

He seemed disappointed at the result of Michael's inquiries; but, after one impatient exclamation, he led the way quietly into the cottage, saying to Michael as he appeared at the door—

" Here's my wife—crying, you see—fit to break her heart because Miss Nora Ambray has just paid us a flying visit."

Michael stood with his cap in his hand, trying his utmost not to look at a large portrait over the mantelpiece, which he could not help seeing wherever he turned, though as yet he had not lifted his eyes towards it.

Mrs. Ambray's was a clear-cut, beautiful old face, noble with shadows of other griefs than her own. When Michael at last found courage to look at it, he saw so much more there than the likeness to another face which he had feared to see, that he felt full of pleasure when it smiled at him, and a voice, like that face as could be, bade him come near to the fire.

The whole of that first evening at Ambray's house was like a dream to Michael. He can only recall the two voices talking at intervals—and that the talk was all George Ambray, Nora, and the chances of gaining the desired end from Mrs. Grist in the morning.

He understood well that evening what the old people were to each other. The miller's wife was to him no wife now except in name, but only the mother of his boy, in whom his very soul was bound up. He could remember and respect her sorrow on her son's account, but in everything else he slighted and ignored her. With her the case was exactly opposite —there was much more of the wife than the mother in her—she sorrowed over George, but chiefly on account of the grief he was causing his father, whose every look and movement Michael saw she watched with a young, suffering, loving heart in her old eyes.

He seemed to understand them both so well that he could scarcely believe he had not known and watched them many years, instead of a few hours.

When it was late on in the evening Michael was startled by Ambray saying suddenly—

" Esther, get the Bible and read me that about the prodigal son."

A shade passed over Mrs. Ambray's clear face, perhaps it was disappointment, almost jealousy; for she had been for some time attending to his comforts, and had thought that he was regarding her with some gratitude and tenderness.

She obeyed him, but began to cry before she was half way through the story, and Ambray took the book from her and himself read it aloud.

As he read, his harsh, weak voice grew stronger—it became almost sweet—his fine eye lit, and filled.

He finished—then looked back over the page and laid the book down.

When he turned again to the fire there were stains in the white dust on his cheeks, and he smiled on Michael as he said—

" It is different with my prodigal. It is I who must go and eat the husks to-morrow, and abase myself for his sake."

Michael said not a word, but bent down very low to pick up a brand that had fallen from the fire.

They put him in George's room, which was fortunately on the ground-floor, for he found it impossible to remain there two minutes, though it was all white and pink, and sweet as an orchard in bloom.

The old latticed window was easy to escape from, and Michael was soon out alone in his world of downs all bathed now in the whiteness and strangeness of moonlight.

He wandered till he was weary beyond the sense of weariness—living through all the day again and again in his restless thoughts.

At last he went and let himself fall prone upon the ground under the little mill, where he could see the stars through its open sails, and the only prayer that he could pray that night was—

"O Great and Merciful, do but visit this little mill with Thy best winds, and I will grind it out—it was no crime- -but I will grind it out."

PART II.

CHAPTER VI

MICHAEL slept in the mill that night, and in the morning stood at one of the little windows and saw the sun rise.

It was a sight to which he was well accustomed, and for which he had spared a few moments nearly every day throughout his busy life. Whether it ever enriched his mind with one poetic thought is not known, for Michael never had the good fortune to be acquainted with any one to whom he could have ventured to impart such a thought, had it been his; and for expressing it on paper, he had never either time, opportunity, or inclination. But it is certain that Michael *felt* nature, rather than thought about it; that he enjoyed, rather than studied it. He had, too, a feeling, that for a man to take no notice of the grand changes on the face of the universe in which he is as but a grain of dust, was to render himself still more utterly dust-like, helpless, and insignificant. So he laid a sort of honest human claim on everything in nature that was great, mysterious, or wonderful. "Where would be his share in these things after death," Michael vaguely asked himself, "if he did not feel, acknowledge, and claim it now, when his eye was clear and his mind sound?"

There were certain times when Michael's work, to which he ordinarily gave such patience and devotion, would suddenly become to him insignificant as the labours of the ant.

His old father had often been amazed and irritated beyond measure that so rational and manly a son as Michael was in most respects, should still be absurd enough to run out on the green and lift his black beard above a crowd of dimpled, infantine chins, to stare at

a rainbow, or hold the mill-sails idle on a breezy May evening, to catch the first notes of a nightingale.

When the light of his first morning at Southdownshire dawned about the High Mills, Michael rose from his bed of sacks and went up-stairs to a window, a mere square hole, which his face nearly filled.

He had better have gone about his work, for this was positively the first time he had beheld the sunrise on any scene but one. On the two nights of his journey he had been weary, and had risen late. So now he found that the daybreak on these fresh fields was not a thing likely to refresh and strengthen him for his morning's work, which he greatly dreaded. It was like an old tune with new words in a foreign language, the music was sweet, but the sense strange, unsatisfying to the thoughts the music created.

The rose and opal lights, the faint cock-crowing, the fresh bird voices, these, indeed, made one part of the morning, but where was the other and dearer part, the familiar sounds of his old home as it began to waken and stir, the familiar sights dawning so pleasantly on his eyes.

The downs shone like emeralds, and the flocks upon them were very plentiful, but the half-bald green at home, and the two veteran horses retired thereon for the rest of their natural lives (or unnatural, as it might please the village boys), these were the pastures and the flocks of Michael's heart.

The little circlet of sea at the end of the valley glittered as no jewel but that one mighty gem of magnitude and depth in its setting of earth and sky *can* glitter, and the sails of the Channel fleet flecked it as the flocks did the meadows. A gallant sight for so true an Englishman as Michael, yet as he looked at it the puny waves of the old pond at home swelled in his memory till they washed all else away, and brought the paper boats of his little brother to make the Channel fleet fly before them.

The sadness of his state of exile was on him, and Michael was obliged to hang his head and own that, grain of human dust as he called himself, the story of that grain was more to him than the story of all creation —the span of its actual existence larger to him than eternity.

Self-pity, however, was a thing of which Michael possessed a very small share indeed, and he no sooner felt it gaining dominion over him than he turned upon himself with a great contempt, and mocked and laughed at himself right heartily.

Mrs. Ambray, when she came to call him to breakfast, thought he was frowning and growling at his work instead of at himself, and said, "Well, poor John has let the mill get in a state; it's no wonder the man's put out about it."

He did not at first see her, and she had to call him twice.

"Michael Swift! Mi—chael!"

She had come up the ladder till she was able to see into the room where Michael was brushing out the grooves of the great wheel.

In an instant his face, all brightness and gentleness, was leaning out of the wheel towards her.

Mrs. Ambray had of late years acquired a cold and stony manner towards every one but her husband, George, and Nora. She had little complaint herself to make against the world, but as these three had much, she had grown into a habit of hardening her sweet old face and voice against it.

But this morning she could not help smiling at Michael, and speaking kindly as she said—"Come—if you've been at work long like this, I should say you're wanting your breakfast."

Michael was too vividly reminded of another dear old face and voice that used to come up the mill, and call him, to be able to answer this.

He crept gently down after her, and as they went out into the warm and dewy field, asked her how the master was this morning.

They were walking side by side, and Michael watched the grief come into her face with a strong compassion as she answered—"Bad—very bad; but can we wonder? It was enough to kill him yesterday."

When they were come into the cottage, Michael saw the breakfast was but for two.

"What?" he exclaimed; "is the master unable to get up then?"

Mrs. Ambray bowed her head with a stately resignation.

"He has tried many times," she said, "but the cough takes his breath as he takes his clothes, and I've persuaded him to give up the strife for an hour or so and lie still."

Mrs. Ambray had as grave a companion at her sad breakfast as she could wish.

Michael was trying to look steadily at the prospect of the old miller giving up the strife for ever instead of for an hour, and was finding his own life utterly destitute of aim or hope at such a prospect.

Guessing nothing of these thoughts, Mrs. Ambray began to be surprised and touched by the sadness of his face, and to wonder about it.

"You're had a bit of trouble in your life, my man," she said in the tone of one making at the same time a statement and an inquiry.

"Trouble—hah!"

It was half a laugh, half a cry, that broke from Michael, and that shook him as he raised his eyes to hers—part relieved, and part frightened by showing her one glimpse of a misery so wild as to cause her to start up and lay her hand tremblingly on his shoulder.

"Bless the poor fellow, what is it?" she cried; "you've had some great loss just now. Ah, is that it? Your mother perhaps?"

Michael shook his head, with a tender gratitude that seemed to say, "No, thank God, not her."

"Your father, then?"

"No," he answered gently and with the same look.

"Not your wife—sure—you are not married?"

"No."

"Some one p'raps that you—that would have been your wife."

Michael felt the rush of grief and despair which had come over him at her first words of kindness subside suddenly, and give place to alarm at what these questions and these answers, simple as they were, might lead to.

His first impulse was to shake his head as he had done before at each question, but he resisted it, and only bent his head, and taking the kind hand from his shoulder, he said with a heightened colour and an awkward laugh—"Ah, trust you women for getting at a secret!"

"I am right then; poor fellow! Ah, what a world it is!"

"It is," cried Michael, with savageness, dashing one clenched hand against the palm of the other. "O yes, it is a world—of liars!"

At this moment a faint voice called—"Esther!" and she was gone instantly.

"And I am the greatest of them all," Michael muttered as she closed the door.

He was in a rage with himself; he could not sit still; he got up and tramped about the room, moving as if he had to push his way through muddy waves or rank grass.

In this manner he came upon the reflection of himself in the mantelpiece mirror, and turned upon it with a sort of snarl, like a dog who does not know his own image. If the snarl had been interpreted it would have been by some such words as—"So *you* are the man who has cheated the grey head, which may be struck with the deafness of death before you can unsay your words."

In a moment or two he looked at himself more mercifully, then coloured, and soon smiled, raising his eyebrows, and saying, "What do you think of yourself, old boy, as a love-sick swain?"

He went back quietly to his chair at the breakfast-table, and his rage was quite spent. Despair itself had come to comfort him by telling him that he had perhaps told but the simple truth in saying he had lost her who would have been his wife. Michael knew not at all whom this might be, yet he believed he would have married some one sooner or later but for the event which caused him to leave his home. And now what woman on earth would have him when his hands and brain and heart were sworn slaves to that purpose which might take his life to accomplish.

Mrs. Ambray, when she heard him, as she went out of the room, declare that this was a world of liars, concluded that the poor fellow had not lost his betrothed by death, but had been jilted very cruelly.

She told the story, with the addition of many romantic surmises of her own, to Ambray when she had soothed his cough, and it led to the old couple falling, hand-in-hand, into ecstasies of admiration and tender, proud delight over Nora's faithfulness to George.

Michael looked a little shamefaced when Mrs. Ambray came back; but her eyes saw only his sadness, and from it took to themselt a fresh shade of pathetic wonder at the world and its ways.

Michael saw this, and was touched, and remained shamefaced still.

They had nearly finished breakfast when the garden gate creaked with a more prolonged noise than usual, as creaking gates will do when hesitating hands are opening them.

A step came up the garden, and a knock at the door, which Michael, with the habits of a family drudge strong upon him, jumped up to open.

The early visitor was Ma'r S'one.

He was looking tired; for early as it was, much of the "heat and burthen of the day" had already been his. He was looking scared, too, and beseeching, like a child who had been forced to go up to a teacher with a lesson that was not half learnt.

He had made himself particularly tidy for his visit, and had, in his clean smock,—so freshly put on as to show the marks of its folds,—the same kind of innocent self-consciousness as a child in a clean pinafore.

"Oh, good morning, Mr. Ma'r S'one," said Michael; "and how might *you* find yourself to-day?"

"Nicely, nicely, thank you, sir," answered Ma'r S'one; but at the same time he stared up at Michael with a humble, self-deprecating gaze, as if he were quite conscious that, however "nicely" he might be, his state was vastly different from that of his kind inquirer.

Backward a scholar in the world's school as Ma'r S'one was, he had yet learnt one lesson of his own setting very perfectly, and that one was—that being so small a creature, with such small capacities, he must rest satisfied with very small things indeed—small wages—small health—small sympathy—small notice of any kind from God or man. When others incomparably better off than himself chafed at their lot, Ma'r S'one could offer a ready sympathy, and he often thought that he must be really the only man in the world who got his deserts. So he always ate his food and lay down in his bed deeply grateful, but timorous of coming trouble.

He was very timorous that morning, as he stood at the miller's door, leaning on his pitchfork, and Michael had not looked at him a moment before he began to suspect him of bringing bad news.

"Be the master 'bout yet?" he asked, when he had replied to Michael's inquiry after his health.

"No," said Mrs. Ambray, who by this time had come to the door, and at whom Ma'r S'one looked very much frightened indeed, and pulled his silver forelock; "he is not up yet—what is it you want, Ma'r S'one?"

Ma'r S'one looked up at her and the patch on the breast of his smock heaved tremulously—his small eyes dilated and his small mouth puckered like the mouth of a child going to cry.

Mrs. Ambray, like Michael, grew suspicious, and her face hardened at Ma'r S'one.

"What do you want?" she said again sharply.

Ma'r S'one shook his head helplessly, as if to express his inability to speak while she made him so frightened; so she waited, fixing her eyes on him with a stony patience.

At last his withered throat began to move, and the small thin voice came.

"Missis is done it. She's let 'em, she has. T' High Mills is let away."

Mrs. Ambray looked at him steadily for a moment or two, then turned and went away, and Michael and Ma'r S'one, following her with their eyes, saw her go straight to the door of the room where her husband was lying.

In an instant Michael was beside her, his arm between her and the door, and closing round her with a son-like support.

"What are you going to do?" he said.

She looked at him, and the look was sufficient answer. He saw that the despair of Job's wife was upon her—that she had been hurrying away to lay her head down by her husband's side, and say—" All is gone, John; let us die!"

Michael's grasp grew firmer round her.

"Come," said he, "if you were my mother I should be ashamed of you. Sit down, and let us talk to Mr. Ma'r S'one a bit. Things may not be so bad as they seem."

He placed her in a chair, and stood behind her, with one hand laid firmly but almost reverentially on her shoulder. He wished to make her feel that help was near, yet dared not tell her so, or let her guess how deeply Ma'r S'one's news concerned him as well as herself.

As they both looked at Ma'r S'one with eyes that plainly demanded a fuller version of his story, he stepped timidly over the threshold, and began at once his explanations, scarcely stopping for breath.

"She never comed 'ome laarst night she dedn't—she ner Ann Ditch—but sent a letter by the red caart to the pos' arffice for Ma'r Simon, and he readed it out to me when I wur fed'n the caarves, and there it wur all about it as she'd let the mills and all this field to Mr. Phillops as had his mill burnt down at Tidhurst. And she dedn't wish fur to shock John Ambray, and thart we'd break it to un fore she comed 'ome."

"When is she coming home?" asked Michael.

"'This marnin', sir, 'bout 'leven, so it says in the letter as Ma'r Simon readed it to me."

Ma'r Sone spoke solemnly as if he were giving evidence about a case of murder before a judge and jury, and indeed the affair was little less awful to him, for he thought that taking the High Mills from Ambray was like the parting of body and soul.

He was much excited, the bit of colour that was usually firm and ruddy on his cheeks had faded and left them very pale, and his eyes looked shocked and aghast.

He stood gazing with Michael at the face of Mrs. Ambray, which despair was making white and rigid.

"'The Lord furgive Mars Garge!" he cried suddenly and with unwonted vehemence.

Mrs. Ambray looked at him, and light came in her eyes, and her lips moved.

"That he never, never will, Ma'r S'one," said she.

Michael's hand grew suddenly heavy as lead upon her shoulder, and he shook her a little as he cried in heavy laboured tones close to her ear—

"Do *you* say that? His mother! Shame! Shame!"

She was much too deep in her sorrow to hear what passed over her—what comfort—what reproach—all could but pass over, not touch her.

Ma'r S'one seeing that they looked at him for no more tidings, and feeling also that he had no more to give, sighed gently, and went his way, closing the door softly after him. In Ma'r S'one's small part on life's stage most of the exits *were* quite ineffective and noiseless. However difficult and laborious, or painful, or pathetic the scene he had been playing, no excitement followed him, no sound of applause disturbed his silence as the end of his little old smock fluttered away.

CHAPTER VII.

MICHAEL was not used to giving advice. His old father and mother, while expecting from him the work of a man, demanded, at the same time, the awe and humility of a child, and would have regarded with deep displeasure any attempt of his at guiding their fast-failing minds.

Unknown to them, however, Michael did direct them very often; but this was only managed by innocent stratagems, at which he was somewhat of an adept. If his father happened to be in a little perplexity, and Michael saw a way out of it, he would give his view of the case by pretending to quote some village wiseacre in whom he knew his father had much faith; or even sometimes profess to remember what he was suggesting as having been proposed by his father himself to some neighbour in a like difficulty. The old man, if he saw the idea was good, would exclaim, "Did I say that, really? Well, I had almost forgotten it; but, upon my word, I think I was very right. What say you, mother?" Then Michael's mother would answer proudly, "What do *I* say? Why that there's none but you could have thought of it, Joseph." And Michael would go back to his work, smiling to himself and whistling softly.

It was, then, no wonder, that though he

had for some minutes felt assured of what would be the best course for the Ambrays to pursue, Michael found himself in much perplexity about how to make known his thoughts to the grey-haired woman, whose mute suffering was inspiring him with more than filial respect and awe.

She sat, with her hands folded in her lap, her eyes gazing straight out before her, her lips closed tightly.

Michael had left her chair, and was standing at the window, feeling her dumb grief go through him as acutely as if she were lifting up her voice in the most loud and passionate lamentation.

It was while her eyes were turning vacantly from their fixed gaze that they fell on him and took in the consciousness of his sympathy.

"Tell me," she said suddenly, "what shall I do? How shall I break this to my poor man?"

"I think, when you come to consider it, you will think that the best thing would be not to tell him yet at all."

"But he is going to beg her mercy. He thinks of getting up in an hour or two and going to beg of her to give him another trial on account of you."

"I think you'll see, when you think over it, that that would just be the best thing he could do still," answered Michael.

Mrs. Ambray shook her head.

"He'd never forgive me if he knew I had let him have the shame of asking for what's gone."

"But is it quite gone?"

"You don't know Jane Grist, my good man, or you'd never doubt it."

She sat silent a minute, her soft brows knit in thought that only turned to pain as it came, and in a little while her tears began to flow down the face she averted from Michael proudly as she could.

"Do we agree that it is to be so, then?" asked Michael gently; "that the master is to go and say his say about the mill and me and changed prospects?"

"Yes, God forbid I should be above taking advice at such a time when trouble makes me helpless as a babe," said Mrs. Ambray.

She rose, and began to move slowly and tremblingly about the room over her household duties.

"I dare say you think I might show myself more grateful," she said, stopping by Michael; "but you don't know, and may you never know, the soreness that comes with gratitude to strangers to such as are like me neglected

and deserted in their need by them who are nearest and dearest to 'em. I often think God only knows what the poor man that the Samaritan was good-to felt in his heart because he *was* a Samaritan, and not the one his soul and his flesh cried out to."

She trembled so that she was obliged to set down the loaf she had taken up to put away, and, burying her face in her hands, she turned from Michael, and gave way to a fresh burst of grief.

"Oh! that heartless boy—why was he born? Then there's Nora, who comes here and kisses me, and calls me 'mother,' yet there she stays fooling her time away at Stone Crouch while we're being turned out neck and crop."

"Then do you think Miss Ambray knows about her aunt letting the mills?" asked Michael.

"I can't tell," Mrs. Ambray answered, with sudden sternness and perplexity. "I can't tell."

For the next minute she was silent and lost in thought. Her face was looking both proud and wistful.

Michael knew she was thinking of her niece—was longing for the girl's sympathy and intercession, but loathing the idea of the lady's patronage and charity.

"I may as well tell you," she said to Michael at last. "I have been thinking of Nora Ambray ever since Ma'r S'one was here. Yes, you are right, she would come and fight our battle for us if she knew, I'm sure enough of that; but what I'm *not* sure of is, that we've any right to accept of her help."

"How so?" asked Michael with gentle remonstrance.

Mrs. Ambray walked to the door of her husband's room, and without bending her head seemed to listen there for a little while. Satisfied apparently that he still slept, she came back slowly to where Michael stood and laid her hand upon his arm.

"I didn't think to speak of this which I *must* speak of, to one I never saw till yesterday; but trouble makes strangers soon acquainted sometimes, and it seems as if the Lord had sent you that we might not be *quite* alone in our misfortune to-day. Well, Michael Swift, the truth is, I dare not look to Miss Ambray to help us, because I feel guilty before her. She calls me mother, and my heart misgives me so I dare not look at her when she kneels beside me and lays her proud head in my lap and will have me talk of George. I know she often wonders why I let it cost her so much humbling of herself, and so many blushes before I do so, but oh, if she knew how the least word that I say of him to her seems to blister my tongue and heat my face—if she knew how I long to go down on my poor old knees before her and say to her, 'Sweet soul, forgive us! my boy cares no more for you than for the father and mother he has set at nought.' Oh, how the girl would rise and look at me!"

Michael's averted eyes became more and more dreary and heavy-looking as Mrs. Ambray made him feel the strength and trustfulness and humility of Nora's love for her son, though it was evident that the suspicion of George Ambray's faithlessness did not surprise him in the least.

"I can—I think I can understand your feelings in this matter," he said, when he had made Mrs. Ambray sit down, and both had been silent a little while; "but excuse me, if I say that I still think you wrong to doubt about letting the young lady know of her aunt's day's work yesterday."

Mrs. Ambray looked up at him searchingly. Michael smiled.

"You think I'm speaking one word for the master and two for the man, I see," he said. "No, begging your pardon, you are wrong there. I could take my lines and get work anywhere. I speak only for your good."

"I don't doubt you," answered Mrs. Ambray, wiping her eyes proudly. "You are not the only one who has been taken with the master at first sight. But as to sending to Nora——"

"It must be done for the master's sake," asserted Michael, with gentle decision; "it must be done."

Mrs. Ambray shook her head.

"It's impossible," she declared. "Who can tell her?"

"Why I can, if nobody else can," answered Michael promptly.

"Bless the man! don't you know Stone Crouch is twelve miles from here," she said; "and Jane Grist will be home at eleven, and it's near ten now, and the master'll be up directly he wakes, and wanting you to go to the farm with him. What's the good of talking in that way?"

"The master has a horse for the little waggon in the shed there?" asked Michael.

"Yes he has," replied Mrs. Ambray gloomily. "Poor old Fleetfoot, who takes an hour to get down the hill to the smithy."

"Isn't there some neighbour who would lend a beast for the master's sake in such a strait as this?"

"No," answered Mrs. Ambray shortly;

"those that would can't, and those that could won't."

"Surely now," said Michael, looking blank; "well, the country's very much like London in some respects. What are we to do?"

"There's only one thing I can think of, and that's ridiculous," said Mrs. Ambray at last.

Michael brightened.

"You heard Ma'r S'one speak of Simon? Well, he is Mrs. Grist's nephew, and is supposed to have the management of things when the mistress is away, though Ma'r S'one really has to do everything and mind Simon into the bargain, who is as frightened at Jane Grist as Ma'r S'one himself is."

"Then how can we expect him to help us?"

"Because he's still more frightened at Nora Ambray; and to please her might p'r'aps be scared into going to her himself or lending us a horse."

"But who's to work up Mr. Simon's feelings to the necessary state? Were you thinking of going to him? Could you go?"

"Me go? I go prowling about Jane Grist's premises when she's away! No, Michael Swift, not quite that, even to save the mill."

"Then shall I take Mr. Simon a message from you," asked Michael, "and manage him as best I can?"

"No, no," answered Mrs. Ambray, "a message from me would do harm instead of good. This Simon hates us because of George. He would only be too glad to see us driven from the mill. It's only the fear of Nora's anger that would make him do what you want."

"Then I must go and find him, and do my best, and take my chance," said Michael, looking round for his cap. "There's no time to lose. Good-bye for the present. When you see me again I hope it will be on one of Mrs. Grist's best horses."

It was scarcely half-an-hour after Michael left the miller's house that he was seen riding on a lazy but strong little cob, which was much stared at by two ladies squeezed closely together in an uncomfortably small and high chaise which Michael met crawling along at a very dignified pace indeed.

He thought that one of the ladies stretched out her neck to look after him as he passed; of this, however, he could not be sure, but he was in no doubt at all as to a shrill and rather a nasal voice exclaiming in tones that the fresh breeze brought very clearly to his ear—

"Ann Ditch! I could ha' swore that there was my horse!"

CHAPTER VIII.

NOT since the days when Nora Ambray used to smuggle him from the farm stables for George's use, had the cob known such a rider as he bore that morning. At first he showed much surprise and temper, and endeavoured by swerving from side to side, making dead halts, and kicking, to prove to Michael his utter inability to go at such a pace as that to which he urged him. In a little while, however, he appeared to be growing interested and excited over his own powers so drawn out and put to the proof by Michael; and before long he entered fully into the spirit of Michael's resolute and headlong haste, and overtook and distanced everything on the road before him with all the vigour and impetuousity of his best days. These, certainly, were not *quite* so far back as long idleness and overfeeding had made them seem to him.

"There, old fellow," said Michael, as he gave him a hasty breakfast at the village below the hill that led up to Stone Crouch. "*You're* not enjoyed a bit as you do this for many a long day, I know. You're like a good many of your betters, you are: you've laid lazying and licking the sugar off life till you've forgot the taste of a good, deep, hearty bite."

Stone Crouch was reached before Michael had satisfied himself in the least as to what he should say to Miss Ambray when he saw her, or what message he should send in to her if she refused to see him.

The house was long, low, and of a greenish white stone, lower in the middle than at the two ends, which formed two square towers newer than the other part and whiter. Before it spread meadow after meadow, swept clean and clear by the March winds right down to the sea. Behind it a line of poplars swayed, top-heavy with noisy rooks.

This much Michael could afterwards remember of the outside of Stone Crouch, and no more. He could never recall the face of the servant to whom he spoke the words he said, or the door by which he entered; for the moment he found himself actually asking for the person whom he had come to seek, his head turned as dizzy as when he first heard the noise of the grindstone and the sails in the lane to the High Mills.

The next thing which he remembered, and which he never forgot, was the sound of music and singing that kept breaking off and being followed by peals of laughter and by a chattering of many voices; from which

Michael understood that a number of young people were practising a song, but growing tired of it, and lightening the lesson by snatches of other songs, by witticisms on each other's mistakes, remonstrances for order and attention, and reckless wanderings into soft dance tunes.

From the voices that called to order, and the voices that laughed, Michael's ear instantly singled out one, and hearkened for it, and to it, only. He had never heard Nora's voice before, but he was certain that this one was hers. It did as the others did—sang, scolded, and laughed; and *how* it said to him, "*I* am the stray bird you have come to seek," he knew not, but it did say as much to him very plainly. It seemed to belong to her name—to her story—to the hope deferred that "maketh the heart sick," and which was hers—to her strong faith in the absent, to her love and her watching, to the little mill, to the names cut there, to the parting that happened there, to the lips that kissed the names upon the bin but yesterday, when the mill-sails on all the heights were resting, and the tenderness of night and silence crept along the downs.

"Suppose Miss Ambray sings it alone once more," Michael heard above the merry confusion, and he thought, "Now I shall hear if this really is the voice."

Entreaties followed, the song was sung, and Michael found that he was right.

He could not at first catch many of the words, but the spirit of the song, the voice, and the accent, made him feel unable to stand. Never had the effects of what had befallen him appeared more fearful than at this moment.

He held the heavy dining-room chair, and prayed that God might mercifully keep him unseen by any eye but his for a little while.

And Nora went on singing—

> "What will you do, love,
> If, home returning
> With hopes high burning,
> The ship goes down?"

Then, as in the last lines her voice rose in triumphant faith and constancy, drops of sweat stood on Michael's forehead, his lips parted and whitened, and he stared before him like one gazing at a mother hushing a dead child in her arms without knowing it is dead, or at warm blood flowing for a cause that is lost.

Michael afterwards heard from Nora that it was old Miss Milwood, the general's sister, who had taken him into the dining-room, and who had been standing by Nora till her song was finished to tell her that a messenger from Lamberhurst was waiting to see her.

It was the same old lady who now came to the door with Nora, and went away again, shutting in the music and voices.

Michael took his hand from the chair, and used his whole strength to keep it steady as he held his cap crushed against his side.

At first he felt surprised and chilled at the brightness of Nora's dress, then surprise at himself for being surprised, and fear at the thought of what folly he might be guilty of next.

She came towards him, and he looked at her and took in her image at once and for ever. He knew her nearly as well at that moment as he did in aftertimes when he saw her every day. He understood at once that this Nora Ambray was a woman whose heart was a tyrant to her beauty—which, fresh as it was, was tried and fretted as May leaves are when cold winds return. Lovely as the blue eyes were, and possessed of little points of light ready to spread and brighten into visible laughter at any moment, Michael saw in them the worn, strained look, telling unmistakably of wakefulness and tears, and over-hasty, heart-hurting conclusions concerning the world they looked out upon with so strange a mixture of longing and defiance. She stood before Michael with all her faults and virtues, all her soul in her face, yet with a certain haughty turn of the chin and lowering of the tender petulant eyelids which seemed to denote most perfect confidence in her own powers of self-concealment, and a calm defiance of the world's scrutiny.

All this Michael saw in Nora when he first looked in her face as she stood waiting for him to speak, her eyes softening with thoughts of home—her lacework frame held laxly by one hand—a great brown tress rising and falling on her heart—restless and eager for his news.

Seeing him so silent and so pale, Nora began to suspect all was not well, and questioned him at first gently.

"You have come from my Uncle Ambray's?"

So George's affianced wife had spoken to him, and must be answered.

His voice seemed gone. He bowed his head.

The brown tress began to stir more quickly—the fingers to tighten on the lace-frame.

"Something is the matter," said Nora. "What is it? Have they had news—bad news?"

He moved his shoulders, he moistened his lips, and tried to look back to his mission, to that morning's history, which Nora's presence had driven far from him, and, in his endeavour to think of it only, he answered clumsily—

"Yes, that is it. Yes, they have had bad news."

"From London?"

He looked at the little lace-frame thrown down, at the hands clasped over the tremulous curl and heart, and saw what he had done, and let his horror show itself in his eyes, looking into hers as they questioned him.

At that moment he seemed scarcely able to keep his reason.

"London!" he repeated. "No. Who said from London? I did not—I am sure I did not!"

"But you mean it!" cried Nora. "Tell me at once what it is. Perhaps you have been told not to tell me. But that is nonsense. I must hear. You must tell me at once."

She looked at him, and took fresh and fresh alarms from his pallor and the suffering in his eyes.

Unable to support herself, she sat down by the table, on which she clasped her hands tightly, and, averting her face from Michael, bent her head like one trying to turn a great agony to prayer. Then she looked up, and asked, with an unnatural calmness in her voice and face—

"What is it? I wish to hear the truth. What have you come to say? You have bad news about George Ambray. Tell it quickly."

She wished to hear the truth; Michael understood that much; in one word he might tell it, and for an instant a passion for truth seized him, and almost made him speak the word that would cover an honest name with infamy, and a sunny hopeful life with despair and misery.

"No," he cried, with sudden strength; "you mistake, I am a stranger. I—I was sent about the mills to you—nothing else."

"Are you speaking truly?"

"My message was, that Mrs. Grist, of Buckholt Farm, let the High Mills yesterday; that Mr. Ambray is going this morning to the farm about it, and your aunt thought you would wish to interfere. This was my message, and I had no other. They have not heard from London—that I know too; and that—is all—I had to tell Miss Ambray."

Nora rose indignant about the letting of

the mills, but with her indignation Michael saw there had come a rush of sweet comfort and fresh hope ; and he hung his head and his face darkened.

"Tell them I am—no—only tell them I shall be there as soon as possible. You will make haste back?"

"I will."

"You should stay and have something, for you look tired; but I think you had better not, as this is very important."

She was putting her hand into her pocket as she spoke and drawing out a little purse.

Opening it, she involuntarily glanced up to see what her messenger might be worth, and, meeting the great honest eyes full of gentle dignity looking at her, she felt half inclined to put it back, but pride caused her to refuse to give way to this impulse, and she held something out to him with an imperious air, as if daring him to refuse it.

"You are very good," said Michael, with

Page 19.

great gentleness ; "but my time is the master's—in the mill or out of it."

He had spoken too humbly for her to be angry—she only looked confused, as she snapped her purse to and put it in her pocket ; but the next instant she looked at him with bright commendation, and said simply—

"Then I thank you for coming ; and you *will* make haste back?"

"I will," answered Michael.

Another minute, and he was once more on the road, looking back at the great wind-swept meadows, clean and ready for their summer wealth, from the house to the sea, and at the top-heavy poplars, swaying their noisy heads against the sky.

CHAPTER IX.

MRS. AMBRAY'S face, when she opened the garden-gate to Michael, told him at once that the miller was up, waiting to go to the farm, and angry at his absence.

"What have you done with the cob?" she whispered.

"I didn't know what to do with him," replied Michael, "so I've given the blacksmith a shilling to take care of him till I'd asked you."

"You must leave him there, then, for the

present. You mustn't keep the master wait-ing another instant; and, mind, I've let him think I saw you asleep through the mill window and couldn't make you hear; he's not surprised, for we've seen that you've not been in your bed at all."

As Michael entered, Ambray was standing up, with his tall Sunday hat in his hand. He chose to wear that, instead of his white cap, not from respect to the lady he was about to visit, but because he wished to assume as much dignity as possible on his much-hated errand.

"Pray, is this one of your London habits," he said to Michael, "sleeping in the day, instead of the night?"

"But I slept in the night too, master," answered Michael, rubbing his eyes. "I've had more walking than I've been used to this last day or so—I suppose that's it."

"And what was the matter with your room that you couldn't sleep there, like a Chris-tian?"

"Why, to tell the truth, I hardly felt like a Christian in it," Michael said, turning to Mrs. Ambray with a look of complimentary apology. "When the mistress shut me in, and I looked at the pink walls and the pink and white bed, all rosetted and beveiled, I felt like a dog in a bandbox with somebody's best bonnet."

The miller smiled grimly.

"You must let him have the attic," he said to his wife, "if—ay, if—he stays. Come," he added, turning to Michael, "are you ready now?"

Mrs. Ambray went with them as far as the mills, and watched them down the White Lane, feeling a great liking for Michael, as she saw how carefully he guided the miller's weak steps without seeming to guide them at all.

The day was fortunately very warm, and Ambray felt that the air, after his long sleep, was reviving and giving him courage.

"It was just such a day as this when my son went away," he said, turning and looking up towards the mill-field. "I remember the wind was west'ly because he turned the mill round for me—last thing. He didn't like me to have to do even that much—then."

Michael said nothing, but he never after-wards turned the mill to catch the west wind without remembering that it was so George Ambray's eyes had last seen it.

The house of Buckholt Farm was about a quarter of a mile from the High Mills, and stood with its side to the road. It had been an old manor-house, with all sorts of quaint irregularities of architecture and green over-growths; but Mrs. Grist, after the death of her first husband, had behaved very hardly to it, seizing upon it as on some happy neglected child, and shearing off its ivy locks, white-washing the fruit-stains from its face, tearing away its flower-garlands, and rendering it miserably tidy.

The white blinds were drawn up to pre-cisely the same height at all the windows, from basement to garret. The door, which in the time of the miller's father had been used to stand open, showing the gleam of the oak passage and silver-mounted stag-horns, was closed, and had an obstinate, inhospitable look.

Some snow-drops shivered in the wintry garden, looking lost and strange like pale spirits who had mistaken the day of resurrec-tion, and come forth before the world was ready.

There was nothing stirring in the yard out-side the garden but a bundle of hay moving horizontally along, with two trembling drab things under it which Michael recognised as Ma'r S'one's legs.

In the field beyond piles of hop-sticks were "weathering," ready to be "cranked" or tarred; and the hop-gardens, where the pre-sent mistress of Buckholt Farm had once picked the hops barefooted, lay sloping south-wards past the little Norman church of another parish.

Against the house at the left of the door a large bundle of birch was fastened by a leather band nailed across it. It looked to Michael so like a symbol of Mrs. Grist's domestic discipline, that he was relieved by seeing the miller rub his shoes against it, and so make known to him its right use. He afterwards found this primitive scraper and door-mat at most of the inland farms and mills of South-downshire.

When Ambray lifted his hand to the knocker, he turned his head and looked up at the High Mills, as if the sight of them should give him the courage that he was evidently lacking; for Michael saw his face had grown paler since they had left the road, and heard, too, that his breathing was be-coming short and hard.

The front windows were partially open, and through them, as soon as the miller had knocked, came the sound of the same voice Michael had heard when passing the ladies in the chaise on his way to Stone Crouch.

"Ann Ditch," cried the voice, "who*ever's* that knocking at the fore door? It's not Nara's knock, I know. Go round and see."

In a minute steps came round from the

back, and looking in their direction, Michael saw a stout young woman with a hard mouth and a squint, who no sooner caught sight of the miller than she ran back again the same way she had come.

She evidently told her mistress who her visitor was; for the same voice was heard exclaiming—

"And why on 'arth didn't you tell John Ambray to go round to the back door? You know I never has the fore door open 'cept when Nara's at home!"

Ambray raised his hand and knocked a little more loudly than before. Michael would have urged upon him the advisability of at least making a pacific entrance; but something in the miller's face forbad him to interfere.

Ann Ditch appeared again and gave her message—

"Will you come round to the back-door, please?"

The miller did not even turn his head and look at her; and his only reply to her request was another almost frenzied knock.

Ann Ditch, in running back, met Ma'r S'one, relieved of his burden, and consulted with him.

He advanced trembling.

"Do'ee come to the back just fur peace an' quiet, Mars John," he entreated.

Ambray turned and looked at him, and Michael saw something deeper than anger in his eyes as they rested on the old man's face.

"What! Ma'r S'one," said he in a husky but not ungentle voice; "and do *you* think that's the right way for your good old master's sons to come into this house?"

Ma'r S'one accepted the bitterness of the reproof with all his little heart and mind.

"No, Mars John," he cried in great distress; "no, no; I don't, I don't; but, O Lord have marcy upon us and 'cline our 'erts to keep this la'!"

Which law Ma'r S'one alluded to was not known, but this was his invariable adjuration when he saw human passions getting beyond control, or sorrow unendurable; and there had been times when his helpless cry had fallen on tempted hearts with more meaning than Ma'r S'one was aware of.

To his great relief, his mistress proved less obstinate than her visitor; for, after Ann Ditch had gone back a second time, she sent her to open the front door, and Ambray, leaning heavily on Michael's arm, went in.

"Missis is in the parlour," said Ann, leading the way, and into the parlour they followed her.

This room was one kept entirely for use, and showed no attempt whatever at ornament, unless it might be in the manner the sausages were festooned from a rope close to the ceiling, almost crowning, like victorious wreaths, the Sunday hats of Simon and Ma'r S'one, which also hung suspended by their brims from the same rope.

Mrs. Grist sat at the table, casting up her accounts, and pretending for a minute to be too much engrossed to look up when they came in.

Michael looked at her face in vain for one remaining trace of the beauty which had been the cause of John Ambray's poverty. It had vanished as entirely as that year's hops which had garlanded and cast the sweet glamour of dancing lights and shadows over it.

Fat, white, and pasty, with small, almost colourless eyes, low brows, insignificant nose and mouth, double chin, black hair jauntily rolled up into a knob at the back of her head—no waving hop-garlands, no mingling of shadows and lights, no glamour could make that face seem lovely for one moment now. The rose had fallen, the perfume vanished, the thorn lived, strong and sharp.

"Twenty pence is one and eightpence," said Mrs. Grist. "Good mornin', John Ambray."

"Good morning, Jane," answered the miller sternly and curtly.

"And four's two shillin's. Ann Ditch, I won't put up t' harse at that there Lion again —it costis me twice as much as it do at the Dorlphin. Well, John Ambray, I wonder as you shud 'sist so on havin' the fore door opened, speshly with a passel o' men's feet with you, to tread all over the place."

"I don't often trouble my father's house, Jane Grist," replied the miller, more sadly than angrily; "but when I *do* have occasion to come into it I shall never do so by any other door than the one he came in at when he came home wounded from Waterloo; and that he went out at in his coffin, with his head on my brother George's shoulder, and his feet on mine."

"Two and three's five, and seven's twelve," continued Mrs. Grist placidly. "I suppose you've come about the mills, John Ambray —of course you have. Well, it's a very okerd thing, there's no doubt o' that, *very* okerd; but same time you caant expect me to keep two great lumberin' mills like that standin' there dead in the wind, and cumberin' the farm for nothing. I on'y wonder as your own sense didn't show you that long ago, and lead you to tarn your hand to something else, speshly as Garge is gone the road to ruin."

"Now leave *George's* name alone, Jane," cried the miller quickly and agitatedly, "whatever you say to *me*."

"I'm willin' enough to do that, John Ambray, and I'm not going to pretend as it's not a great marcy for Nara's sake as he's kept away. It's natural as I shud be thenkful to see her prospec's all right again, and I am thenkful. As to that Garge, I always said as you wouldn't lose much if you was never to see him again."

Ambray, quivering with anger, was turning upon her, when Michael stopped him by a monitory touch of his foot.

He paused, and his cough took away the strength of his passion.

"I told you before, Jane," he said at last faintly and with a great effort at calmness, "I did not come to talk of my son, but about the mills. It's quite right what you've been saying; of course I know I could not expect you to let us go on in the way we have been doing, and I came to tell you I have made up my mind to take a man, and get things all straight again; and I am sure I needn't say how Esther and me'll pinch and live on a mere nothing till we've paid off the long score you have against us."

"Now, what *are* you talking about, John Ambray?" cried Mrs. Grist, looking up with her pen in the middle of a column of figures; "one 'ud think you was pretending you *didn't* know the mills was let, which is nonsense, as I wrote off about it last night, and Ma'r S'one went up this marnin', and everything behindhand in consequence, a purpose to tell you."

"What does she say?" said Ambray, turning to Michael, and passing his hand over his face with a sort of laugh ; "she's let the mills? Hah! I'd like to see her do it."

Ma'r S'one had just been putting wood on the fire, and was creeping out again, shaking his head ; and Michael caught as he passed by him, murmured in a solemn patient sigh the words—"To keep this la'."

"Ann Ditch!" called Mrs. Grist. "*Do* come here and tell me whether you meant this for a eight or a five. I *never* see such a girl for figgerin' in all my life!"

Before Ann could approach the table, the miller's fist had descended upon it, close by Mrs. Grist's ink-bottle and account-book.

"Look here, Jane," said he, leaning over it and bending down to make his face even with hers, "I've worked in the High Mills, and they've been looked on as mine since I was seventeen, and now I'm seventy-one. Now look me in the face, I say, if you dare, and tell me that you—you—YOU—who came from starving in ditches to fatten on the plenty of this house, have let 'em away from me, have beggared me!"

"It's a five," said Mrs. Grist. Then closing her book, she added, "Really, John Ambray, how vi'lent you are—there's the ink all over the table."

Ambray slowly drew himself up and stood erect, while despair and anger strove with equal strength for possession of him.

Suddenly, as he stood staring before him, Michael saw his eyes soften, his head uplifted wistfully.

"Never mind, Ma'r S'one," said the voice Michael had been listening for ever since he entered the house, "he will have a long rest, for I'm not going back to-day."

"Why, Nara!" cried Mrs. Grist, "it's never you?"

As Michael's eyes fell on her when she came in from the passage—the three farm dogs licking her trailing habit, and making frantic, but hesitating, leaps at her hands—he saw instantly that some great change had come over her.

The strained, wan look had gone from her eyes, which seemed to fill the room with light and sweetness as they came into it.

The sight of this new joy and peace in her startled Michael, and filled him with a vague alarm, and set him questioning himself fearfully as to what it could mean.

Seeing Ambray, Nora went straight to him, and laying her hands on his breast, looked up into his face, and smiled such a smile as Michael never before dreamed of.

The miller also looked half afraid of Nora's happiness. Placing a trembling hand on her shoulder, he uttered her name, half questioningly half reproachfully.

"Nora!"

She bowed her head twice, as if unable to do more, then laid her cheek against him, and sobbed out—

"Yes, yes ; we will kill the fatted calf and make ready. The dear, dear prodigal is found, and I know that he will soon be here."

PART III

CHAPTER X.

IN the mill where Michael had first worked, the machinery which regulated the sails to the variations of the wind was reached at an arm's length up the grinding-floor wall. The habit of stopping noise and confusion by stretching up to touch this had so grown into him, that in any mental tumult, even when he was far away from the mill, Michael would often throw his arm up its full length against the wall, door, or tree he might be standing near, and feel with his fingers, as if he thought that something should hang within reach by which he could restore calmness and order to his mind.

When Nora, after one vain attempt to keep her joy from bursting upon Ambray in his sorrow, like a too vivid gleam of light on eyes that have been long in the dark, gave way to it with the twofold force of tears and laughter, first making with this rain and sunshine a bow of promise on his darkness, then more than fulfilling the promise with her words, Michael's arm was flung up against the wall, and his fingers groped over the slippery oak with a passionate and desperate persistency.

What had she said? The prodigal was found? Whom could she mean, save George? but how, then, could she say that he was found and was coming home?

Like the builders of Babel, Michael's thoughts were struck with confusion. Was he, like them, to be shown by some miracle that the work he had begun, and in which lay all the peace the world could give him, was too daring to be permitted? Was this hope, this vein of gold which he had found and followed in the very pit of despair, to prove but a deceitful thing, that should lead him deeper into the same pit?

As he asked himself this, a sudden change came over him. The first throng of wild thoughts Nora's words had sent rushing into his brain were banished as cowardly—as base.

What had he been fearing, Michael asked himself. The very thing he ought most to hope for—if it were possible. Could he not bear it? Could he not rejoice at it?

His eyes, full of a desperate and tender courage, looked at the doorway, and he told his God he *could* endure fearlessly the sight of a Lazarus-like face if it might appear there, the sound of a Lazarus-like voice if it might speak answering to a father's and a lover's cry of welcome.

Yes, he *could* endure it even though the face and voice spoke of him such things as should make the man at whose feet he had come to offer a life's service, and all the country in which he was so helpless a stranger, turn upon him and without trial hurry him before that Judgment which he feared so much less than man's.

By Mrs. Grist's clock Michael experienced such thoughts, such sufferings, but for one moment, by his own face they might have had possession of him for ten years.

During this moment Nora remained with her face resting where she had hidden it, against Ambray's, when she saw every one looking at her as she cried out her news.

Ma'r S'one, who had followed her in, picked up the riding hat she had thrown down and stood gazing from it to his own and Simon's, as if its similarity of shape suggested to him the idea of hanging it on the beam beside them, a proceeding which his respect for Nora evidently made repugnant to him. So he stood holding the hat in a state of helpless indecision till Mrs. Grist snatched it from him, and with a push sent his weary little feet tottering hastily back to the path of duty which he had in his timid gallantry permitted himself for one moment to abandon.

Ambray stood looking down at Nora. He had taken his hand from her shoulder, and both his hands and his face seemed eloquent of an instinct warning him against taking her and the hope and joy of which she told him his longing heart.

At the instant when Michael, with his arm thrown up against the wall, was trying to realise how much he could endure if George might indeed come back, the miller caught sight of a letter crushed in Nora's hand as it rested on his shoulder.

He recognised the writing. The patient suspense and doubt passed from his face. He held Nora off, and spoke to her gently and half banteringly, as if his own faith in his son had never been shaken, and he only had *her* joy to think of.

" He has written to you then, the bad boy? He has written at last !"

Had such a face as Michael had been trying to picture really appeared before him, his own could not have shown more terrified amazement than it did when Nora looked up and answered proudly and delightedly—

" Yes, he has written to me !"

" I may read it ? I may read my son's letter ? " Ambray at once entreated and demanded.

She put it into his hands, holding them a moment as she said—

" I stopped to ask as usual, feeling so sick of the little shop. And when they gave me this just now, *I* don't know what I did. I emptied my pocket for the children, and I think I gave Tommy my whip ; yes, that I did."

" O Nara ! Nara !" cried Mrs. Grist. "Did ever anybody see such a girl ! I gave a guinea for it ony laast Jenuwery," she added, appealing to Michael as the only person likely to be unengrossed by George's letter.

But Michael's eyes were fixed upon his master as he perused the letter, now reading bits aloud triumphantly, now in tender silence, and sometimes looking up and speaking from the fulness of his heart.

" Hah, this *is* humility ! This is coming to his senses indeed. *' Scarcely daring to hope that you will even read this.'* Listen to this, Jane Grist," he broke out after a minute. " My son tells Nora he is painting two great pictures to send to the Royal—Royal what is it ? O *' Royal Academy,'*—that's a place where all the world goes to see 'em. And this is why he has neglected to write lately, he's so short up for time—George always was, you know. Well, his friends tell him they're sure to get in, and yet he says to Nora—where is it ?—*' I work—I work hard, though I have nothing to hope for, whatever my success may be, but your forgiveness. Nothing else from you have I now any right to dream of.'* That's a right spirit, though, isn't it ? *' As for father and mother, I can send them no message. I cannot ask them to forgive me till they know what will perhaps make forgiveness impossible.'* Tush, bless the lad, I never saw the debt yet in our

family that couldn't be ground out on an honest millstone. O why doesn't he come and put his shoulder to the wheel, and let his pictures be—— S'h'sh, what am I saying ? But I don't seem to care a rush now whether they get in this fine place or not. Let him come, and hang 'em on his grandfather's walls !"

" Nonsense, John Ambray," said Mrs. Grist. "*I* don't want 'em. Let him turn an honest penny by 'em if he can."

" What's this ? " continued Ambray, frowning. "*' Remember that you are free—that I feel myself too vile even to look back on the times when we were so happy.'* Ah, I see ; right spirit, Nora—it's the right spirit. I should say as much myself, or more, if I was in his place."

Nora, with her eyes full of tears, smiled, and waved her glove impatiently.

" You are coming to his dream," said she. " Go on—read his dream."

Ambray read :—

" *' I was thinking about father last night, many hours.'* There ! who says that lad's heart isn't in the right place ? *' And as I remembered all that I was to him before I left home, I came to believe that he will forgive me, even when he knows the worst.'* What, did it take hours to sum that up, George ? *' And I fell asleep, miserably comforted. Then, Nora, I had a strange dream about the mill, that made me wake wretched again. I dreamt that I was going home ; I don't know where I was, but I could hear the mill, and the sound made me try to hurry on towards it.'* Bless him ! There's nature now," cried the miller, much moved. " It's been his lullaby often and often, that grinding has. *' But I could not stir. My feet seemed turned to stone, and the more I tried the heavier they grew. And then I thought that people from here passed me, and I knew they were going to tell father all which I have been too cowardly to tell him or you yet. I tried to shout to them to let me go first, but either I had no voice, or they did not heed me. And I saw them go on to the mills, and I heard my father's voice in the noise of the sails. O, Nora, I was not sure but that he cursed me ! And yet I could not move.'* Cursed him ! Bless the lad ! As if I'd hear him slandered behind his back."

He finished reading the letter in silence, then looked back over it with something shining at the end of his white eyelashes.

" Why, it's enough to make you jealous, Nora," he said, with a tender pride. " He's writing to *you,* yet here's 'mother' and 'father' in nearly every line—mostly ' fa-

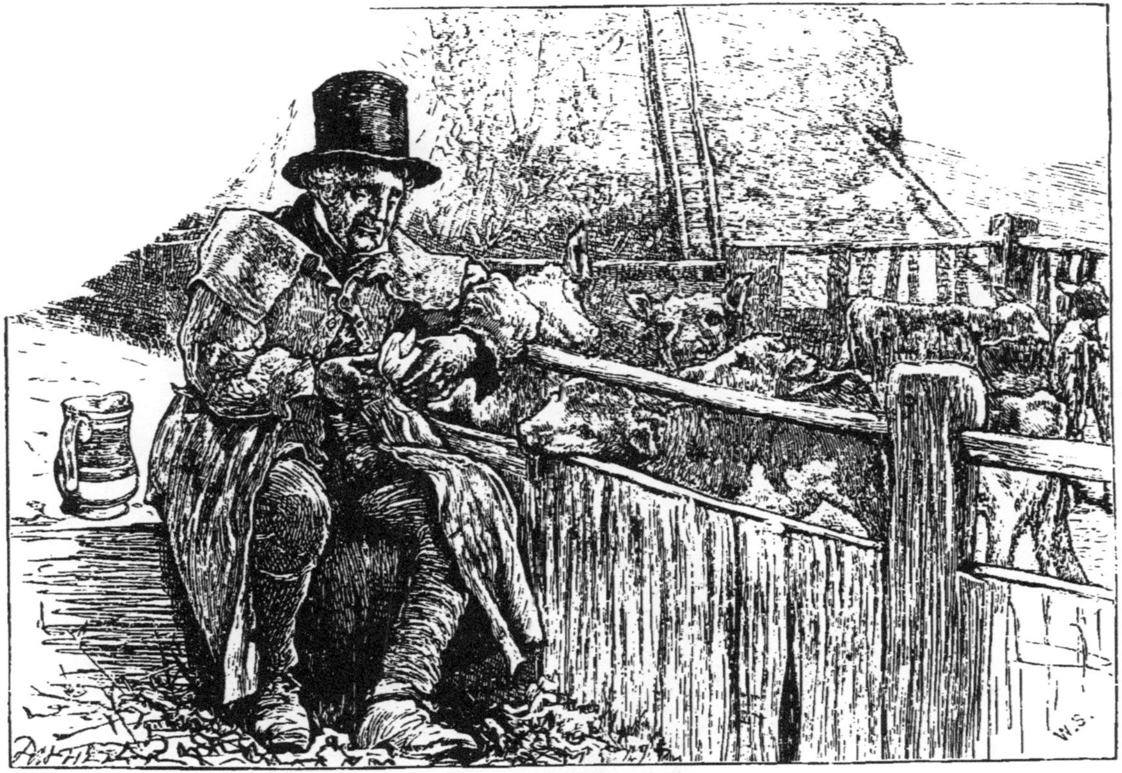

"MA'R SONE WAS THERE SITTING BY THE LOW PEN, TAKING HIS EARLY TEA."

Page 33

ther' though. Ay, my child, this *is* repentance indeed. You are right—how can we do enough for *such* a prodigal? We have no robe to put on him—except it's his little old white coat that hangs in the mill—well that was a garment of innocence, God knows—and he might do worse than put it on again. We've no rings for his fingers, but we will com—comfort him—won't we, my child!"

Nora fell into his arms with a cry, and he clasped her to his heart, trembling very much.

A hand—too heavy to be Nora's—touched his shoulder. He looked round and saw Michael with one arm thrown up against the wall, while with the other he pointed to the letter Ambray still held.

He was very pale, his eyes were wild and blood-shot, but had a gentle expression in them. As Ambray faced him he seemed unable to speak, though he still pointed to the letter.

"What now, Michael Swift? What have *you* to say on the matter?" asked the miller encouragingly, thinking that perhaps Nora's presence confused the man, and not noticing half the strangeness of his look.

"The date," Michael said, speaking with his breath, and without voice. Then aloud, and with a vehemence that had solemnity as well as passion in it, he repeated—

"The date, I say!—the date! Do you read a letter like that, and feel it like that, and not care to know when it was written and what has happened—I mean what time has passed—since?"

"The date?" said Ambray, looking at the letter. "Why, George hardly ever *did* date his letters, and I don't suppose he's dated this. No, not a sign of a date. But what's the matter with you, man? A date's not a thing of life or death, is it?"

He turned fully, and looked at Michael, and Nora also looked at him in a sort of vague annoyance and surprise.

Michael lowered his head, and dragged his arm slowly from the wall.

"I—I beg your pardon," he said, scarcely audibly. "I only wished to—I—I myself once made a great mistake through—through this same thing. A letter that——"

"There, there! of course you meant well," Ambray interrupted him; "I know that. Where are you going?"

Michael was gliding quietly past him.

Without turning his face towards him, Michael answered gently—

"To the mill, master. I am not wanted here now, I think."

The miller made no objection; so he went out through the door that led into the yard.

Ma'r S'one was there sitting by the low pen full of calves scarcely a month old, in whose society he was taking his early tea.

There was an air of peace and innocence about the simple little picture that made it seem as balm to Michael's blood-shot eyes.

He looked at it for some time, then approached the pen, and leant his arms upon it. Ma'r S'one's elbow, as he cut his bread with a clasp-knife, came just over the top of the pen, and was causing a soft, dreamy contention among the velvety heads there, each of which sought to rub against it.

"You find these creatures pleasant company, Mr. Ma'r S'one," said Michael, after watching a little while.

"That they be, sir," replied Ma'r S'one, looking down at them tenderly. "I'd leiver get my vittles with 'em than up at the Team any day, though it's mighty improvin' there sometimes, bein' gen'ly a scollerd there as can read the noospaper right arf without spellin'; but then it's gen'ly 'bout murders, and I caan't abide murders—they makes me creep, they do. 'Cline our 'erts, I say, to keep this la'!"

Michael was gazing vacantly into a sun-blinded velvety face that, baffled in its attempts to reach Ma'r S'one, had come to be fondled by the stranger. At Ma'r S'one's last words, Michael's eyes dilated and swam, his hands clutched each other over the side of the pen, and a hard breath came labouring from him, with the words—

"Amen, Ma'r S'one, Amen!"

CHAPTER XI.

MICHAEL'S existence was apparently forgotten by all Lamberhurst till near sunset, when Ambray burst the mill-door open, calling his name.

"Michael Swift! what on earth have you done with yourself all day? Hollo there! Swift!"

As the miller looked round on entering, it seemed to him a good week's work had been done.

His grey eyes lit with hearty approbation, but, falling on Michael, became instantly hard and suspicious.

As he came forward, his face pale, his hair flattened close to his brows by the sweat o. his hard work and the pressure of his cap, which he now held in his hand, there was something in his look and attitude which struck Ambray as being almost abject.

The miller immediately put his hard work to the balance against him.

He stood, looking him full and steadily in the face, with undisguised severity.

When Michael understood the look, he quailed more, and caught hold of the steps.

"Look here, Michael Swift," said Ambray. "Look me in the face, and tell me you are not keeping anything back that if I knew it would prevent my taking you."

Michael remained quite motionless for some time.

At last he raised his eyes with difficulty, showing Ambray nothing in them but the simplest honesty and sorrow.

"Master," he answered with much effort, "I shall tell you nothing of the kind. I don't know you well enough yet to know what might or might not prevent your taking me. All you have any right to ask is for a good character of me. If you don't trust what I gave you to read—you have only to write to the man who has put his name and address on it. I have never done a dishonest thing in my life. I have no more to say for myself."

"Would to God everybody could say as much," Ambray retorted quickly, his doubts dispersed by the light that flashed from Michael's weary eyes as he spoke;—"and with as much truth as I believe you can. You will have a master given to suspicion if you come here as my servant—I don't disguise that from you. I've had enough to make my right hand doubt my left. But come. I must tell you that Phillips's agreement is torn up—done for. My niece has won the day. The mill and the grist both secured for three months certain, and how much longer depends on you."

"This is good news, master," answered Michael, turning away to tighten the knot in one of the bags hanging down from the shafts. Deep gratitude and relief had brought the blood to his face more eagerly than he cared for Ambray to see.

"Shake hands on it, man," cried Ambray, kindling under the influence of his father's old port which he had been drinking freely at the farm.

Michael turned and stretched out his hand heartily, but instantly withdrew it again as if it had been stung.

"No," he stammered confused, but resolute, "not till you know me better, master."

"What," cried Ambray, "you bear malice, do you?"

"I don't—I swear I don't—but I will not shake hands with you till you know me as—I wish you to know me."

"I know you already for a man one must pick and choose one's words for," said Ambray impatiently, "which I'm not used to do for any man alive—so I warn you—but come away and have a glass of wine of a sort that'll put you in a better temper."

Michael smiled as he opened the door He looked back with a glance of involuntary pride on the improvements he had made on the ground-floor.

Ambray looked too and nodded.

"Very well indeed," he said, "and you can fetch the corn to-morrow. Ma'r S'one is to have it ready for you down in the hop house by six in the morning."

Ambray rose the next day about breakfast time in feverish spirits, and nothing could keep him from going up the field far enough to see the mill, with Fleetfoot and the waggon at the door.

A strong north wind was blowing—the sun made all the fresh downs look yellow—the mill sails swept round against the bluest sky of the year, Michael's face came and went at the windows, a very sun of brightness and content.

Old Guarder, the mill dog, ran incessantly too and fro between Michael and his master, and did his best to keep Fleetfoot from wasting his oats through a hole in his nosebag by barking at him from all sides, and even mounted to the driver's seat in front of the waggon to try whether his voice would have more weight from that place of authority.

Ambray and his wife went together to the mill in the afternoon to see the improvements Michael had already made there.

Michael, looking down from the stone floor, saw them standing by the meal bin watching the meal as it came pouring down. The mill was going so fast that it came down warmer than usual.

Old Ambray took some up in his cold, trembling fingers, and felt it with an exquisite pleasure.

"Here it comes once more, old girl," Michael heard him say; "plenty and warm, ay, warm from the Almighty's hand!"

CHAPTER XII.

Several weeks passed without bringing Ambray any reason to repent of his bargain.

He was much within doors during that time, the weather being changeable and his asthma bad; but he heard from all quarters of the industry and civility of his servant.

When the wind served, Michael worked by night as well as by day.

Far and wide over the country, and far and wide on the sea, people began to look for the light at the High Mills every windy night.

The little waggon, with Michael standing a few yards in front of it, smiling at Fleetfoot's slow advance with a kind of placid despair, became one of the most familiar sights on the road and in the lanes about Lamberhurst.

He had as yet made no friend but Ma'r S'one ; and there were days, when Ambray was confined to his bed, that Michael passed without speaking or being spoken to from morning till night ; and this to one who had not been used to walk a dozen yards without receiving a greeting from familiar lips was a very strange experience. It was the more so to Michael, because of his having always been possessed by a strong interest in his fellow-creatures.

Sometimes in the spring evenings, when Ambray was suffering more than usual, and his wife scarcely left his side a minute, and when there was nothing doing at the mill, Michael found his time of leisure—brief as it was—hang very heavy on his hands.

Once, when he looked in at the Team by way of a change, the company, unable in his presence to think of anything but the High Mills and their owners, conversed all the evening about " Mar's Garge " and his feats in running and wrestling, his handsome face, his good humour, his pleasant word to everybody, his popularity among rich and poor, his looked-for return.

Michael never spent another evening at the Team.

He tried several times to make the acquaintance of Mrs. Grist's nephew Simon. He went down to the farm and made polite inquiries about him every market-day after he had seen Mrs. Grist and Ann Ditch go off in the chaise with the butter. But the answer he received from Ma'r S'one was always either—that " Ma'r Simon " was asleep, or that " Ma'r Simon " was "arf," which last Michael had come to understand meant off to the Team, and for that reason would be deaf to the voice of friendship or duty for the rest of the day.

When he had been a fortnight at Lamberhurst, Michael had a letter from home. It was short and cool enough, but he was as agitated over it as a little schoolboy whose dimpled fingers tremble round the seal of his mother's first letter.

Michael's letter was from his father.

" The Green, Thames Dutton,
April 19, —.

" DEAR MICHAEL,

" I am very glad to hear you got the place you was after, and your mother is glad you are quite well and comfortable. We are pretty well, thank God, except for rheumatis in the same leg as before. I posted a letter the day after you left, which I found directed but not stamped in the pocket of poor Grant's coat. We supposed you meant to take it with you, as it was directed to the same place as you are at, and forgot it. I dare say it will have reached all right. Your mother pertic'lerly hopes you go to church reg'ler, and has your things mended weekly, as your brother Tom has just come home in a shocking state.

" Your affectionate father,
" JOSEPH SWIFT."

Michael felt that there was a great necessity for this letter to be destroyed ; but he could not do it. It was read, laughed, and sighed over, as if it had been the most brilliant and moving epistle that ever was penned, and when it had become worn almost to tatters in his pocket, it was placed between the leaves of Michael's Bible, where it remains to this day.

Nora rode over nearly every morning. Her visit at Stone Crouch was coming to an end, and her aunt was busy with preparations for her return.

Michael dreaded this return beyond everything. Ever since she had looked at him when he spoke of the date of George's letter, he had felt as if he would rather face anything than meet her eye again.

Even if he chanced to be seated with Mrs. Ambray at dinner or tea, when she came he would disappear at once, leaving not only the room, but the house, and sometimes while it was raining heavily. The Ambrays were always too much excited by her visits to take any notice of Michael ; but Nora saw and noticed him, and wondered he should have so much delicacy, and wished Simon was more like him.

No more letters, dated or undated, had arrived from George ; but as he had said that he should not write again until the fate of his pictures was decided, this caused no surprise or disappointment.

The three loving and expectant hearts kept each other full of happy restlessness with the idea that he might arrive any day, any moment.

Every night Michael heard his master remonstrating against the house being shut up so early, and he knew he kept awake an hour or more, sometimes many hours, after all was still and dark, straining his ear for the step, the knock, the voice, till his heavy eyelids fell and shut away the world and its vain hopes, and he was stilled with a foretaste of death's tranquillity.

Michael knew all this because the walls were so thin he could hear every word that was spoken below almost as well as if he were in the same room with the speaker. And often Ambray, long after all had been silent, would ask his wife if she did not think there was a sound like wheels or horses' feet coming up the White Lane, or tell her that Guarder had barked, or the gate had creaked. There were times when the consciousness of these grey heads lying awake far into the night in such trembling and tender expectancy became almost unendurable to Michael. Starting up, he would half dress himself and steal barefooted down the steep, narrow stairs, stand with his palms against their door, and be within a breath of bursting it open and falling on his knees before them, his face scarcely needing language as an interpreter. But before anything else was done, when only his noiseless feet had stood there, and his noiseless palms touched the door, he would turn and fly back, leaving upon the walls that shut in the stairs the prints of his moist hands dying away in the moonlight.

Back in the thin-walled solitude of his little room, where he was forced to be so quiet and careful, he would cast himself upon his bed, thanking God he had gone no further, and telling himself he must not, could not, make known to these poor, weak, loving creatures the full extent of their sorrow, till they had learned that they had at least a more faithful servant, if not a better son than George, to support and comfort them.

CHAPTER XIII.

AMBRAY was suspicious of enthusiasm. He could understand and honour a man doing his duty honestly and to the full; but such work as Michael gave for wages, which, as the miller said to his wife, "the man had not yet seen the colour of," was a marvel and almost a trouble to him.

Work that went beyond duty was regarded by him as a kind of conscience-offering.

It was Michael's duty to give his best attention to the grindstone, to turn all winds to good account, to keep the mill clean and free from damp, to carry the meal and flour

to the villages and farms from which it had been ordered, to be civil and obliging to his master and his master's wife, and to be considerate of the age and nerves of two such valued and venerable servants as Fleetfoot and Guarder. A grinder who neglected any one of these things would have fallen into great disfavour with Ambray.

But here was a man, who, not content with making good use of the day and the day winds, must needs spend most of his nights also, laying in wait to catch and yoke to his master's service each wind that moaned across the dark and solitary downs, or came sighing up the valley, moist and heavy from the sea.

On breezeless days, Michael devoted his time to the cultivation of a piece of ground belonging to the mills, and lying between Ambray's cottage and a pasture-field of Buckholt Farm.

The half-wild, half-barren state in which this had lain for the last five years had troubled Ambray sorely, being a constant theme for Mrs. Grist's calm satire, and a cause of dissension between himself and George; for George had disliked gardening as much as "millering," and his father's strength by the mill alone was greatly over taxed.

It was therefore no small pleasure and triumph to Ambray to see, and have others see, his unprofitable little wilderness thus brought to order and use; and claiming its small, sweet share in the universal bloom and promise of the spring.

All April possessed no touch of green so fair to his eyes as the buds that opened on this spot, nor any note of music so sweet in his ears as the singing of the birds above the soil Michael had cleared and refreshed.

Yet as he crept along, leaning on his stick, wrapt up, and keeping as much as possible in the patches of sunshine, he would watch Michael at his work with more suspicion than gratitude.

Sometimes Michael would look up, and meet his strange gaze with eyes so perfectly frank and honest that the miller felt ashamed of himself, and would go home and abuse his wife for not having provided a better supper for Michael.

But once or twice Michael had encountered his master's look in a very different manner— his eyes had turned to the earth, sick and confused, his hand had trembled on the spade. Then Ambray had looked at him hard—he was not a merciful, though he was a just man. He had looked at him as if he would search out the secrets of his soul, and Michael, when he next sat down to eat in the old people's presence, knew that they were regarding him as one who had come into a strange place to ride him from the shame of some dishonest act.

Sometimes Michael bore this treatment with exceeding patience and meekness; sometimes he chafed under it with subdued but visible passion, dashing the mill keys down when he went to bed, and treading the floor as if he would grind it to powder.

These fits of temper did more to reassure his master as to the wholesome state of his soul than anything else; yet Michael hated himself whenever he had been possessed by one of them even for a minute, and did his utmost to retain that very gentleness and forbearance which roused the miller's suspicions.

But more and more often, as the spring came on, Michael saw upon his master's face the look which said as plainly as look could say—" I shall find you out soon, my man; you cannot deceive me long." Yet, in spite of all his obstinate suspicion, scarcely a day passed without Ambray deriving some ray of comfort, cheerfulness, and renewed love of life from that very study of Michael's character to which his suspicion moved him and which strengthened his suspicion. The glow of a spirit more healthful, more honest, more fervent than any that had lived near him before was warming and comforting him, and he knew not whence the warmth and comfort came. It was the sunshine of the spring, the prospect of his son's return, Nora's bright, brief visits, the certainty of keeping the High Mills for yet three months more—anything, in fact, but the companionship and service of the man whom he was determined to "find out."

Nora came home about the middle of April. On the same afternoon that she arrived with her boxes at the farm, Ma'r S'one toiled up to the miller's cottage holding—with the edge of his smock between it and his fingers—a little note. It was an invitation to Ambray and his wife to drink tea with their niece and Mrs. Grist.

The miller was for refusing it, but Mrs. Ambray and Michael overruled him, and prevailed upon him to let Ma'r S'one carry back a grateful acceptance.

After that day Michael never left the mills without taking a long look from the little terrace to ascertain that Nora was not on her way to or from the cottage. When he reached the door he stood still and listened, and if he heard her voice within—as he did several

times—he would return to the mill, or go and work in the garden till she left.

The first time that he saw her face after her return was at church. She and Mrs. Grist now sat alone in the large old pew, where Ambray used once to sit with his father and mother, his old grandfather, and all his brothers,—while he was yet too small to know the weariness of having to dangle his feet a few inches above the hassock they could not reach,—while indeed he was still too little to dangle them at all, but could only turn, direct towards the pulpit, a pair of tiny soles, which perhaps pleaded his small cause eloquently enough by thus simply and mutely offering evidence of their very recent and slight acquaintance with the earth, among the sinners of which their owner was called upon thus early to proclaim himself.

The grey head which now bent beside Ma'r S'one's and others as lowly, on the most backward of the free seats, told a very different story, offered very different evidence as to its need of mercy.

It was during the sermon, when Mrs. Grist slept soundly with her fat hands folded on the large pocket-handkerchief spread over her claret-coloured satin dress, and when Ma'r S'one and a curly-headed ploughboy, between which two Michael sat, were requiring constant reminders from each shoulder that he was neither a pew wall nor a bundle of hay, it was at this time that he ventured to look at Nora.

He had scarcely done so when his eyes fell full of perplexity and wonder.

Why was she so pale, so different from when he had last seen her face in the parlour at Buckholt Farm?

He dared not look again, because her eyes had been gazing straight towards the seat which she shared with the Ambrays and her aunt's servants, yet he would have given much to know whether her face was indeed so altered as it had seemed to him; whether it really wore that look of vague suffering, that desire for divine guidance and help, a desire which had appeared to him to be expressed there as humbly as it was on Ma'r S'one's face, when he prayed that his heart might be inclined to keep his Master's laws.

If he had been right, if her face had really looked so, what had caused the change?

Had George Ambray's letter, read many times, begun to have a different meaning for her at last? Was she beginning to suspect that something worse than debt, and long absence without explanation, had wrung from him those expressions of repentance which had so moved her and gladdened his father's heart?

While he was trying for courage to look once again at Nora's face so as to be better able to answer himself these questions, the voice which Mrs. Grist had found so soothing ceased; and she woke with a start, and fixed instantly a look at once appreciative and critical on the old vicar, as if, on the whole, she approved of the sermon, but could decidedly point out a flaw or two in it if closely questioned on the subject.

Ma'r S'one also woke, sighing and shaking his head, and murmuring very self-reproachfully—

"'Cline our 'erts," and finishing his prayer upon his knees.

The plough-boy, too, lifted his curly head from Michael's shoulder, turning upon him as he did so a look of surly indignation, as if requesting him not to take such a liberty again.

Now comes the blessing, the silence, the rush of fresh air and sunshine through the door the beadle has noiselessly opened, mysterious sounds among the Union boys as they are trying to persuade each other, by nudges and kicks, to begin the general uprising; mysterious sounds, also, among the old men in the free seats, a gentle fumbling for sticks and crutches, patting and coaxing of stiff, gaitered legs, that apparently have mistaken this for their last journey here, and gone to sleep. Silence again, then suddenly, and at its full, the noise of the rising of a large parish in a little church; the mingling of rustling silk and creaking old limbs, the roll of the organ, the light fall of well-to-do feet, and the grinding and clattering of myriads of little hobnails. Down sails Mrs. Grist, the richest woman of the parish, placid, self-conscious, doffed to and nodded to by high and low.

Will he see Nora once more? Michael wonders. No: the crowd hides her, the Ambrays are waiting for him at the tiny side door.

One more glance across the motley little mass, moving all one way, across the smart bonnets, the files of tiny corduroyed figures; but it is a vain glance. He sees no more of Nora, and in another instant finds himself again by his old master, the old duties, the old sickening necessity of listening to the old story pressing upon him.

How sick he feels this morning of these glittering downs and the old mills that seem to look loweringly upon him from the hill as he toils on towards them, supporting his master, who leans so ungrudgingly upon him,

because he thinks his arm unworthy of giving him support! How sick, too, of the thoughts of seeing again that door of George's room standing open to show him directly he enters the miller's house, its almost awful air of expectancy and waiting!

CHAPTER XIV.

A WEEK of wet weather, with scarcely a gust of wind from Monday to Saturday, had improved neither Ambray's cough nor his temper.

Michael was beginning to look habitually scared and downcast at his approach, and at the sound of his voice.

On Saturday evening, more as an excuse to escape from the cottage than from any other motive, Michael pretended to remember that a hinge of one of the mill windows was loose, and might be letting in the damp if left over Sunday.

It had just ceased raining when he went out, but all the world looked as if it could never dry up and brighten again; and the mill had a stark, dead stillness and lifelessness about it by no means cheering to a miller's eye.

Michael entered and went up to the stone floor, where he stood looking out half vacantly from the window of which he had spoken.

He had pushed it open, and was watching the smoke rising, or rather being held down by the damp as it came from the chimneys of Buckholt Farm.

He had been standing there for nearly ten minutes, not thinking so much as being overgloomed by thoughts that came like the clouds passing above him without any working of his mind.

There had been no sound since he stood there but the water dripping from the mills and the pale trees; but now he was startled by hearing a loud bark from Guarder; which was immediately answered by a bark from another dog, and then there was a noise, as if challenger and challenged rolled over on the stones together.

Michael looked down from the window. He did not see the dogs, but he saw a figure walking along on the grass by the side of the path, and after his first glance at it he fell back a step or two and stood watching its approach.

His own face had changed in that moment; had lost its look of sadness and vague foreboding, and taken on it the blank, breathless air of one confronted suddenly by a new and an unexpected calamity.

The figure came too near for Michael any longer to see it.

The bell fastened to the ground floor door rang loudly; an instant after he heard the lifting of the latch.

Michael turned and looked at the opening in the floor where the ladder was, and breathed hard.

He knew his delay must be but momentary; he *must* go down, whoever, whatever waited him. That was Ambray's door at which the summons had come; he was Ambray's servant; there was no help for him.

He was a stranger, there were none to take his part.

His eyes, turning slowly and heavily about in a despairing search for aid, fell on the grindstone.

He went and stood before it, and looked down at it, and the panic and despair in his eyes softened and kindled to sorrow and passion.

Without moving his lips, and while keeping his eyes, misty, and burning, and still, cast upon the stone, he pleaded mutely with God.

Was the stain which his hands had inno-

Page 35.

cently brought upon this stone, and which none saw but him, *not*, after all, to be ground out by his hands, though he was willing to make that work the aim and end of his life?

Had he not for this purpose deserted, in their old age, his father and mother? And had any one seen the pathos of Michael's eyes as he set this deed before his Maker he might well have believed these two to be little less than angels, instead of being the most selfish old couple in the world, as in truth they were.

Had he not been patient since he came

here, and was his patience, and was all his work to go as nothing? Had the end indeed come? Was Ambray to hear all now—this day—this evening; was his fury to come upon him in this dull rainy light, while the mills were standing still, and every one's door was closed on the drenched world?

Slowly and with a certain faint trustfulness in his face, Michael at last approached the opening, set his heel on the ladder, and went down.

He did not pause an instant in the grinding-room, or on the dressing-floor, where he threw one quick glance at the sketches on the bin, but went on down the broader steps till he came close to the open door and the person who had admitted himself.

The visitor stood with his hand still on the latch, and his face turned in the direction from which Michael came ; though his eyes were not looking in the same direction, but were turned to the ground with an attentive expression.

He was an old man, of medium height, dressed in patched and ragged clothes, the appearance of which a thorough drenching had not improved. He had a long white beard, and a high forehead, and was superficially venerable looking, but to eyes that rested on his face many moments, it was evident he was not wanting in the low-cunning and brute strength of nerve natural to the born vagrant.

His blindness—for Michael knew it was this affliction which caused him to keep his eyes on the ground while his face was lifted towards the steps—his blindness, no doubt, kept him unaware of how plainly his mouth revealed the half pitying contempt with which he regarded the world in general. Why, it was difficult to tell.

All that was unpleasant in the old man's face struck Michael now for the first time.

When he had seen that face before—the only occasion on which he ever had seen it before, it was under a flaring gas-lamp, in a crowd—and all that had struck him in it then was its age—its white beard, its blind eyes rolling and straining in their sockets in helpless and yet awful anger—he had seen it thus, and for one minute only, and the image of it had never quite left him since. He had never wished it to leave him. He had cherished it in his memory that he might say to himself, when he grew faint-hearted and sick of soul over that minute's history, " Could *any* man have looked on this blind face, and stayed his hand just then ?"

Would the old man know him ? He had heard his voice that night, and Michael knew the wonders of blind men's memories.

The old man, far too dignified to lift his hat, pushed it further off his forehead, and assuming a proud meekness of voice as well as some vague sort of emotion, inquired—

" Sir, do I—do I stand before — Mr. Ambray ?"

" No, Mr. Ambray is not in the mill," Michael answered without hesitation, then watched, searched the face before him with patient intentness for any sign of recognition of his voice.

He saw none. The blind man was evidently aware of something that made his senses very attentive over the voice itself while it spoke, and for an instant or two over the recollection of it when it had ceased speaking.

This, however, might be his habit when hearing, as he must so often have heard, voices which perplexed him for the moment through their resemblance to other voices.

Not the least curiosity or excitement followed his very careful study of Michael's voice and its vibration.

Having learnt that the master of the High Mills was not present, he became less ceremonious. Letting go the latch, he stepped briskly in and took off his hat, and shook the wet from it in Michael's face.

" He'll be here some time to-night, old Ambray, won't he—eh ?" he asked, rubbing his knuckles, which, while shaking his hat about, he had knocked against a shaft.

" No, he won't," answered Michael.

Again there was the same attentiveness over the voice while it spoke, and after it had spoken ; and again the same lack of excitement followed the consideration.

He put his hat on, and Michael was half hoping, half fearing, he would go without making known his object in coming there.

But the old man, after feeling about, touched a sack of flour, on which he immediately seated himself, wet as he was, with a grunt of satisfaction.

Michael only wished he had been an utter stranger, that he might give him his opinion upon this proceeding.

" You Ambray's man, eh ?" inquired the blind tramp, adjusting himself comfortably on his yielding seat.

" I am, and I am going to the house. Can I take the master any message ?"

" No, thank yer, young man. Must see him. Must see him. Come another day. I'll have a rest now. So this is a mill. Never was in one before."

If he were never to be in one again, Michael thought, so much the better. " I like the smell of it," said his unwelcome visitor, lifting his nose and sniffing vigorously. " By-the-bye, where's my dog ? Just look out and see, will yer ? Here ! Jowler ! Jowler !"

Before Michael had made up his mind whether to obey this command or not, a miserable animal, who looked as if he had a share in all the cares of the world, rushed in with a string attached to his collar, and entangling his legs as he ran.

" Come, Jowler," said his master with unaffected feeling ; " come and let us see if that clumsy country brute hurt you. You shud keep that beast chained up," he added to Michael, as he carefully felt Jowler all over; "he flew out very savage upon Jowler, and I'll let yer know, my man, if he'd a hurt him it ud bin as much as his life's worth. A retriever—yours *is* a retriever, ain't he? Well, you've just to ask and pay to git another, exactly like him; but I'd like to know the name by which you'd find another such as Jowler."

As Michael could not deny the difficulty of such an undertaking, he made no answer.

"Your young master's at home now, ain't he?" asked the blind man suddenly.

"*Who?*" said Michael involuntarily, and understanding what was meant the instant he had said it.

"Young Ambray—your master's son—George Ambray—he's at home here now—eh—ain't he?"

Michael laid his hand on the shaft, and looked steadily at the blind face.

There was a world of covert meaning in it—a world of secrecy and cunning; but Michael drew from it, in spite of this, the belief that the question had been put in good faith—that the man was really ignorant as to the thing he had asked about.

From that moment he drew freer breath. Why, he asked himself, should he fear this man if he neither remembered meeting him that night nor knew of what had happened since?

Why was he here, then, inquiring for Ambray? No doubt to bring some charge against George. If this should be so, he must keep the man at all hazards from meeting Ambray.

For the next few moments Michael suffered a great contempt for himself for having thus been overwhelmed with fears for his own safety, and keeping his eyes closed to what might prove danger to the name which he had sworn to keep as unsullied as he might. Was it selfishness or great unselfishness that made Michael feel suddenly cheerful and courageous when he found he had to do battle on George's account instead of his own. It was a question Michael found himself unable to answer when he thought of it some hours after the mill was closed and he had gone home.

After considering a little while, and looking with puzzled eyes upon the blind man and his dog as they settled themselves more at their ease on his sack of flour, Michael thought the best thing he could do would be to try and remove the impression of extreme disrespect and inhospitality his silence must have given.

"Might you have been born blind, now," he inquired, "or was it an accident?"

"Accident! no, thank yer, young man. No, I'm happy to say I'm a so-born. Don't know nothing about sight at all. Never seed in my life."

"Well," said Michael, trying to keep his patience as his saturated guest stretched himself on the flour sack, pommelling it to make a comfortable place for his ragged elbow, "it's a blessing to be contented, certainly."

"Contented! Why I wouldn't have sight at no price; it 'ud be like a hextra arm or somethink o' that kind—I shouldn't know what to do with it. Here, p'r'aps you'd like to have a look at my stiffikit."

While Michael was wondering what on earth that might be, the blind man drew from his pocket a small parchment roll, which having untied he held out to him.

"There," said he as Michael took it; "I wears that 'ere round my neck, but most folks in London might be as blind as me for the notice they takes on it. Not as your country bumpkins are much better. They will read it, it's true, stand before yer, a concealin' of yer from the public thorerfare, and spell it out to the last letter, then walk away as coolly as if they'd bin a readin' it on a dead man's tombstone."

Meanwhile Michael was reading on the card, written in a schoolmaster-like hand, the words, "Christian charity is solicited on behalf of Richard Bardsley, born blind, who at the age of seventy-three walked from York to London, where he waits his end in the full reliance that his generous-hearted fellow-creatures of this city will not see him starve."

"And you find Jowler a pretty fair guide?" asked Michael, venturing to pat the queer head as he returned Mr. Bardsley his card.

"Well, yes," he answered, turning towards Jowler, who was showing the whites of his eyes as he lifted them to his master with an expression which seemed to implore that he would please say the best he could of him; "Well, yes, leavin' out o' the question one or two little failin's which all sight-gifted natur', human and otherwise, is invariably addicted to—and namin' which I must, I really must"—shaking his head at Jowler, who gave a little whine, and twisted himself as though he knew well enough something not altogether pleasant was being said of him, and he entreated his character might be spared as much as possible—"*must* specify POUNCING as the most wicious, and apt to trip a person up unawares, specially when it's after a sparrer on the edge of a curbstone, or a rat in the bottom of a ditch. I might mention fixin' his mind on perticler streets, and always tugging in them particler directions, as ilconwenient to a person who happens to have a will of his own likewise ; but tugging is a ilconwenience only, pouncing is a wice—a wice !" And Mr. Bardsley shook his stick at Jowler with one hand, while he felt a large bump on his forehead with the other.

As Jowler looked depressed, and gave a melancholy yawn, after this account of him, his master felt it incumbent on him to put his hand in his pocket and draw forth and snow to Michael the little money-box he usually carried, and which was heavy enough when holding ever so few coppers, Bardsley assured him, to try the teeth and temper of any dog living.

"And what is more, sir," said Bardsley, "there is a haction of Jowler's life, which did ought to a won for him a respect above coppers, as makes the box heavy about little, and *is* trying to his teeth. It is a haction I should have had recorded on the stiffikit, only the young man as wrote the present stiffikit in this here beautiful hand was caused, by circumstances over which he had no control, to leave the country—that is to say, sir, he was transported for forgery ; and I was afeard, as two different handwritin's on the stiffikit might look unprofessional, consequently Jowler's haction is still between hisself and me and the Almighty. It was a time, sir, when bad luck did seem, like a bloodhound as 'ud tasted our blood and meant to have the last drop. My little grandchild had come into the world a few hours or so, and was a crying at it still with all her might and main. My poor son, a so-born, like myself, was a waitin' on her and her mother, and blubbin' with joy as his little child was born to see, and which she were, sir, with sorrer as she shud see such trouble in the beginning. I lay on a mat in the corner, racked with rheumatis, and Jowler hard by, a growlin' out now and then in his sleep with

hunger. Not a crumb had any of us had for more hours than would be credited. Every mornin' since I 'ud bin bad had that there dog stood waitin' with the box in his mouth a tryin' to coax me out. His own feelin's taught him how badly money was wanted in the box, for he had always been used to bite short when it was empty. His respect for the box though is nothing in regard to his respect for the stiffikit ; for, seeing people stand and stare at it *afore* they drop money in the box makes him naturally look on that as the most important. He wouldn't by no means let me go out without it, as I used to be goin' to do sometimes in my flurry of mind when my poor son's wife was in her tantrums. He'd go back and stand at the head o' my bed where the stiffikit was hung on a knob, and there wait till I come and took it down and put it round my neck. On this mornin' I'm speakin' of he wakes up all of a sudden, gits the box, brings it to the head of the bed, and sits looking up at the stiffikit, and giving little pitiul howls. Presently he begins makin' jumps at it. Then it all came to me what he was after. 'Come here, old boy,' says I ; 'have yer own way, and the Lord guide yer.' So I twisted the stiffikit string round his neck short, and he dashed out. He hadn't been gone a quarter of a hour before he came back tearing like mad, rattling something in the box, and the stay-lace woman, and the match gal, and two or three more from the steps where I used to sit, comin' up the stairs after him to tell me how he come there, and how they all knowed old Bardsley was in trouble."

"Well done, Jowler," cried Michael, patting him, "*he* carry coppers ; why he deserves to have nothing but gold in his box to the end of his days."

"Come, old boy, we must be on the tramp, or little missis 'ull wonder what's come of us. Well, young man," he added, turning to Michael as he took Jowler's string, "I shall look in on yer master agen on Monday. Now, Jowler, not there. No pouncing, you rascal ! Out, sir, out !"

PART IV.

CHAPTER XV

"ND then I saw them go on to the mills, and I heard my father's voice in the noise of the sails."

It was Tuesday morning, and the blind beggar's visit had been on Saturday, and had not been repeated; yet Michael found it impossible to think of him without those lines from George Ambray's letter ringing in his ears.

He knew well that Bardsley was one of the people whom George had seen in his dream going to the mill with evil tidings of him. He had been unable for the last two days and nights to put from him a sense of George's being near; watching, as he had told Nora he had done in his dream, the threatened mischief to his name and the pure memories of him which lived about his home.

Michael could scarcely conceive an image more tragic than that of the returning prodigal held back by some implacable hand, while his sins alone should arise and go to his father.

Each day since he had first come to the mills his friendship for George had been strengthened. He had known him only in his shame and sorrow; but now the reality of what he was before was felt by Michael almost as well as if he had been familiar with him from childhood.

Bright and healthful memories of George were incessantly gushing up from the past and veiling Michael's stained image of him; gracing and purifying it as the waters of a fountain grace and purify a discoloured and mutilated statue over which they play.

Lamberhurst was full of him. There was scarcely a spot known to Michael which Ambray had not pointed out to him as the scene of some wonderful performance of George's, or connected with him in one way or another.

That knoll between the pines was "where my son threw Marsham, the greatest wrestler in the country." And after hearing this, Michael never saw the knoll without seeing also a dim sculpturing of forms, among which one only stood out distinct—gladiator-like—beautiful, as the pale face he knew so well must have been in its bright health. The Long Ridge fields were where "that young rascal won the foot-race," and where now Michael could never look and not see the flying figure, the feet scarcely touching the sunny grass, the flushed face certain of success.

It had truly become to him more like an actual than an imaginary object, that figure which haunted Michael's paths, stealing upon him in all places, gliding over the grass in his white cricket shoes. At one time it would be as the admired young athlete, his eyes downcast with the graceful modesty of unrivalled power, at another as the calmly triumphant lover of Nora—so handsome that the vaguest smile, the simplest remark from his lips must needs, it seemed to Michael, be more winning than a year's courtship from one less gifted than this young ideal of his, this wonder growing upon him from the past, for ever increasing and strengthening those claims he already had on him.

Michael had made his hero out of somewhat common-place materials; but owing to the life he had led, which apart from his hard work, had been a very child's life, there was, perhaps, no kind of character so fitted at that time to fascinate his untaught imagination as George Ambray's.

Michael had read so little, had associated so little with minds in a better condition than his own, that he was unfit—not through any natural grossness, but through simple inexperience—to understand, without help, a character whose worth was veiled under misfortunes, either physical or mental. Delicate shades, subtle intricacies were lost upon him; his mind required an idol made on the commonest principles of strength and beauty, and in George he had found this.

To him the ruin of such a man was more tragic than the ruin of a thousand ordinary beings—a thing to be tenderly hidden from the world, and most of all from the eyes of those who loved him.

With such feelings in his heart for the absent and helpless, Michael could but regard the blind beggar's appearance at Lamberhurst with much dismay and foreboding, even after he had felt reassured as to his own identity remaining unrecognised by Bardsley.

On Monday night he began to hope that the rain, which had fallen heavily all day, would continue, and perhaps weary out the old man's patience, sicken him of his errand, whatever it might be, and cause him to return to his old quarters.

On Tuesday morning, however, he woke to disappointment, for he no sooner opened his eyes than he saw the upper half of the poplar at the corner of the mill-field stirring in golden light, tremulously—exultantly, like the wand of some wizard alchemist in a crucible when a long looked-for change has come. The first warm weather of the year had set in.

It was market day: and Ambray, Michael, and Ma'r S'one were going to the town on Mrs. Grist's business. In addition to her farm, mills, and hop-gardens, the miller's sister-in-law carried on a small corn-trade, to which Ambray had for many years lent a managing hand. Since his illness Mrs. Grist and the person whom she had put into the little corn shop at the Bay had so mismanaged things that on the day Ambray and his wife went to take tea at Buckholt Farm she begged quite humbly that he would resume his old duties. At first he declined doing so, but the remonstrances of his wife, Michael, and Ma'r S'one caused him to change his mind, and he promised to go to the Bay and look into things as soon as his health would allow him. This Tuesday was the first market-day that he had found himself able to undertake the journey.

The three set off in Ambray's waggon drawn by two stout farm horses, Michael driving, and Ma'r S'one sitting at the back.

Ambray was very nearly as silent and depressed as his father's old servant, because as they started he had seen the meeting of Nora and some of her friends who had ridden over from the Bay to visit her, and the miller had thought she had blushed and brightened overmuch when General Milwood's nephew stood talking and laughing with her as he held down the fine, angry little head of his black horse. Reports of how much more time than usual this young gentleman had spent at Stone Crouch during Nora's visit there had come to Ambray's ears, and he did not forget them as he watched Nora beating her pink palm with a rose and talking so animatedly.

Ambray had felt very angry with her as he drove out of the farm-yard, and during all the journey was as gloomy and jealous for George's sake as ever George could have been for his own.

" Look at her," he had muttered to Michael. " Silly flirt ! How do I know but what my boy's prospects are going to the ground, being fooled, chattered, trifled away with every leaf of that rose ? *Such* a jackanapes too ! Ha, I'd like to lay my whip about his shoulders."

" It would be a bad move, master," answered Michael; " they have all their flour from us."

" I wish it may choke——"

" 'Cline our 'erts !" murmured Ma'r S'one.

The thought that Bardsley's next, and perhaps last, visit to the mill would probably be while they were away was a source of so much satisfaction to Michael, that he enjoyed the journey as he had not enjoyed anything for many months.

CHAPTER XVI.

IT was four in the afternoon by the market clock, when, the business of the day having been concluded, Ambray and Michael drove to the spot where they had arranged to meet and take up Ma'r S'one.

They found him waiting there. Ambray had fetched his coat, and was crossing towards the waggon, and Ma'r S'one was doing something to the harness at Michael's direction, when all three were caused to turn their faces up the street by a sudden cry.

It was not a cry of acute pain, fear, anger, or entreaty ; it was not a cry wrung out by any sharp and sudden aggravation ; it was rather such a cry as might come from a creature who, in the loneliness and darkness of night, when no earthly ear can hear, and when God seems further than the stars, sets free some misery that has lain gagged all day, and lets it wail aloud.

It was a girl's voice, and its youth made its anguish the more penetrating and strange.

It did not soon cease, but went on minute after minute till every one in the street stood still and turned and listened, while several hurried towards the spot from which the sound came.

Thus a little crowd soon shut from Ambray, Michael, and Ma'r S'one the object which they had seen when they first turned their faces and looked.

This was the figure of a girl standing at the edge of the kerb-stone with her hands stretched a little forward, the palms outwards, as if she were feeling for the wall on the wrong side of the pavement.

By the time Michael had consigned the reins to Ma'r S'one, and pushed his way with his master through the little crowd, the girl was sitting on the kerb stone where she stood a minute before, and the cry that still came from her lips seemed duller and more monotonous.

She appeared to be about sixteen years old, and at a first glance Michael thought her but a commonplace, slatternly, ragged creature, differing little from thousands of others he had seen selling fruit and flowers in the London streets.

She was very slight, her ragged clothes hung on her as on a reed; but her face, though it was small, was not thin or pinched with want. The cheeks and lips were at this moment colourless, but it seemed as if colour had only recently left them.

The head from which the bonnet and hair-net had fallen was thrown back, the eyes were closed, the face was uplifted with an expression of intolerable misery.

The girl's clothes were dark and travel-stained, and her hair, of a pale and rare flaxen shade, looked strangely out of place upon her drawn-up brows and over her shoulders, which were pushed up by her hands being rested at either side of her on the low kerb-stone where she sat.

These hands were red and black, as were also the little bare feet resting in the road.

The outline of the up-turned chin was singularly perfect. It seemed, indeed, touched—as the sunshine fell on it—with a most tender spiritual beauty, which made one imagine that some unseen, angelic hand supported it; and kept this creature, so young and so helpless, from sinking utterly in those depths of anguish from which the voice—flowing drearily through the parted lips—appeared to come.

"What's this about? What's the matter with the girl?" asked Ambray of a commercial traveller who stood near him.

"Oh, she pretends she's just been struck blind."

"Pretends?" echoed Michael, indignant, though whether with the speaker or the girl he hardly knew.

"Struck blind," Ambray repeated; "what, just now?"

"Hush," said the commercial traveller. "Let us watch,—I fancy there'll be some fun presently: that policeman has his eye on her. I fancy, from what he said, he knows her, and has seen this game before."

"Ah, the young baggage; is that it?" murmured Ambray, beginning to feel resentment at having been duped into a feeling of pity but for one instant; and, with a stern satire in his eye, he set himself to watch with the rest of the crowd—to watch and judge this most wicked impostor or most bitter sufferer, whichever she might prove to be.

She had arraigned herself, or fate had arraigned her, before a set of judges which, perhaps, represented the world about as faithfully as an ordinary court of justice does.

The larger part of the crowd had collected since Ambray and Michael had arrived at the spot; but those standing closely round the girl were simply the passengers through the street who had been all simultaneously stopped in their different pursuits and thoughts, and compelled, by this sad voice, to turn and fix their minds, one and all, on the same subject.

The number of these was about fifteen, and consisted of the commercial traveller, standing by Ambray; three friends, two of whom were poor-law guardians, and one an impressionable old gentleman, who boasted of never being deceived in his first impressions; the watchful policeman; a little tailor, going home disappointed of some money he had expected; a party of young ladies and gentlemen just returned from a yachting excursion; an old farmer and his wife; a clergyman; a tramp of doubtful character; and a little child about three years of age, standing with its finger in its mouth, and the exact same expression of rueful pity in its face as Ma'r S'one had on his as he turned round while standing holding back the powerful cart-horses, meek as lambs against his feeble arm.

The commercial traveller did not put any question to the girl, as most of the others did in turn, but stood prepared, as he had said, to enjoy the fun of seeing an imposture detected, an impostor hunted down. He was a hard-working, honest man, who lost something considerable yearly in actual pounds, shillings, and pence, through not departing a little from his own ideas of honesty. This loss was never absent from his mind, and the only compensation he found—for the world offered him no other—was dwelling on the sufferings of those who had not, like himself, chosen the straight path. His virtue was as a wolf within him, demanding for its food the tears of detected vice. He was one of those men whom if placed among the sheep on Christ's right hand would find less reward in hearing the words " Come, ye blessed " than in listening to the " Depart, ye cursed " uttered to the goats on the left hand.

Next to this man stood Ambray, who hated law for the simple reason that it had always gone hand in hand with Mrs. Grist against him. This caused him, though his own judgment was hard against the girl, to regard the delighted excitement of his commercial neighbour with much disgust; and he could not help comparing him in his mind to a great blue-bottle fly buzzing with delight as he watched some feeble and pretty creature of his own species entangling itself in a spider's web.

The three friends stood nearest the vagrant —and of these it was the impressionable-looking gentleman who spoke to her most often, and who always appeared more and more convinced of her sincerity and innocence each time he spoke to her, whether she answered him or only continued her bitter crying.

His friends the poor-law guardians did not seem greatly impressed by his opinion. One —the perfection of whose health and toilet showed who and what had been his chief care through life—had clearly written on his handsome face an intimation to providence that, after such a winter as the parish had undergone, he should certainly expect this to prove a case for the prison authorities, and not for the poor-law board.

The person who leant upon his arm was also a rich man, but one who had grown cadaverous and hollow-eyed, and had sickened of his sumptuous fare, his purple and fine linen, in considering the sores and cries of those who came to ask for the crumbs that fell from his table. He was a charitable man whose charity had been much imposed upon ; and as he stood looking at the girl none in the crowd doubted her more, and none were so anxious to believe in her and to give her assistance and comfort.

The policeman stood just behind the commercial traveller, whom he had taken into his confidence. With his hand on his hip, he listened with a smile of supreme contempt to all the questions, sharp or gentle, that were put to the miserable girl, and to the answers that she gave.

The disappointed little tailor, with the black cloth—in which he had just taken home

the work for which he had not been paid— twisted round his arm, stood a little aloof from the others, lost in thought. He was too humble-minded a man not to have accepted instantly the verdict of his betters; and one glance at the poor-law guardians, the policeman, and commercial traveller, had convinced him as to the depravity of the creature whose cries had stopped his feet on their sad journey homewards. But though he accepted the verdict undoubtingly, there was a furtive, frightened, but an almost fierce anxiety in his eye as to the judgment that was going to be passed on the offender. He had never seen her before, yet he was possessed by a feeling of which he was greatly ashamed, but which none the less held him to the spot—a feeling that there was no one in the world so well able as himself to offer evidence as to how easy might have been the slipping of these young feet, how terribly hard it is to resist the slime on want's steps when the head is giddy with hunger and the heart sick.

The yachting party had evidently enjoyed a gay little cruise, and were rather glad to hear and believe that the girl was an impostor, and that consequently there was no need for them to put aside their gaiety and look on the matter in a serious light.

The old farmer and his wife took the whole affair as one of the amusements of the town —a visit to which was an utter failure, unless it afforded some such sight. They only removed their spectacles from time to time to wipe them and put them on again, and begin the study of the town impostor with renewed zest.

The tramp of doubtful character apparently had many if not good reasons for keeping behind the policeman as much as possible. He looked very haggard and weary, and carried his boots over his shoulder on a stick that had as vagabond-like an expression as his face. His eyes remained fixed on the young girl, wistfully alert to meet her eye, and signal to her with as much force as could be thrown into a wink that, stranger as he was, he considered her game was up, and that the sooner she made off the better it would be for her.

The clergyman appeared also to have come to the conclusion that the girl was acting, but he seemed to be watching the little crowd about her with almost more interest than he looked at her. Perhaps this was because he knew most of these persons pretty well, and was wondering with melancholy interest which among them was fitted to cast the first stone.

He had not the pleasure of the commercial traveller's acquaintance, or doubtless he would have wondered no longer; for, though that gentleman was really too good-hearted to do personal violence to any one if he could help it, yet, as far as *right* went, he would assuredly maintain that he could take up the largest stone at hand and smite with clear conscience and unerring aim straight through the hypocrite's young bosom to her heart.

The little child and Ma'r S'one were the only ones who regarded her simply as being in trouble—who, without inquiring as to the why or the wherefore, turned to each other with faces that said only, with rueful sympathy—" Here are tears !"

" Come, my poor girl," said the impressionable gentleman, trying to control his excitement, and to speak calmly, as he bent down to her, " try and tell us more plainly how this came. Were you crossing the road —or were you here ?"

The cry, without stopping, uttered the word—

" Here."

" You were standing or walking here a few minutes since, and could see plainly ?"

The crowd closed a little to hear the words with which the cry, still unaltered in tone, was now burdened, and caught such sentences as—

" Oh this darkness ! O father ! father ! Where is my father ?"

" I shouldn't wonder if that ain't the old man's cue for coming on," whispered the policeman to the commercial traveller. " You'll see, sir, it'll be as good as a play afore long. The old raskill 'ull come fumbling along with his dog, and pretend to hear her all of a sudden, and call her, and find out she's just gone blind, and there'll be a fine scene between 'em. They've carried on the exact same game at Manchester, Birmingham, and half a score of other places; but we've got 'em now—*we've* got 'em !"

" You'll be fools if you haven't," observed the commercial traveller. " But the girl *is* blind, isn't she ?"

" Yes, sir, bless you, blind as a bat, and always has bin."

" Can you tell us what there is opposite ? What you saw just here before you lost your sight ?" asked sharply the poor-law guardian, with the florid face.

" The gentleman might be sure she'd been well put up to all that," sneered the policeman.

" Rather !" agreed the commercial traveller.

It so happened, however, that both found themselves mistaken in this matter, for the girl began to murmur about things that were not in the street, and that, in fact, seemed to belong to another place altogether.

The policeman rubbed his whisker with a puzzled, uncomfortable air, these mutterings of churches and factories were not in his programme. He could not understand them.

The bitter voice, dull, monotonous, wailing, still flowed from the parted lips, and for a minute all again listened to it without interruption, while the sea, moaning at the end of the little street, seemed offering solemn attestation as to the truth and depth of its misery.

All this time Michael Swift had been looking on and listening with feelings more strong than any one's in the crowd.

Like the little tailor, his experiences had made him merciful and slow to condemn. Like the impressionable gentleman he was susceptible to the charm of soft flaxen hair and a lovely profile, and like Ma'r S'one and the little child, he could not unmoved see tears pour down like rain.

These weaknesses in his nature acting upon one another caused him to be seized more than once with a very strong wish that the commercial traveller or the policeman might do something that would give him a fair excuse for knocking one or both of them down.

" Now," he heard the policeman whisper as he stood watching them, " here comes the old scamp, sir. Now see if it don't all go just as I said."

Michael, turning to look in the same direction they were looking, saw coming quickly down the street a blind man and a dog, whom, with a sense of vague alarm, he instantly recognised as Bardsley and Jowler.

He glanced hastily from the old man to the girl, and fancied by her face she heard him coming. Her lips and closed eyelids trembled, and she grew much paler.

At first things went exactly as the policeman had prophesied.

The old man came along with a swinging, agitated step, stopping now and then to listen and tremble, and turn himself about with an air of great confusion and distress of mind.

At last he cried out passionately—

" It *is* her voice ! Polly, my child, where are you ?"

Then suddenly wringing his hands and appealing to the crowd, he cried—

" What is this ? Why are you all gaping here ? What has happened to my child ?

Why is she crying? Let me come to her. Oh let me come to her!"

The policeman and commercial traveller exchanged smiles as they parted to let him pass between them.

The impressionable gentleman hurried forward to meet the old man, and staying him by laying his hand on his tattered sleeve, explained to him hastily but gently what had befallen the girl.

To the infinite amusement of the policeman and commercial traveller, the profound admiration of the tramp, and the disgust of the little tailor, the blind man appeared to be terribly stricken by the story. He interrupted it constantly with bitter exclamations, by which he managed to make known that this calamity had been the great dread of his life since he had had his grandchil1 left solely in his charge and dependent on him; that she had been blind once for several years when a little child, but had been cured, though the doctors had warned him she might at any time lose her sight again suddenly. And now the dreaded blow had fallen! Now when he had not a farthing in the world to help her with.

"Let me pass, sir; let me go to my chil.1!" he cried, waving his arms wildly.

"When are you going to put an end to this?" asked the commercial traveller. "To me it's a sort of blasphemy."

"Wait a bit, sir," whispered the policeman. with superior calmness. "Now hasn't it been almost word for word as I told you? Now, you'll see, sir, when he says, 'Polly, Polly, what is this?' the girl 'ull throw herself in his arms and shriek out, 'Daddy, I'm gone blind?' and make everybody cry."

"I have my pocket handkerchief ready."

"Well, I can tell you, you may want it, for she does it uncommon well, sir."

"I am ready."

So likewise is old Bardsley ready. He has made his way to his grandchild, has cried in his best style, "Polly, Polly, my child, what is this I hear?" and stands with his arms outstretched before her.

But here comes something that is not in the policeman's programme.

Polly does not apparently recollect her cue.

Instead of throwing herself in her grandfather's arms and crying, "Daddy, daddy, I'm gone blind!" she does no more than raise herself a little from the pavement by leaning on her hands; then seems to stiffen in all her limbs, while her white face stretches towards the old man, and her lips turn blue in trying vainly to speak.

Another instant and she has fallen to one side and rolled over in the road at Bardsley's feet.

With far less effective dramatic action than he has previously shown himself master of, the old man goes on his knees and raises her. The "Polly, Polly, what is this?" that he mutters in her ear now is not nearly so touching. The voice is sharp, husky, scarcely audible.

The crowd presses nearer. Bardsley turns his sightless face about wildly, for Polly is uttering strange shrieks, strange words. He tries to shut the voice up in the blue lips by holding them against his face, but it rings out wildly—shrilly.

"No more! No more! O daddy, I can't do it never, never, never more!"

"Hush, hush, Polly; Polly, hush!" mutters Bardsley. "She raves, gentlemen, she raves. This sudden affliction has turned her brain. There; quiet, Polly, quiet."

But Polly's fingers begin to clutch about him like a drowning creature's, and her lids open and show her sightless blue eyes rolling.

"Daddy, daddy!" she cries in great labouring breaths. "I seed fire I did—inside me eyes. Oh, I'll never, never! Oh, let me beg—beg all day—but never that —never!"

"Hush, Polly, hush! You wouldn't ruin— you wouldn't. Ah, gentlemen, her brain is gone!"

"Where's all them people? Where am I? Am I mad? I thought I was a-going mad, daddy, I thought—"

"Hush, child! Dear, good Polly—so good—so good to me. She wouldn't ruin me—she'll be quiet. Gentlemen, we will go home. I will take her home. She will be better at home."

Suddenly he seems to grow suspicious, and waving his disengaged arm with a passionate vehemence, cries hoarsely—

"Stand back, I say, and let me take her home! I want nothing of you—not I! I want to take my child home. What are you crowding for? Let me pass!"

The policeman looks back at another one who is waiting a little lower down the street, and who joins him when he has made his way to the blind man and girl.

The crowd closes round the group.

No outcry is heard, only an indistinct flood of protestation from the old man, and soon the little crowd parts, the four go very quietly down the street in the direction of the prison, the girl clinging to her grandfather, and looking white and terrified, but quiet and stricken with remorse, as if her

"STAND BACK, I SAY, AND LET ME TAKE HER HOME."

mind had, under this new shock, recovered itself and become conscious of all that had happened.

The little tide of street life that had been stopped by Polly's voice flowed on its way again.

The impressionable gentleman, who had several times declared that he would stake his life on the truth of a girl with that face, went home too much depressed to speak to any one, feeling himself to have been thoroughly taken in.

The handsome poor-law guardian took his rich, cadaverous-looking friend home to dine with him, and rallied him with much lively grace of manner on his low spirits and poor appetite.

The commercial traveller went away with a smile on his face and Pope's line about an honest man on his lips.

The yachting party went home satisfied that there had been nothing worth making themselves miserable about.

The old farmer said to his wife—
"Now that's over, old woman, let's come and have a look through the telescope."

The clergyman went to wait for the policeman, that he might ask some questions about the prisoners.

The little tailor rolled his cloth round his arm very tightly and went quietly home, where he surprised his wife by sitting up the whole night, keeping her awake with his "stitch, stitch, stitch," and by being for many days so gentle, sober, and industrious, that, as she told her neighbours, she suspected him of having had a fright or a dream.

The tramp, when he saw Polly and her grandfather led down the street, had turned and looked after them till they were out of sight, then dabbed his palm flat against his eye, and went on his way muttering an oath.

Ambray, Michael, and Ma'r S'one, in rather dreary silence, got into the waggon and rattled away over the jolting High Street stones.

The little child left alone suddenly began to wonder what had made it cry; but failing to remember, sat down in the sun and began to sing and play with its toes.

CHAPTER XVII.

JUST twelve years before her cries had thus interrupted the business of the High Street at Bulver's Bay, Polly Bardsley had made one of a very different assemblage, and had had very different opinions passed upon her.

It was the day when her fate had been decided—a day when after merciful hands having led her into a better path than she had yet in her blind infancy trodden, her wilful little feet had recklessly and passionately of their own baby will turned and fled back to the very path from which she had been drawn, and which had now led her to the prison where she sat—darkness in darkness stamped on her young face.

It was a grand day at the house where the child's kind patrons had placed her, and where she had been three weeks—that great house the space of which caused her to feel ready to cry whenever her small voice ventured forth and made known to her sensitive ear how very far the walls and floors and ceilings were asunder from each other.

A concert was being given by all the blind scholars for which this great house was built, and of which Polly was by many years, many inches, and many degrees the youngest, smallest, and most useless. She was the lowliest, too, by birth—a very sparrow of humanity, whose fall from light to darkness had been thus mercifully seen and noted by a Divine eye.

All the morning Polly, sitting winding cotton for the blind knitters, had heard the preparations for the great occasion going on. The biggest room of all, where the great organ stood, had been filled with seats, and the two rooms leading out of that were arranged like a bazaar with the wonderful things Polly's blind schoolfellows had made — the mats, the brushes, the baskets, and the needlework, much of which was too delicate for her little fingers to be permitted to touch, and which she could only hear about till she cried with curiosity.

The blind girls and women had done each other's hair with ever so much more carefulness than usual, and chattered and laughed and wondered if this person and that person would be coming to the concert, till Polly likewise began to have small thoughts and hopes and fears of her own about the coming of a person whose existence in the outer world made that world seem all home to her, and whose non-existence in this place, where she was, made the comfortable house a wilderness.

She had gone into the great room with the others, and taken her place with the singers, under the organ; and all the seats were filled by the patrons of the place and their friends, and other ladies and gentlemen, and poor people too. The organ played, songs and anthems were sung, and speeches were delivered between whiles, setting forth now much had been done for Polly and her schoolfellows, and how much more was going to be done; yet Polly's heart never knew one throb of gratitude, knew nothing, indeed, but wild throbs of wonder as to whether a certain wicked old man was here—was coming to her when all this should be over, to take her in his arms for one minute.

The old man was there, and was making himself a nuisance to his neighbours, by repeated inquiries as to whether they did not see a little child among the singers.

"Look agen, miss, *if* you please," he urged anxiously to the young lady sitting before him. "She *is* so uncommon small you'd hardly see her at fust."

To please him, the young lady rose, and said, as she sat down again—

"Oh yes, I do see a tiny child, quite a baby; a young woman is holding her hand; but she cannot be four years old, I think."

"Ah, that's her, miss, sure enough," said Bardsley. "Her years ain't took up much room in her. My little grandchild, miss."

Page 41.

When the concert was over, and the people went to look at and purchase the school-work in the outer rooms, the same young lady and her blind brother encountered Bardsley buying himself a pair of warm socks and waiting—he informed them—till he might obtain permission to visit his little grand-daughter. They found the old man much distracted between parental affection and anxiety for the safety of his dog, whom he had left in charge of a boy outside the door, and whom he urgently commended to the notice of several persons as they left the building.

"Beg pardon, sir," he was saying to some one as they came up to him, "but would you kindly cast your eye round the toll-gate as you go out and tell the lucifer boy in charge of a small, long-legged tan dog that he's bein' watched, and 'ad better mind what he's about with that ere animal.'

Half an hour later, when Mr. Bardsley's new acquaintances were waiting in a little parlour to see some one in the establishment with whom an appointment had been made, a blind lad appeared at the door with old Bardsley.

Not noticing their presence, he told the old

man to sit down, and his grandchild should be sent to him. Directly he had spoken, however, he knew that the room was already occupied, and apologised for the intrusion ; but the young lady said she should be glad to see the little girl.

"But why is she here ?" she asked. "Surely she is not blind with those pretty eyes ?"

" Ah, but she is, miss," answered the beggar, and added, with a sigh, " and what makes it worse, miss, she ain't exactly a so-born, little Polly ain't, so it don't come nat'ral to her yet ; but as she begins young, we must hope in time she'll overcome the dislike she 'as to it, and come to look on life as a step and a feeler—which as yet she don't, but runs and falls and knocks her precious little self about, and frets for her eyes as if they'd bin her mother and her father."

"But has she not a father and mother ?" they asked.

" Father she's none, sir and miss," repl'ed Bardsley ; " and if I could say the same of her mother, better would it be for little Polly, though besides her she's got but me and Jowler in the world."

"She isn't kind, then— little Polly's mother ?"

" She beat her, and would have starved her if that 'ud been easy, which it wasn't while Jowler and me could drag our limbs along. But for Jowler's box and my stiffikit, God knows where little Polly would a bin. Under the ground belike along with her father, my poor son, m'ss, a so-born like myself ; took a fancy to ly a sight-gifted young woman, as I was myself afore him. She broke his heart, miss—mainly with bad language to me and Jowler, and unpleasing reflections on the box and stiffikit in hard times. When Polly was born, and he heard she was sight-gifted, he took heart again wonderful, and made mats enough to carpet Jerusalem. We all strove for her, but it's hard work striving against a tartar, a drunkard, and a thief. At last she got herself took and transported, and Polly's sight went, and her father sunk under it all, and——"

Here Mr. Bardsley was interrupted by the opening of the door, and the entrance of little Polly herself.

The blind girl who brought her put her timidly into the room, and closed the door behind her.

Polly was indeed a small creature, whose every garment was in itself a wonder. A mere frill of preposterously few inches seemed her black skirt from her waist to the tiny

socks which, tiny as they were, found them-selves too large to keep up round the little leg, in despair whereof they fell over the tops of Polly's well-worn boots, where they lay in a limp and helpless state. Little Polly as-suredly did not possess the attractions which her grandfather hinted as having been the portion of himself and son. It might be said with some truth, perhaps, that the child's affliction was the only thing which then gave her significance.

Her grandfather had risen at her entrance, and now stood, hat in hand, waiting, listening for her approach as impressively as if she had been a duchess.

The child still remained on the same spot where she had been left, and where she stood with uplifted listening face and little hands clasped before her, patiently waiting that guidance without which she had not yet learned to move. It was touching to see them facing each other without knowing it, and waiting passively each other's assist-ance. At last the smallest voice imaginable inquired, with a sweet patience, " Is my daddy here ? "

At this old Bardsley went to her as direct as if led by the truest of eyes, stooped, took her in his arms, and returning to his chair sat down with her while she lay upon his neck, an arm cast loosely over each shoulder, her face flat against his old coat, in what seemed to be an excess of peace and contentment rather than any childish emotion. Mr. Bardsley prided himself too much on his personal dignity to give way long to the feelings which had overcome him at the meeting with his little grandchild. Drawing down her hands, and seating her on his knee, he began to stroke her light hair with one hand, while he held her small chin in the other.

"You see here, sir, and miss," he said, " you see here a little creetur born to trouble if ever a creetur were."

And if ever a creature looked it, Polly did, with her meekly drooping head, her useless blue eyes, and her small mouth drawn up so tightly as if every breath of life had too sour a taste for it to take more than it found posi-tively necessary.

" And is little Polly happy in this place ?" asked the lady, scarcely knowing in what manner to reply to Mr. Bardsley's introduc-tion of her.

A slight turn of the head and a faint flush showed Polly's ear as sensitive as her eyes were dull. She looked for one moment em-barrassed and timidly inquisitive, but the next the remembrance of the value of the few brief minutes she had to be with her grandfather came over her; and turning a stubborn little back towards the strangers, she devoted her whole attention to caressing his hands, his buttons, and his long grey beard.

"Come, come," said Bardsley, vainly endeavouring to make her turn her face, "speak up, pretty. Polly's nice and comfortable here, ain't she?"

Polly leant upon his breast that he might feel the meek little nod which was her answer.

"She has good wittles, eh?"

Polly nodded again.

"And she's a learnin' to 'read with her fingers?"

At this Polly lifted her head up with the injured dignity of one whose powers had been undervalued, and said, "I can 'ead a lot, daddy, 'out my fingers, 'out a book at all, 'bout Jesus and Herod and Judee."

"Oh, ah, that ain't readin', that's knowin' by 'art, Polly," rejoined her grandfather. "But Polly's agoing to learn to read with her fingers all off pat without stopping, like old Ames that sits in the square with the big Bible, and mumbles the Scriptures when he hears anybody comin'. I dunno how his dog stands it. I know Jowler wouldn't. Well, and Polly stands up and sings with the rest of 'em. My gracious!"

Polly flushed with pleasure, and kissed the button she was fondling.

"Did hoo 'ear me, daddy? I sung in 'Joyful, joyful.'"

"Did I hear her! I shud say so, rather. Well if Polly didn't ought to be a proud and happy little girl!" said Bardsley. "Why, she's not got a thing to wish for."

This last proved an unlucky assertion, as it invariably is even to the most happy and grateful. It was certainly too much for Polly, "born to trouble." The little fingers engaged in trying to coax the worn covering back over one of Bardsley's buttons, of which they had felt the brassy nakedness, were slowly withdrawn. Slowly they clutched the wee skirt of Polly's black frock, and drew it up and found beneath it, safely attached by one corner, and illustrated with the legend of the rats who decided to bell the cat, a pocket-handkerchief.

It was a handkerchief which, in Polly's sight-gifted days, had been an inexhaustible delight to her and to Jowler; whose sagacity in discovering that it was *that* handkerchief and no other which he was expected to scratch and bark at when she shook it and

said, "Rats! rats!" had always concealed from Polly his utter want of appreciation of the artist's truth to nature. Now that the little washed-out relic of happier days could gladden Polly's eyes no more, she was content to keep it to dry them of their tears, of which they knew no few.

Trembling with that bitter charge of having nothing to wish for, Polly lifted the rats in council to her cheek, and, pressing close to her grandfather, sobbed with more passion than one would have thought sorrow had left in her—

"O daddy, daddy, I tood 'ike my eyes! I *tood* 'ike my eyes! and I wants to go home, and I can't stay here!"

The old man was much disturbed. He clasped her with arms that trembled, and rocked her against his breast, and the eyes which had never shed a tear over their own darkness, let fall some heavy drops for Polly's. Recovering himself very soon, and trying to make her sit up, he said—

"Come, come, Polly. Why, I never would have thought it. Fie, for shame; what will the young lady think of you?" And turning to her, he added apologetically, "She'll be herself again in a minute, miss. This is what comes of not bein' a so-born, you see."

It did not seem that Mr. Bardsley's prophecy was likely to be very soon fulfilled, for Polly continued crying bitterly in spite of attractions offered her in the shape of a watch held against her ear, a cake put into her hand, and sundry articles from her grandfather's pockets picked up in his street wanderings. Her crying would probably have brought some one into the room soon and caused a sudden and sad ending to her grandfather's visit, if there had not presently arrived a comforter whose loud scratching and barking outside the door made everybody start, and was instantly recognised by Polly.

"O daddy," she cried, sitting up joyfully, "it's Jowler! it's Jowler!"

"Upon my soul if I don't believe it is," said Bardsley with much alarm; "there'll be a nice set out!"

The young lady, who was not so fearful of offending against the rules of the establishment, opened the door, and in burst Jowler.

Polly slid from her grandfather's knee, and meeting her old friend half-way, sat down on the floor to receive his wild caresses, which she answered with smiles and soft little pats. She seemed to think his frantic joy quite accounted for by his possession of that sense of which she was deprived; for as she gently restrained him she said with a tender envy in her voice :—

"Jowler, Jowler, dear Jowler, you are pleased. You see me, don't you, Jowler?"

By degrees she got him quiet, so that she might feel him all over, to assure herself he was in nowise changed from the Jowler her eyes had loved.

Jowler stood with lolling tongue gazing round from the corners of his eyes with unutterable affection on the little hands that were so inconveniencing him, and submitted to their examination with quite superhuman patience till they came round to his tail, when he offered a gentle but decided resistance.

"And he's bin a good Jowler, has he?" inquired Polly, holding up her favourite by the front paws.

During the twelve years that had intervened between this visit of Bardsley to the blind-school and his visit to the High Mills, some three or four Jowlers had worn out their lives in the old man's hard service. Of these it was in all probability the Jowler of Polly's infancy who was the true hero of the story that had been related to Michael Swift, though Bardsley was in the habit of applying it to any dog who happened to be in his service. The vices and virtues of a live dog must, he reasoned, inevitably be of more interest to the public than those of a dead one; and if he could amuse the public, and even edify it, as he sometimes believed he did by his anecdotes of dog-life and dog-character, he did not see that he harmed any one by letting his hearers believe that they had the true hero of those anecdotes before them. For this reason he had found it necessary to keep to the same name.

When Polly asked about Jowler's behaviour since her absence from home, Bardsley told the story of the "pouncing" and the "stiffikit" in nearly the same words in which he told it to Michael twelve years later.

While he did this Polly sat quiet with a patient, half-weary look on her face. Even in those days it was an old, old story to her.

At the moment when Jowler, after the recital, was receiving the pats and applause of all present, the young woman who had brought in little Polly came back to summon her to tea, and to inform Mr. Bardsley that the doorkeeper was waiting to see him out.

The little one had her arms round Jowler's neck when the summons came. In an instant she was up, kneeling on her grandfather's knee, her hands clutching him tightly.

"Tea, eh?" said he, making a bold effort to quiet her emotion by seeming not to share or

perceive it. "Buns, too, I bet a penny, as it's high day and holiday. My little Polly havin' tea and buns along of a lot of ladies and gentlemen. What yer think o' that, Jowler?"

Jowler only wagged his tail with a preoccupied air, for he was intent on a bag of biscuits on the table.

"I doesn't want tea, and I doesn't want buns—I wants you and Jowler," was Polly's cry of misery; and she clung and pressed against the beggar's tough old heart till its slow beating quickened painfully.

Afraid of trusting himself to comfort her, he rose and gave her into the girl's arms just as she was, in her tears and struggles, and she was carried out.

Her grandfather adjusted the string round Jowler's neck, and gave him to understand, by the roughness of his touch, that he was again on duty; that sentiment had been banished with little Polly, and the hard business of life was now to begin.

Polly was put to bed long before it was dark. She knew it was not near night by the talking and the laughter in the workrooms, and by the vague red glare she saw when she turned towards the windows, for as yet Polly could tell light from darkness, and sometimes see a form or a colour suddenly, and generally but for a moment.

She could not rest. The day's excitement, the joy of meeting Bardsley, the sorrow of parting from him, the playing of the organ, as she had stood so close under it, the over-much wandering and ruminating alone which she had had that day, the crowds, the many voices, the unusual influence of strong tea and coffee which had been given her instead of milk and water on this great and confusing occasion, all acting together on little Polly's weak brain and passionate heart, made sleep impossible—bed a rack.

She got up and crept to the door, from the door to the top of the stairs, and stood listening.

People were walking about still, the organ was playing, the great front doors were open, wheels were noisy in the streets, little children shouted and laughed there—ah, how free and happy Polly thought them! Why should she not go down the stairs and slip away through the great doors—away for ever from this grand place with its awful organ—this wide-roomed house so clean, so good, so dull, so miserably strange? Would any one notice her? All seemed so busy. There were many little girls come with the visitors;

she might be taken for one of them if she slipped out quietly, but then she must put on her clothes, for no little girl would be there in her night-dress, Polly remembered.

She ran back and dressed herself as well as she could, then went to the stairs again, and listened.

Bardsley shared the room which he had occupied since Polly's birth with a bird-seller, known among his friends by the name of "Traps." It happened that on the night of Polly's grand day this person was obliged to be up late, painting two green-finches to sell in the streets as valuable foreign birds. Bardsley, being nothing loth to have some one to whom he could describe the grandeur of Polly's school and Polly's prospects, had kept his friend company; while Jowler, a miracle of patience and self-sacrifice, sat winking and gaping between the two, and trying hard not to look at the birds, which he had had the mortification of seeing fatten-ing for sale on hemp-seed for the last week.

"Traps," said Bardsley, suddenly inter-rupting himself in his description of Polly's delight on meeting him, "that's the second time I've heerd it."

"Heerd wot?" inquired Traps, holding off the painted finch by the feet, and con-templating it with the eye of a connoisseur, while Jowler retired, sick with temptation, to the farthest end of the room.

"That noise," said Bardsley, rising; "like a lot o' people down at the door. There! they're on the stairs; they're a-coming up; they're coming here."

Traps uttered an exclamation which implied their coming was the reverse of welcome to him, and, thrusting the bird into its cage, covered his paints with Bardsley's old woollen comforter, and took up his pipe.

Meanwhile Bardsley opened the door, and found the whole houseful of lodgers crowded round a policeman, who had something in his arms.

It was Polly; and Traps, listening sulkily, made out from the confusion of tongues that she had been found feeling her way along by the pailings, half a mile down the road where the school for the blind was, that she had given her grandfather's address with extreme exactness, and demanded with great energy to be taken there and nowhere else.

Bardsley, with a strange expression on his face, came and took Jowler's money-box, and emptied out all its contents into the police-man's hand.

He then brought Polly in, and shutting the door in the face of all who would fain have entered and heard the story of her return, stood her on the floor, and seating himself remained for a moment with his face buried in his hands.

Traps caring only that the people had gone, and that the door was shut, opened the cage and resumed the bird and the paint-brush, observing with complacency—

"If this ain't took for a Java sparrer, it'll be 'cos there never was no Java sparrer to come up to it."

"Polly," said Bardsley, suddenly lifting his face, "come here!"

She went and placed her hands upon his knees.

Polly had in her hasty dressing been un-able to fasten her clothes round her shoulders, so that Bardsley drawing her to him found them bare. He began to beat them with so heavy and passionate a hand, that Traps in his astonishment obliterated a scarlet spot he had made with great effect on the green-finch's wing, and stared round.

"Traps!" cried Bardsley, almost fiercely, as he stood trembling over Polly when she had cast herself, stricken with terror and ex-haustion, at his feet. "Traps, you are a witness as I have done my dooty by this child. I moved the world to get her in that place—you know it, Traps—and now when she's wickedly run away, I've beat her—I've beat her till she's dropt. You see it, Traps, if that ain't dooty I'd like to know what is! But now that's over come to me, my precious —my darling! and let what can part us two agen.

"Ah, Traps! it's no good goin' agen fate. She was born to trouble—which means to me. I tried to put her away from trouble and from me, but it don't do, you see, Traps —it don't do."

The old man put forth the same plea on that night twelve years afterwards, when Polly had cried herself to sleep upon the prison straw, and his own heart and brain were restless and tormenting.

"I tried to put her away from it all," he kept crying inwardly, "but it didn't do— Traps knows it didn't do."

PART V.

CHAPTER XVIII.

BEFORE it was light the next morning Bardsley was disturbed by his granddaughter being brought to his cell. She had been locked in for the night with three drunken and riotous women, who towards morning had quarrelled so violently that Polly had been frightened, and had wakened the gaoler by her entreaties to be let out; he, not knowing where else to put her, and remembering Bardsley was alone, had brought her to him.

Polly was much too weary to be capable of showing her gratitude for the change in any other way than falling into a peaceful sleep.

When this had lasted about two hours Bardsley began to have little fits of coughing, to walk about and stumble, as if he wished to waken her without seeming even to himself to do so purposely.

It was necessary that Polly should begin without loss of time to receive her instructions as to how she must behave when they should be taken before the magistrate, how she must swear to having suddenly lost her sight at such a time and in such a place, and how she must guide her statement according as the evidence for and against them should go. Perhaps she would have to swear to having lost he sight before in one or more of those towns which might send witnesses against her, and consequently swear to having recovered it again as many times as might be necessary.

Bardsley had during his sleepless night thought out all Polly's lesson with much diligence, and was impatient to teach it to her before they were disturbed.

He had never felt himself so much to blame before, as he did for having been so carried away by the repeated successes of Polly's street scene as to venture it here, so near to the High Mills, which formed the real aim of his and Polly's pilgrimage, whereon they had found their daily bread in this fearful manner. The story that he had come to tell the miller of Lamberhurst would assuredly have to remain untold if Polly and he were to be proved guilty in this town. There would have to be months, or, likely enough, years of waiting, until the case should be forgotten—and perhaps it might never be forgotten in such a place as this. He felt, on considering all these things, that his hopes and the future he had pictured for Polly must indeed be ruined unless his own cunning and good luck should bring them safely out of the dangers into which his hardihood and Polly's "fit" of yesterday had thrown them.

But if Polly would learn her lesson well, if she would but wake free from all the excitement and confusion that had seized her yesterday, Bardsley believed he could so manage their case that, however much might be suspected, nothing could be actually proved against them. It was the old man's besetting fault to put too much faith in his own wits and the gullibility of the world; and sharp experiences of its dangers had not in the least degree tended to cure him of this fault.

The straw on which Polly lay was spread upon the stone floor, and on this Bardsley at last sat down beside her, to wait for her awakening, and gently to hasten it by passing his hand over her face and hair.

He had not done so many times when his fingers began to tremble. He withdrew them, and sat with his head bent and his face darkening.

It was not that the coldness of Polly's cheek had made his heart misgive him for her health's sake; he knew by her gentle breathing, and the moisture on her brow, she was recovering from the shock of yesterday, as she had recovered from so many similar shocks before. It was, that his fingers had gone to her face as, but for his blindness, his eyes would have done, full of the question—Would it all be well with Polly when she should wake? Would she perjure herself this time meekly and obediently as she had done before? He had asked this as he touched her, and had taken a chilling answer from her face. He had seemed to feel something like severity in the cold and still repose of the eyelids and the mouth—something that made him fancy Polly had not wholly returned to her usual meek and dependent spirit—that she had things in her mind, in her dreams, strange to him and against him.

Again he touched the mouth he had fed so long with the wages of his blindness and beggary, and again it seemed strange to him and chilled him. Its perfection felt to him like the seal of truth upon it—cold, firm, unbreakable. Bardsley was imaginative and superstitious, but he thought this had nothing to do with his fears concerning Polly. He thought, with his usual self-conceit, that he had the power of feeling expression, and that Polly's face was expressing some thought or dream injurious to him.

He got up and moved to and fro in the cell with confused and unsteady feet, but in less than a minute came again to where his grandchild lay, and crouching down beside her, his hands clutching each other tremblingly, he uttered her name in a voice hoarse with superstitious fear.

" Polly !"

She woke, and rose up on her elbow.

To see Polly's awakening on this or almost any morning was to guess at what was generally regarded as another misfortune in her almost as great as her blindness, but which was perhaps the chief blessing with which the child had been endowed.

Polly had not nearly an ordinary share of sense. It was as if her Creator, considering into what evil and unclean company her mind would fall, had mercifully kept it as a bud never to expand; closed tightly to all cankerous things and baleful airs, so that day after day it might be steeped in mire which should fall from it, leaving it unsullied and pure at heart; for with Polly it was very seldom that anything sank deep or rankled. She scarcely had even memory to trouble her. Sleep would generally banish from her any day's sorrow, and leave her spirit fresh and bright as a blade of grass which the drop of dew all night upgathered on its point has fallen over in the morning and left glistening.

There were times when it seemed, as by some magic touch, to open for a little while and be penetrated by a mysterious vague sense of the misery by which it was surrounded. It was one of these unwonted fits that had seized it yesterday and filled Polly's cry—begun in hypocrisy—with such true and bitter anguish.

When Bardsley called her, she woke at once as innocently and brightly as anything on earth might wake, rising towards him, smiling, and stretching her little hand, the substitute for her blind eyes, to his face.

He could know nothing of how sweet her pretty, rich-fringed eyes were, or how the sunshine glorified her hair, claiming it—all abased and trailed on prison stones though it was—as one of the shining treasures of the morning and the spring; but her waking and her touch comforted him greatly.

" I'm glad you've slep' well, Polly," he said, trying to maintain a dignified composure of countenance under her attentive fingers as he sat down at her side, and laid his hand on her shoulder. " I'm very glad, indeed ; for there ain't nothing like sleep to shake a person together agen, when they've shook theirselves to pieces, as you did yesterday—both your own self and me, Polly. I ain't slep' at all, now, all night—not a wink ; it warn't in me ; but I'm truly glad as you could, Polly—truly glad."

And Bardsley sighed with a sort of philosophical resignation, as if adding mentally, " So is it ever in this world—the innocent must suffer for the guilty."

His voice and his words brought all the bitter truth at once into Polly's mind. With it came also one of those strange, brief flashes of inner sight which allowed her to see herself and her life.

Her morning freshness and cheerfulness were gone. Horror and self-pity came over her, her eyes filled with tears, and she threw herself face downwards on the straw and began a dreary wailing, which moved Bardsley with impatience and irritation.

" Oh well, if that's to be it, Polly," he said in a voice sternly contemptuous, " I must let things go as they will. It's no good one strivin' and strainin' while t'other lays down and howls. Now I tell you once for all, Polly, if this goes wrong with us, as you seem set on letting it, I'm done for. I could ha' wished to see you better provided for, afore I meets your poor father, but my efforts for you, Polly, is come to a end, if the worst comes to the worst on this occasion. I'm an old man, Polly, which on account o' the energy I puts out for your sake you're apt to forget ; but age is age, and can't stand a blow like this."

Here Bardsley tried the effect of a little smothered but very audible sobbing himself.

Polly's wailing ceased ; the weary, downcast little form drew itself up and nestled at his side. The hem of Polly's wretched gown was applied with gentle vigour to Bardsley's eyes—an attention as unpleasant to him as it was unnecessary, but which he bore with Christian fortitude, and rewarded Polly for by receiving her somewhat stiffly in the arm against which she leaned.

" I don't want to scold you, Polly. I'm

well aware as you're not strong, and can't reckon on your mind in 'he right place and the right time, and it ain't for *my* sake but your own hintirely as I could wish for you to break off this sort o' childish way you has of roaring out over a bit o' trouble which, as I've told you often, is a thing as we're all born to, an' as runs in your own family most perticklerly. I ain't bin able, it's true, to give you such a edgercation as you'd a had if you'd stayed at the place I moved the world to get you inter; but I do take credit to myself, Polly, for trying to keep you well up in one lesson as I've learnt by harder ways than I've tried to learn it to you—a lesson, Polly, as the teachin' of is much neglected in all circles—and that is, the *accepting* of trouble as a *fact*, as a thing you must expect to meet anywheres and everywheres, as certainly as a party you might 'appen to owe a small sum to—as take the case of the ketch-'em-alive-O man I borrered sixpence of last June, where could I turn a corner without finding myself stuck to his fly-papers? But I expected him, Polly, and dodged him as I'd have you expect and dodge trouble, which is as real and sticky as fly-papers, and, no doubt, set by a judicious providence as knows it wouldn't do for us to be all in the sugar-basin at once."

Polly listened meekly, thankful to hear the old man fall into his habitual preaching tone to which she was so well used. But Bardsley, at the first pause he made, became aware of how he had been wasting the few precious moments which remained for him to teach Polly her part in the day's performance.

He erected himself with as much dignity as he could in his lowly position on the floor, and assumed a brisker tone.

"But what I was goin' to say to you, Polly, is, as it's of the most vital importance as you shud rec'lect to-day, you are no longer a child, but a growed-up young woman with responsibilities, with more responsibilities— some desirable, others not—than most young women of your age."

Polly sighed. She knew that it bode:l no good to her when Bardsley began to speak of her responsibilities—knew well it was a token that some unpleasant task was about to be assigned to her.

Bardsley began at once to make known to Polly what he had so carefully considered as best for her to do and say. He restrained his usual volubility, and managel to convey his thoughts and wishes, or c'mmands, very simply and clearly to Pclly, so that she could not fail to understand him.

When he had finished he did not feel any surprise at finding her silent and motionless for some minutes, for he knew that Polly often hesitated to speak too quickly, for fear he should charge her—as he often did, and justly—with answering from her quick heart without having received the sense of what he had said into her slow mind at all.

He waited patiently.

At last the thought of how many minutes must have passed since the ceasing of his own voice, troubled him suddenly. The doubts he had felt, the strange fear he had had when he touched her face, as she slept, returned to him all at once as the strange-ness of her silence came over him like a bitter chill.

Why, he wondered, did he hesitate to speak to her, to stretch his arm towards her? He could not tell, but he did hesitate till the silence lengthened painfully.

At last he moved his arm, and found that she had gone away from his side. Then a cry with anger in it as well as fear broke from him.

"Polly, why don't yer answer me?"

Straining his ears as he half sat, half lay with his face stretched forward, he heard her quick, excited breathing.

"Answer me, Polly," he cried less angrily, more beseechingly. "Tell me as you'll do what I said you must do. Answer me."

From the corner towards which a vague instinct had caused him to turn his face Polly's voice came at last, low, so low he could but just hear it, and heavily burdened with misery—

"I can't do it, daddy. I can't swear as I see.l the light."

The voice seemed to creep tremblingly along the prison floor, so that he knew Polly was cast down in great distress in that corner to which she had taken herself.

"Who is it," he asked hoarsely, "a-speak-ing to me like that? It's never Polly?"

"I can't swear as I seed the light; it *is* me as ses it, daddy."

"It is!" cried Bardsley, quivering on his elbow, and speaking in a voice of solemn anger. "Then what evil speret is a-tempting of you to speak and to be'ave like this, Polly, in return for all I've done for yer?"

Polly was silent. She could not tell him what spirit it was. She could not understand herself, and was still less able to describe to him these moments of mental and spiritual seeing; when she beheld her wretched little life with such passionate consternation, counting up her miseries, and making moan over herself as some opium-dulled mother, free for a few moments from her stupor, might wail over her starving and ill-used babe.

Polly was not moaning now; her tears were falling fast and silently on the thin little arms that pillowed her face as she lay cast down upon the stones.

"Come, Polly," said Bardsley in a conciliatory but intensely anxious voice, "you've got one of your crazy fits on—throw it off, Polly, throw it off."

It was one of Polly's trials to have these times of terrible sanity called madness—for Bardsley never thought them anything else, though often during them she wailed out some bitter truth to him.

The only answer that she could make now was a repetition of the cry—

"Daddy, I can't swear as I seed the light."

"So," said Bardsley, after remaining some time in angry silence, "Polly is a-goin' to ruin her old grandfather, is she? And for a whim—a fit o' nonsense?"

"No; it's 'cos I can't, daddy—I can't swear as I seed the light."

"And why can't yer, you unnatural, wicked gal? Why can't yer? Don't roar; but answer me why can't yer?"

"'Cos I'se afraid as God a'mighty won't never again let me see if I do—if I swears I 'as when I 'asn't."

By the burning of Polly's cheeks in uttering this it might have been a most shameful confession. It required no little bravery on her part to utter it; for she knew it would bring Bardsley's ridicule upon her, as indeed it did, promptly and bitterly, in a laugh and an oath together.

At this she sobbed aloud.

"'Nough o' that row, now!" cried Bardsley sternly. "I see wot it is—it's that confounded school nonsense a workin' in yer 'ead. Now, Polly, is it possible as you can't yet bring yer mind to understand wot I've told yer so many times as to the subjec' of the same religion not being conformable to all speres o' life? Now, I arst yer to put it to yerself like a sensible gal, Polly. Take the case of a—a—a statement of a fact as isn't a fact. Well, now, do you mean to say on yer honour, Polly, it's the same thing whether it's done ter save a person from ruin, or whether it's done by a fine lady in her drarin'-room 'earin' a double knock at the door, and reflectin' she ain't got her best cap on, or fancyin' she got a glimpse out o' winder of an old gown as she gave seven year ago to a poor relation as may ha' come

down thinkin' it's time the bounty was renooed? Now, I arst yer, Polly, do you think it's the same?"

As Polly at the best of times was incapable of argument, she did not attempt any answer to this perplexing question.

"Depend on it, Polly," continued Bardsley, "God a'mighty 'ud a great deal rayther you'd save your old grandfather from ruin than be a-puffin' up yer 'eart with religion at such a ilconwenient time as this. I'd always have yer say yer prayers, Polly, and believe in a Providence above as wisits awful retribution on all as furgits the blind, or in anyways worrits 'em, and as is something to look to when all else fails. But fur people in our station to be expectin' to keep to a religion which I've heered is as much or more than them in the 'ighest circles can live up to, why it's rank presumption, Polly, and nothink else."

If continuing in the same determination might be called presumption, Polly remained presumptuous still, for Bardsley had no sooner ceased speaking than she again put forth her feeble, drawling, but obstinate cry—

"I can't swear as I seed the light!"

"Then don't!" shouted Bardsley fiercely. "Ruin yerself and ruin me, you——"

And he launched at Polly such a selection of epithets as none but one brought up like herself, with very free and liberal ideas of language, could hear without horror. Even with these ideas Polly was much shocked and shaken; for it is certain that the accepting a vocabulary as being right and proper, and the having its hardest words hurled at oneself, are two very different things. A more piteous lamentation arose from her corner, and Bardsley's fierce abuse smouldered down to a low and ominous muttering.

Suddenly he got up and felt his way to the corner where Polly was.

"Polly," he said, holding his rage in strong control as he stood over her, "as nothing else can turn you from this wicked state o' mind, I shall be compelled to tell yer what I didn't wish to say nothing about to yer yet, but now I can't 'elp myself; so set up and stop this howling, and I'll tell yer what I have brought yer down to this —— place for."

Polly sat up.

"Are you a-listenin'?" asked Bardsley sharply.

"Yes, daddy."

He paused for some time, leaning his shoulder against the wall.

"I 'spose you ain't guessed at all wot I did come down here for, Polly?"

"No," answered Polly with a sigh, which

seemed to express a heartfelt opinion that, whatever the journey was for, it had been a great mistake.

"Well, I've come after that scamp," said Bardsley, "that's wot I've come after, Polly."

He bent his head, endeavouring to detect by breath or movement any effect his words might have had on Polly.

An unnatural stillness was over the little form at his feet. Whether it denoted surprise, consternation, pleasure, or indifference Bardsley could not tell.

"Did you hear me, Polly?" he asked. "Do you understand where we're a-goin' when we git out of here?"

"Jigh Mills," answered Polly in a weary voice that might have come from one thrice her age.

"Exactly so," said Bardsley.

He waited then for something more from Polly, but she remained silent.

He was clearing his throat preparatory to giving her more information concerning the purport of their journey, when he felt Polly's hands flung on his feet, and heard her voice choked with sobs, crying—

"Don't, don't, don't, daddy! Don't go there; don't go there, and I'll swear I seed the light; only don't go there, don't go there."

Bardsley drew back a step.

"Polly," he said sternly, "I don't know you: there's nothink of you left but whims."

He was agitated, and spoke only to hide his agitation. He *did* know her at that moment as well as he knew himself. He understood, much too well for his peace of mind, the kind of struggle that was making her writhe at his feet.

He knew that every instinct of self-respect or honour which her hard life had left in her would be moved to strong and bitter rebellion against the threatened visit to the Mills—and he knew how much too simple she was to perceive that, remaining true to her purpose of not swearing that she had recovered her sight, was the surest way of preventing this visit.

But though for a little while Bardsley was moved by this simplicity in her, he did not scruple to take cruel advantage of it, as it was for this very thing that he had made what would appear to be so unwise a revelation to Polly.

"Very well, Polly," he said, crouching down and patting her shoulder, "then that's our bargain, eh? You swears us out o' this like a brave good lass as you are, and has yer own way ever after."

Polly submitted to his conciliatory pats like a lifeless creature. She was so strange

that he judged it best to say nothing for several moments.

He had no pangs of conscience in thus cheating one whom it was so very easy to cheat, but reasoned with himself that weak things like Polly were not to be managed at all without such stratagems.

What was she doing, he wondered, with her face down against the stones, so silent and so still? Taking leave, perhaps, of that far-away, strange thing she called the light, which she thought she must no more hope to see after this day when her lips were to swear falsely concerning it.

"Innercint little fool," thought Bardsley, sending up his ragged coat-cuff to do his eyes a necessary service, "as if—if there *was* anythink to pay for this sort o' thing—Providence wouldn't send in the bill ter *me;* and a long un it 'ud be—Lord 'elp me!"

While he was waiting and listening for Polly to move, he heard the sound of keys rattling and bolts being drawn in the direction of the front of the building. Apparently some doors were opened, for immediately afterwards the sound of a fine organ penetrated to the cell where they were.

Bardsley knew it was the old organist practising in the church on the other side of the narrow street in which the prison stood. He and Polly had been humbly admiring listeners to this early performance every morning since their arrival at Balver's Bay. Indeed, the old man had found it rather a profitable kind of amusement, for the organist was only too happy to buy a pennyworth a day of such profound and ecstatic admiration as the blind man's face and waving hands testified, while Polly drooped and wept with childish memories, or lifted up her face sweet and smiling with a renewal of childish hopes, and Jowler outside in the churchyard stood first on one tombstone and then another in sculpturesque attitudes, trying to see in at the windows, wondering what was going on, and having a gnawing suspicion of breakfast.

When Bardsley heard the grand sound coming as the angel came to Peter, calmly triumphant over bars and bolts and all prison fastnesses, he growled a curse upon the white-haired player, for he knew it would disturb Polly again with thoughts of her babyish school-days.

He was not wrong. In a minute she lifted her face from the stones. She rose to her elbow—to her knee—to her feet, pausing to listen between each movement.

She stood listening, her arms crossed, a hand laid on each shoulder, hugging the memory of that little pure white cape of the blind-school uniform, which might have kept the wilful heart as pure, had she not cast it off so wantonly.

Bardsley knew, felt fully how excited she was growing, and expected each instant she would cry out to him and give him more trouble.

She did cry out, in mingled passion, misery, and triumph, but not to him.

"O our Father!" cried Polly, "Our Father 'chart'n 'eaven! I won't swear as I seed the light!"

At that moment Bardsley heard the rattling of keys close outside the door, and voices, from which he made out that the gaoler had brought himself into trouble by placing them together.

The door was presently opened, and then the glory of the angel that had come to Polly's succour rushed in and filled the cell. Bardsley leapt to his feet, blaspheming and stretching out his arms, more in impotent desire to wrestle with those sweet and powerful sounds for possession of Polly's tender spirit, than to offer any resistance to the men who had come to take her weary form away from him for but an hour or two.

Another moment and the door was closed again, and a lonely mass of rags lay heaving on the prison floor.

CHAPTER XIX.

ONE evening, about a week after their visit to Bulver's Bay, Michael shut up the mill early, whistled to Keeper, and went some miles along the Tidhurst road to meet and walk home with Ma'r S'one, whom he expected to be returning about this time.

The old man had been sent off to Tidhurst cattle fair early that morning, greatly over-burdened and saddened by the charge of a fine hog of fourteen stone, which, in consequence of a suspicion of measles, Mrs. Grist had desired to have sold immediately, and at its fullest price.

He appeared to be greatly surprised and touched by Michael's attention in coming to meet him and relieving him of some heavy farm implements which he had had to purchase at Tidhurst and carry home.

As they walked along together, Ma'r S'one's repeated sighs and solemn shakes of the head led Michael to fear that he and his errand had met with the very worst of ba l luck, and that he had real cause for being alarmed at meeting Mrs. Grist. He forebore questioning him, feeling sure it would not be many minutes before the old man would confide his trouble to him. Without seeming to loiter for him he suited his strong step to Ma'r S'one's uncertain, plodding trot.

"Stopped at th' aarf-way 's' aarfternoon, Ma'r Michael," he began presently, evidently finding walking and talking at once a great labour, and more than his breath could manage without much trouble.

"Ah," said Michael, well knowing that Ma'r S'one alluded to the old half-way house between Lamberhurst and Tidhurst, where the coaches used to stop before the railway came to Bulver's Bay. "Well, you're no bad judge, Mr. Ma'r S'one. Old Piggot's ale's the best in Southdownshire. When I go by every Wednesday I have a glass regularly."

"Ay, ay, I thart ye did," said Ma'r S'one, with a little sudden, sprightly mischief in his eye and voice. "I thart ye did, Ma'r Michael."

"You thought I did? Why, how in the world should you know?" asked Michael.

"I wur round there with your maister in the waggon o' Friday mornin'," answered Ma'r S'one, shaking his head slyly; "and Fleetfoot he drared up grandly at th' aarf-way—grandly, he did."

While Michael wondered for some minutes why Ambray had not spoken to him concerning Fleetfoot's revelation, Ma'r S'one relapsed into his former sadness—the sighing and the shaking of the head recommenced.

"Yees," he began again after a little while, "I stopped at th' aarf-way 's' aarfternoon."

"Ah, by-the-by, so you said," answered Michael encouragingly.

"'Arry Piggot carled me in, and there were a chaap there a-read'n' out the noospaper. O they be arful, they papers—arful."

"What was the matter this afternoon?" inquired Michael.

Ma'r S'one sighed heavily, and answered in a trembling voice—

"T'wur 'bout that poor blind cretur'."

"Who! The girl we saw on Tuesday?"

"Ay; they've give 'em six weeks ave it, Ma'r Michael."

"Six weeks of it!" repeated Michael. "Have they now? Well, I suppose that old rascal deserves it. I suppose they both deserve it—don't you think so yourself, Mr. Ma'r S'one?"

Michael spoke quickly, and while his thoughts were far away from what he said. He had not paused to think whether old Bardsley and his grandchild deserved their sentence, or whether it was an unjust one.

His only feeling on hearing Ma'r S'one's news had been one of glad relief. For six weeks he need not be expecting any disclosures to Ambray concerning George. He had seen a two-days' old paper at the Team every day since their arrest, and had searched in it vainly for any news of the blind impostors.

Six weeks! Who could tell whether by the end of such a time that might not be known at the High Mills which would render the worst Bardsley could have to say stingless and trivial?

They had walked on for nearly ten minutes in silence, and Michael had forgotten the question he had asked Ma'r S'one, when he was startled by the old man saying,

"You never arst me 'bout th'og, Ma'r Michael."

"No; but I've been wondering all the way what luck you've had, Mr. Ma'r S'one."

"Arful—arful," groaned Ma'r S'one. "Arful luck!"

Michael uttered an exclamation of sympathy and condolence.

"But what did you get for him then?" he asked.

Ma'r S'one looked up as one aghast, and answered in a choking voice—

"Just what missus said—two pound eighteen and fourpence—Ma'r Michael."

"What? four and twopence a stone! Well done!" cried Michael.

"Ah," said Ma'r S'one with much difficulty and catching of breath, "but you shud a see th' old chaap as baught it, Ma'r Michael,—arl bent, an' gray and saarft in th'ea.l he wur, and grinny-at-nothing like, and aarf a score older 'an me, Ma'r Michael, he telled me esself."

Michael tried to comfort him by assuring him he had acted but as any one else would have done, but his words had no power to remove the old man's conviction that he deserved imprisonment tar more than Polly Bardsley.

Michael parted from Ma'r S'one at Buckholt Farmhouse.

He was carrying his purchase down the yard for him, and had nearly passed the front door before he noticed that Mrs. Grist was standing there.

No sooner did Ma'r S'one also become aware of this fact, than he made a nervous attempt to possess himself of what Michael was carrying for him.

Mrs. Grist, however, had already seen them, and Ma'r S'one was soon shaking at the sound of her voice, and looking helplessly at Michael.

"Well, Ma'r S'one," she called out, "I shud ha' thart you hadn't so much to do to fatigue you but what you could a ca'ied your own little harrants 'rom Tidhurst without having a pz ,sel o' men to bring 'em home for you."

Mrs. Grist invariably spoke of Michael as plural, often to his perplexity, causing him to look round to see who might without his knowledge be accompanying him. He ha l grown used to it by this time, and gave her a civil "Good evening" as he put down Ma'r S'one's little errands, which consisted of two new pitchforks and a heavy horse-collar.

"I tell you what, Ma'r S'one," cried Mrs. Grist, without deigning to notice Michael's respectful salutation, "when you're out for your own pleasure you go into what company you like—I'm not going to look after you at your age—not I; but when you're on business o' mine, you'll please to keep yourself to yourself, so let that be a understood thing, or you and me will farl out."

"Yes, missis," answered Ma'r S'one in a great tremble, and signing to Michael by imploring jerks of his elbow to go and leave him.

"And I shud like to know how much longer you are going to stand there," she continued almost in the same breath, "without a word o' 'pology for bein' so late, an' they caarves left without bite nor sup this nine hour. It's a deal o' use me keepin' a elderly man as wants constant physicking and pampering—o' purpose to be responsible and stiddy, to feed the animals, and he behaving just for arl the world like a giddy lad. Do you hear me, Ma'r S'one, or do you intend to stand there sett'n' me at defiance arl night?"

The "physicking" to which Mrs. Grist alluded had been the administration by her of a black draught on one occasion, about a year ago, when Ma'r S'one, from the effects of overwork, had been unable to rise in the morning; the "pampering" had been the swallowing of a little gruel the next day, when he was too sick to take anything else.

The idea of setting any one at defiance was so terrible to Ma'r S'one that he shook like an aspen as he protested, in a voice full of distress—

"I wur goin' to 'polergize 'bout bein' so laate, missis, but you was tellin' me 'bout th' caarves. I wur laate because I gits along so slow; and 'Arry carled me in th' aarf-way just ter arst me how you was."

Ma'r S'one did tell small untruths sometimes for "peace and quiet." And this was one, as Michael knew by the faint flush that came over his hard little cheek.

"But I 'polergize humbly, missis," he added. "And I——"

"When you've done these parltry s'cuses, Ma'r S'one," interrupted Mrs. Grist sharply, "I shall be glad if you'll please to recollect I'm waiting arl this time to hear about the business you was sent on."

Ma'r S'one, after much fumbling, drew the purse from his bosom, and with a guilty glance at Michael, gave its contents into Mrs. Grist's fat hand.

Her face expressed so much satisfaction that Ma'r S'one began to feel a little consoled for all his misgivings of conscience.

"Come, that's arl right," she said, putting the money into her pocket; but the next instant her eye and voice were as sharp as before, when she looked at Ma'r S'one and observed—

"But you know this is just a proof o' what I'm arlways sayin', Ma'r S'one, as you *can* do much more 'an you chooses to do."

Even Ma'r S'one's patient spirit was stung by the injustice of this remark.

"I does arl as lays i' my power, missis—"

Page 57.

"There, don't argue at me, Ma'r S'one," cried Mrs. Grist; "I wouldn't ha' that if you was as old as Thuseler. Come now, I shall be glad if you'll get th' yard cleared o' your friends. You know it's a thing as I never allow no one; a pack o' strangers on the premises arfter dark, speshly from London."

Michael, who had had reasons of his own for waiting, came forward at this, and pretending not to have heard any of the doubtful allusions to himself, inquired if he could take any message to the High Mills for her.

As Mrs. Grist also feigned deafness, and

turned her back upon him, Michael went up the yard with Ma'r S'one, who let him out at the gates with many expressions of humble gratitude for his company. He also apologised to h'm for having tried to hasten his departure.

"But you see I didn't want fur to aggrawate missis." He explained—"She's arful haard to-night, but it's best not to aggrawate, but to do arl we can fur peace and quiet."

And as Michael turned away he heard the old man murmuring to himself—

"'Cline our 'erts to keep this la !"

CHAPTER XX.

THE spring continued fine. The children came up in troops to the mill-field to look after their floral types, the daisies. The beauty of Michael's new world increased around him with such soft but marvellous speed, that often when he came in the morning to look out at the mill window, he would, after his first glance at the earth, push back his cap, murmuring aloud some word of wonder, and throwing upward, as if straight into God's eyes, a smile of irrepressible lowly, but full-hearted congratulation, as intensely real as that with which some humble workman in a great sculptor's studio might turn to his master after beholding a night's progress of the inspired hand.

Michael loved the summer, and throve in it so well that it was now only the sorrow of those amongst whom he lived that kept alive his own.

As it was now known that George's pictures had not been accepted,—if they had been sent,—and as he still did not come or write, every day which passed seemed to increase the probability that ties stronger than those of home were holding him. For this reason Michael knew that Ambray and Nora regarded these sweet summer days only as lovely thieves stealing wealth from their treasure-house of hope.

Nora little dreamed who knew her best in those days of outward sweetness and inward bitterness,—whose honest eyes watched her from afar when she walked in her aunt's garden, or stood trying to interest herself in seeing the hops tied to the sticks,—whose thoughts followed her at evening up to the old drawing-room,—whose ears listened to the music to which she tuned the sorrows of her heart there in the twilight, when the cows were lowing to Ma'r S'one as he softly shut door after door in the yard, and tottered gratefully to his bed in the stable, a little and yet a little more weary each day than the last.

One evening when Ambray was alone in the mill, and Michael was returning from a journey with Fleetfoot, he suddenly saw passing by the smithy two figures, which he felt certain could belong to none but Bardsley and his grand-daughter.

Long before he came into the village they had disappeared.

Michael stopped at the smithy, and called the old smith out to look at one of Fleetfoot's shoes which he had put on that morn-ing. The smith saw nothing wrong with it, and disagreed with Michael as to the necessity of doing his work over again.

Michael, however, insisted in a voice and manner almost menacing, and turned away up the White Lane, leaving the waggon standing there, and the smithy loungers staring after him open-mouthed.

CHAPTER XXI.

WHEN Michael reached the top of the White Lane, and the mill-field lay level before him, he saw nothing of the two figures.

They must have gone into the mill.

Michael set off running and burst in at the mill door, breathless and with a tiger-like fire in his great eyes.

First he saw Ambray, who stood with folded arms looking towards the door, as if he had heard his hurried steps and watched for him.

He turned to look in that direction which Ambray fronted, and then he saw Bardsley standing with his hat in his hand and Polly leaning at his side looking giddy and scared with the noise of the mill.

They were considerably thinner, paler, and more ragged than when he had last seen them. In that hurried and excited glance it seemed to him that Bardsley's face showed less cunning and satire, more bitterness and desperation than formerly.

"You are in a hurry, Michael," said Ambray, with a look and tone of peculiar meaning, of which Michael could understand nothing, and at which he could only wonder vaguely.

He attempted no reply, but returned Ambray's look, quite incapable of hiding his great excitement from him.

"Here are some friends of yours, you see," Ambray said, still looking at him with the same searching expression.

"Friends of mine?" echoed Michael with a laugh, scarcely knowing what he was saying.

Bardsley showed the same kind of interest in listening to and considering over Michael's voice as he had done on the occasion of his former visit to the mill. Now, as then, he seemed to feel he was mistaken in thinking he had heard it before.

Michael too watched as he had watched then for the effect his voice would have upon the blind man. And this time he thought, as he had thought before, it was not remembered by him.

Seeing this, he was but the more amazed

5

at the thought of Ambray's evident suspicion of him in connection with Bardsley.

All possible conjectures passed through his mind startlingly and rapidly. Was Bardsley cheating him? Had he recognised him from the first? Did he know the secret of George Ambray's absence, and inquire after him only to mislead Michael as to the purpose of his visit?

"Well," said Ambray, turning to Bardsley, "and I am to understand, then, that until this man came in your way you were prosperous and comfortable?"

"We was so, sir," replied Bardsley; "the talk and envy of neighbours. Our means was not large, certainly; but neither was our wants, sir. I would have had you see this child in those days, sir."

"Let the girl sit down," said Ambray, himself touching her shoulders, and guiding her to a low bin. "She looks bad enough now," he added.

"So I am told, sir," answered Bardsley; "the truth is, sir, her spirit is broke by these ewents as I have told you of. In them days of which I was troubling of you with some account of it, was often remarked to me what a pictur' of 'ealth she were, and what a pictur' it was to see her, gay as e'er sighted on earth, sir, a-sitting at the door platting away at her baskets and a-singin' to the bird over her 'ead—as they say ud look down out of it's cage all in a heap and sulky at bein' outdone in it's own pertickler line of hart, which I have observed, sir, is a thing tryin' to the feelings of most on us, and to many as is of a 'igher moral tone than birds. But I detain you too long, sir, over these recklections of 'appier days."

"Yes, yes, be quick," said Ambray; "you were telling me, before the door opened just now, that some of your neighbours blamed *you* for all this."

"They did, sir," replied Bardsley; "they blamed me for havin' allowed his wisits; but I am a simple old man, sir, of a trustin' nature, and for seemin' honesty and straightforradness of character I never met one like him. *I* shud 'a trusted him to the last, sir. Ah, you see, sir," sighed Bardsley, drawing his sleeve across his eyes, and speaking in a voice broken with sobs, "it's so easy to deceive the blind."

"The villain!" cried the simple old miller, trembling with rage and turning his back on Michael.

"Yes, sir," whined Bardsley, proud of this stroke of success, "it is so very easy to deceive the blind and 'elpless."

"Easy to who, to what kind o' man is it easy?" asked Ambray, looking at Michael with eyes full of angry scorn. "Tell me who this scoundrel is, and what I have to do with him, that you come to me with this tale —that's all I want to know."

Bardsley hesitated.

"I—I feel for you, sir," he stammered; "it will be a shock to you, sir. You mustn't be too hard on him, sir."

"Who is he, I ask you, and what have I to do with him?" repeated Ambray with stern impatience.

Bardsley appeared to be seriously disturbed by the task before him. His face grew flushed, his eyeballs rolled, and his fingers worked nervously.

"Indeed, sir," he said, "I feel for you— I do, sir, with all my heart—in making known, sir, that this young man is your—is no other, sir, than your—"

"What now?" cried Ambray, for Michael had seized the beggar by his coat-collar, and was holding him off and looking into his master's face with a gaze that puzzled and amazed him.

"Your—your servant, he means," cried Michael, in a voice so deep and thick Ambray scarcely recognised it.

There was one in the mill who did, however, for no sooner had Michael spoken than Bardsley became too excited even to remember the indignity he had received.

"Ha!" he shouted, throwing his hands upon Michael's shoulders. "*Now* I know the voice!"

"Then mind it," muttered Michael close in his ear. "As you value the life I saved, a word more now and you shall repent it."

He turned towards Ambray, with eyes that had never looked more true—more full of devotion and courage.

"You have found me out, master," he said, scarcely above his breath. "Isn't that enough? Have I any right to ask you to leave me alone to satisfy this man. If I have I would."

Ambray gave him a look in which there was almost as much disappointment as contempt, and went out, closing the door violently after him.

"What lies are these you have come here with?" demanded Michael.

Bardsley was shaking himself, pulling up his collar, and gradually recovering from the effects of Michael's somewhat rough handling.

"You saved my life," he answered, "otherwise I might offer objections to the term.

You saved my life, which is a haction as ought to ha' won you universal gratitude and respect, consequently I will *not* offer objections to your havin' seen fit to come between me and George Ambray's father, as I've come from London on purpose to see. I will only ask you *why* you did it?"

When the old miller had gone out, Michael's overwrought excitement had left him suddenly, and the consequences of what he had done oppressed him like a nightmare.

After his first half-frantic question to Bardsley, he had turned dizzy and gone to lean against the steps.

Glancing at Bardsley as this question, with all its suspense and fear, forced itself upon him, he saw what he had not before noticed, that the old man was very far from sober.

His grand-daughter, a picture of weariness and stupor, had fallen asleep where Ambray had seated her.

Bardsley was standing, sulky and perplexed, evidently waiting with no slight misgiving some explanation of Michael's conduct.

"So here is a second time," said Michael suddenly, "that I've saved your precious life for you."

"Eh?" cried Bardsley, lifting up his face in much alarm.

"Well," answered Michael, "I can tell you it would have been about as much as your life was worth to have let that old man know that the rascal you had been telling him of was his son. I wouldn't answer for what might have happened if I hadn't been here to stop you."

"I've always heerd as this old miller is a just and a honourable man," asserted Bardsley, "as wouldn't see the blind and 'elpless imposed on."

"He's one who wouldn't condemn his only son on the evidence of those who he's seen making imposition a business," said Michael quietly.

"Do you mean he wouln't believe me?" cried Bardsley, clenching his fists. "If it's proofs and witnesses you want, I could overrun your parish with 'em any day."

"Then why do you come here without any—with nothing but your tongue to tell your tale with?"

"Because I was driv' by misfortchins to come as I could. But trust me, young man, *I'll* make this place ring with his rame aiore I've done with him. Friend as yer are of his, I tell you that."

"How do you know I'm a friend of his?"

"Wasn't you with him that night? Wasn't your cry, 'Hold, George! hold!' my sen-

tence o' life, as I may say? Ha! I knowed your woice from the first, though I couldn't, so to say, lay my finger on where I'd heard it before—not till you pitched me agin the wall just now, and calls to the miller, 'Your servant!' in just the woice as you said, 'Hold, George! hold!' Then I knowed yer."

Michael had become very pale while Bardsley was speaking, and had more than once started as if passionately to silence him.

For a moment or two he remained without saying anything, his eyes fixed steadily on the beggar's face. After this he rose from leaning against the steps, and approaching Bardsley with folded arms, said—

"Now, what was it you were saying to my master before I came in?"

"It's a weakness o' mine," answered Bardsley, "to like to know a person's right to ask such a question as that."

"Haven't I a right to ask it as George Ambray's friend?"

"If you are George Ambray's friend, friend enough to give yer a right to ask such a question, you are friend enough for him to have told you all about my affair with him without my doing it."

"Then I should be all the better able to know if your account of it is true."

"Then I shan't repeat it," cried Bardsley impatiently. "I didn't come here to dispute —I ain't got my case ready to dispute. I came here t' appeal, not to dispute—though I'll do as mucn as you like o' that when I has things ready."

"Now, Bardsley," said Michael, laying his hand on his shoulder, "let me give you a bit of advice."

"It's a thing as don't generally agree with my digestion," replied the old man, trying sulkily to jerk the hand from his shoulder.

"But you'll find that this will, and I give it to you, Bardsley, as well out of consideration for your affliction, and"—looking round at Polly—"hers, as for *him*. I mean George Ambray. You are right, I *am* his friend, and I would like to do the best I can for him now that he is—not here to receive you and defend himself. My advice is, say no more to Ambray. Tell me the whole truth, prove it to me, and I will do the best that can be done as to making you amends if amends are due to you. What good can Ambray do you? He has barely enough to live upon, any one here will tell you that. I have the means of giving you some help if I see that you ought to have it."

Bardsley considered for some time, rubbing his hand over his face.

"Look here," he said, with decision : " I shan't tell you to-night what I'll do, except as I'll promise you to do nothing one way or another till you come to me at the Bay, that's to say, if you'll come to-morrow some time before evening."

"Why not tell me now? you know my time is not my own," said Michael.

" Well, if you must know why," answered Bardsley, " I should prefer as my head was a little clearer than I find it at present, owing to having had to let Polly rest rather oftener than usual on our way up here."

"At least let me know what you told Ambray," said Michael ; " it didn't take you very long to tell it to him."

Bardsley was obstinate. He could not trust his head to tell anything that was to be disputed, he informed Michael.

" Arst for me at the Barge Aground," directed Bardsley, " and I will leave 'em acquainted with my whereabouts."

It was about half-an-hour later when Ambray returned home from the mill.

Michael, when he came in, was sitting at the table bending over a letter for home which he had been writing by snatches for the last week. He looked up in patient expectation of the storm that was to burst.

The gaunt old miller had a look of triumph in his face, as well as sadness and contempt—the triumph of a man vain of his judgment who finds a favourite prophecy fulfilled.

Michael returned his look with great gentle eyes, full of resignation and courage.

Instead of closing the door after him, the miller stood holding it open.

" Come," he said to Michael, pointing out. " March I I'll have no scoundrels here."

PART VI

CHAPTER XXII.

"COME," said the miller, seeing that Michael did not move; "take yourself off. If my son was here you would not wait to be told twice. Out with you, you hypocrite!"

Michael sat still, his hands locked on the table before him. He was too much confused and stunned to be able even to guess as to what kind of disgrace he had taken from George's name to his own. He felt as yet like one fallen from a height —too breathless, too much paralysed to know his own injuries.

The word hypocrite stung him a little; his shoulders heaved rebelliously. He drew a deep breath, and looked at Ambray with heavy and perplexed eyes.

Mrs. Ambray, alarmed on her husband's account by his expression, laid her hands upon Michael in weak command and strong entreaty.

"You've never deceived *me*, Michael Swift," declared the miller in triumphant severity. "I've known you for a different man from what you seemed since the first time you darkened my mill-door. I've suspected something between you and this Bardsley, too, ever since I was told you sent him away without letting me know he had asked for me. Ah, you can't keep these sort of things in the dark *here*, you see; this isn't London."

As Michael drew another hard breath, Mrs. Ambray tremblingly gave his head a push, at the same time commanding that he should not be insolent to his master when he saw him in the heat of passion.

"Who is in a passion?" asked a voice at the door; and all three turning to look, saw Nora Ambray standing there.

Mrs. Ambray hastened to meet her; Michael went and stood hesitatingly at the foot of the stairs that led from this room straight to his attic. The miller's eyes followed him sternly, avoiding Nora's, which were fixed on her uncle with gentle, smiling accusation, as knowing none other would dare to be in a passion under this roof.

Coughing and trembling, the miller threw himself into the wooden arm-chair by the fireplace.

In doing this his elbow knocked a little slate hanging near the mantelpiece, and made it swing and clatter against the wall.

Ambray turned and looked at it; then resting his elbow on the chair-back, leant his head on his hand and sighed bitterly.

It was on this slate that his debt to Michael had been recorded from the day of his arrival at the High Mills in the second week of March.

He rose and supported himself by leaning against the table near where his niece stood.

"Nora," he said, "I would do almost anything rather than ask you to intercede for me with your Aunt Grist again, but there's no help for it. I must give this man his wages and be rid of him. I can't and won't, while there's life in me, let such a rascal fall into George's very footsteps here — taking his place in this house, at chu.ch along with us, and everywhere. No, I will not bear it."

"Why do you stand there, Michael Swift," demanded Mrs. Ambray sharply, "irritating your master by holding your tongue when I dare say you could explain if you liked, and pacify him?"

"Not he!" cried the miller, turning upon Michael defiantly. "Explain! I don't know any explanation a man can offer for cheating and misleading the blind but that he is a worthless wretch that nothing better can be expected from."

Michael at that moment knew none of the inward peace or confidence supposed by some people to be the portion of the falsely-accused. He was, on the contrary, finding himself every instant less and less able to endure with patience or resignation the consequences of his rash impulse. The anxiety with which he waited for the nature of the sin he had claimed as his being made known to him, was intensely painful. The shame which had already fallen on him was probably twice as hurtful as it would have been to one that deserved to be ashamed, and that was not so utterly unused to such a burden as was Michael, who had led the life of a child and a slave, and had been kept so sinless by his simplicity and his fetters together, that even calumny had forborne touching him.

The most spitefully disposed in his own village would as soon have thought of slandering the babe of a week old, or the white-haired Methuselah of the place, as " honest Michael ;" who, of course, being somewhat more sound and purely healthful of mind and heart than most men, was accounted a little " wanting ;" and looked after by the village loungers with taps of the forehead and sympathetic winks, especially when he had just parted two furious dogs, or walked out on a Sunday with the plainest girl in Thames Dutton, rather than she should sit alone, and watch her pretty sisters parading their swains before her window.

So Michael's head hung down with as heavy a shame as the greatest sinner's could have done before these three pairs of eyes all looking at him at once, and deciding with deep worldly wisdom that because the cap did not fit him at all, and he carried it with so ill a grace, it must be his.

Suddenly he raised his head and looked at his master as he stood holding the little slate at Nora's elbow, then turning went heavily up the stairs.

They heard him tramping hastily about.

" He is putting up his things, John," observed Mrs. Ambray in alarmed but meek remonstrance.

" What do you say, Nora ?" asked the miller, taking no notice of his wife. " You see he takes me at my word, as indeed he had better. Do you think Jane Grist will manage this for me ? I believe I would rather cut my hand off than let it touch her money, but I can't keep a scoundrel in my house."

Nora, having received an admonitory twitch of the sleeve from Mrs. Ambray, understood she was not to appear too sanguine on the subject. She therefore averted her eyes with an expression of profound consideration and dubiousness ; and when the silence became so long as to be embarrassing, looked up with an affectation of sudden hopefulness, inquiring briskly—

" What's to-day ?"

" Thursday," answered the miller, looking at her anxiously ; and Nora echoed—

" Thursday ?" lifting her brows with a look that seemed to say that of all days in the week Thursday was the most unpropitious one that could have been for obtaining what they wanted.

A firm, light step came down the stairs—unnaturally light and quick, the miller thought, for Michael's ; his movements being generally a little ponderous and slow, steady and sure.

His cap hung behind Ambray. He stretched his arm out and got it. Mrs. Ambray silently drew her husband's attention to this. The miller turned and scowled at him.

Michael returned his look with troubled, almost fierce, eyes. A panic was upon him ; a wild desire to cast down the idol of this household ; and he wished to escape while he yet had strength to control himself.

In turning to Michael, the miller had knocked the slate against him, and it had fallen to the brick-floor.

Michael looked down on it, then put his foot upon it twice, breaking it to pieces.

" Let my wages be forgotten, as my hard service has been," he said, in a voice that made Nora turn and look at him in amazement—it was so full of bitter and despairing solemnity.

" They will not be forgotten. I know where your father lives," answered Ambray. " I shall send your wages there. You deserve them, as you deserve this usage ; which you, no doubt, think hard, though I should treat my own son worse if he had acted as you have done."

At this Michael, having his hand upon the latch, turned, his eyes wild with the passion of some desperate reply ; and he must have then spoken words which would have cost him a lifelong and bitter regret had it not been for one of the most faint but subtle of influences.

The door of George's room opened out of this. It was open at the moment that Michael lifted the latch of the other door, and as he turned round in his passion a slight breeze blew from it bearing the scent of the flowers with which Mrs. Ambray, after country fashion, daily filled the little fire-place ; wondering each morning whether those she placed there might be destined to greet the eyes of him for whom, like disappointed revellers but just arrived in gay robes, and with sweet stores in bosom and sachet to make merry through the summer's day, they were taken in their first freshness of floss and odour, honey and dew, to deck this little temple of vain hope.

They were roses there now, whose breath seemed to proclaim them the rich heirs to all the sweetness of the flowers that had lived and died since the year's beginning; but to Michael, as the breeze brought their odour, it seemed like a sigh of bruised and patient love and hope, reminding him how long the vain watch had been kept there, and might still be kept.

He could not bid the watchers watch no more, and tell them that the tardy feet for which they listened would never reach their threshold, that the voice they longed for could never speak to prove to them how much sweeter is a dear sound heard afresh than one remembered ever so tenderly.

These things Michael could not tell them for reasons he thought good; but he remembered that by refraining from uttering the words that had risen to his lips ere the breeze from this still-sad room had touched them like an angel's finger, he might at least save the watchers from much bitterness.

So his tongue was stayed even while his heart was hot within him, and he left his master's house without another word.

CHAPTER XXIII.

MICHAEL had decided on walking to Bulver's Bay and spending the night there, that he might lose no time in the morning in seeking Bardsley, and learning the truth, or as much of it as possible, from him.

The sunlight was still lingering among the pine-stems when Michael passed the knoll, and his heavy heart knew a throb of pleasure as he looked at it and remembered that in spite of all that had happened this day, Lamberhurst was still ignorant of how easily the proud wrestler, the hero of this spot, had allowed the world to throw him.

The Long Ridge fields also received from Michael a more peaceful farewell look than they would have done had he yielded to his temptation to make known how grievously the bright runner, whose feet still seemed to him to press and spurn the summer grass, had swerved and slipped.

The evening was breezeless; its lull was without rest; its shade without dew; it seemed still day with all the sun's heat, but without its colour; the blue of the sky was blanched and faint; the sun burned down in pale, fierce fire, leaving no crimson pall to cover the slow hearse. All the mill-sails on the heights were still.

Michael stopped and looked back.

The white mill being nearest to the edge of the hill, he could see it and it only.

The sails had fallen to rest in a position that made them appear like a huge cross.

The instant Michael looked up and saw it, the feeling came over him that this mill and this valley were not to be departed from and borne only in remembrance by him. That with these things, already so familiar, he was to have yet a nearer, deeper acquaintance.

The great grey-white cross prophesied to him: or rather Michael hung his fears upon it and read them freshly from its face, until, as the heat came down between his eyes and it, he could fancy that it grew and spread, darkening half the valley.

He turned away with a deep certainty that one day he must return to suffer here perhaps the worst that he had ever feared since his great sorrow which led him to this place had befallen him.

A skylark darted from the corn close to him and rose, sending up into the heat-misted skies, and letting fall to the heat-blurred earth, a fountain of song, bright as morning, fresh as rain.

Michael, at this voice of gladness starting up out of the silence and languor like a sudden sweet deed from a stagnant life, looked up and laughed, and muttered while his worn upturned eyes danced in light—

"Well said, little silver-pipe! and I believe you too."

What was said, and what believed in, lay between Michael and the speck growing more and more minute against the blanched blue of the evening sky.

CHAPTER XXIV.

WHEN Michael, early in the morning, called at the Barge Aground, no one there knew where Bardsley was to be met with. On making a second call, an hour later, he heard he had been in for his morning draught, and had left word for Michael to join him on the beach beyond the Fish Market.

Michael, going in that direction, soon saw him in the distance, sitting alone, contemplative, ragged, solitary.

Bardsley knew his step, and listened to its approach, smiling with gratified vanity at the keenness of his ear.

As Michael looked at him, it struck him with some surprise that, as he sat there, his grey beard and rags the playthings of the wind, he appeared less repulsively wicked than pitifully, almost pathetically, insignificant and helpless. Perhaps, Michael thought, it could hardly be otherwise than that any form of evil *should* shrink and appear to diminish and wither here in these grand front ranks of nature merging into heaven, from which they seem curtained only by excess of light.

Or might it be, Michael wondered, that even the man whom he had thought as unlikely to change his sins as the leopard his spots, had not been able to sit here without receiving inwardly *some* cleansing touches from that spirit of strong, fresh purity that breathes here always, making the sands so fair, and revealing the thousand faint, sweet tints, and tender graining of the pebbles?

"Well, sir," said the blind beggar, as Michael stood still near where he was sitting, "here I am, you see, monarch of all I survey!"

His face, as he uplifted and turned it slowly from side to side while speaking, was not without a certain sadness and grim satire.

Michael looked at him, and was constrained to address him in a manner different from what he intended.

"Bardsley, you are an old man," he said. "You have a child that I suppose you care for—*one* child? This miller, *he* had——"

He stopped suddenly. Bardsley noticed the stop, and the word at which it was made. He did not, however, choose to let Michael perceive he had done so; but to prevent him from thinking this, altered and finished the sentence for him as if involuntarily.

"Yes, the miller has one child—one son—a very fine young man he is, too. As he's a friend of yours, may I ask where he might be at this present time?"

In his eagerness to come at some idea of how Michael received the question, the blind face was not sufficiently guarded, but showed Michael it was listening intently to the very change of his breathing, to the turn of his foot in the shingle.

Michael stepped back, looked at it hard, and grew pale.

"As I am George Ambray's friend," he said, commanding his voice as well as he could, "you may be sure I am not likely to have much patience to answer your questions about him. I may as well tell you at once that he will not meet you, or have anything to do with you in this affair, except through me. If you ask me why—I say, remember your last meeting."

"Well," said Bardsley after some hesitation, "you was saying about the miller having this one child like as I have Polly. What do you want to make of that? 'Do unto others as I'd be done by,' is that all the tune of it?"

"Whatever I was going to say, I say this

now," answered Michael, "that the nearer I find you keep to the truth in telling me about this affair, the better it will be for you and your poor child. Come, Bardsley, try it for once in your life, try it for her sake."

"What *you'd* call truth would be nothing but repeating word for word what young Ambray's told you, I suppose."

"No," returned Michael, "I can make allowances for both of you. I can see both sides of the story."

"Which is never alike," observed Bardsley, "to any of us, sighted or blind."

He remained for a moment or two silently digging into the beach with his stick. Suddenly he lifted his face towards the other with so savage an expression on it, that Michael began to hope he might be growing truthful.

"No doubt, young man," he said, in a tone of suppressed hatred, "you thought it a fine thing in your friend that he should be so good as to have such a intention for a day or a hour, though it was for a day or a hour only before he lived long enough to grow wiser. *He* marry Polly? Of course the intention alone ought to a' bin grand enough for us; what right had we to expect to see it carried out—or what right had my gal to faint dead in the church? or such as ud knowed her from her birth to cry out agin him? no right, of course—no more 'an you think I have now to come to his father when I'm starving and she's starving, and gets six weeks of it for bein' obligated to beg."

"Well," said Michael, fearful of letting the old man perceive his breathless interest and surprise, "don't waste your time in that way; tell me the simple facts—your side of the story, as you say; and depend upon it, I shall know if you try to deceive me in anything, and make it the worse for you."

"First of all," said Bardsley, "did he dare to breathe a word agin Polly as first he knowed her?"

"I answer nothing till you've told me all."

"Well," continued Bardsley, "at the time these artists first see Polly a-selling flowers and came a-clamouring to me tor to let her be a model, I take my oath as the child had more friends in 'igh circles than I can reklect to count. There was all the ladies connected with the blind school she'd bin in as an enfant, and run away from; not as she didn't feel herself a equil with any there, but quite the contrary through feelin's of independence such as always kept her family from risin' as it might otherwise have done. Well, these ladies, at the time I'm speaking of, had took fresh interest in her, and got her ever so much basket-work and straw platting to do. Others give her different things to do; she was as busy as a bee, and had so many fine friends a-calling on her and bringin' one another to see her, I was forced to give up out-door business and stay at home a purpose to answer their questions, which Polly was not quick at, and didn't used to give satisfaction with. Altogether I was not the only person as declared there hadn't bin so many visitors in our court not since Sally Cole, as you've no doubt seen represented in the travelling wax-works, lay in a trance at number three for seven months, never waking but only once when some gentlemen from the Temperance Society was there, when she expressed a wish to sign the pledge, and fell asleep agen as they put the pen into her hand. But you've read of it in the penny papers, as rose to tuppence on the day she spoke. Polly never rose the papers —her case was considered striking—as being a blind person as could work so hard and be so contented ; but simple industry and contentment can never, of course, be as taking to the public as the case of a young woman in a trance, as only wakes once in seven months to observe she is going to heaven, and consequently wishes to sign the pledge."

Bardsley pause l and rubbed his head with an old handkerchief he found somewhere in the recesses of his hat, blowing contemptuously with his lips, and in other ways expressing his impatience at the depravity of the public taste.

Michael in listening to him found it not at all easy to follow him in his many changes of mood. He would without any kind of warning pass from a bitterly truthful manner to one of grossly affected simplicity, which would in its turn glide almost imperceptibly into a tone of intense sarcasm and mockery.

"However," he went on, "since the young woman I have named retired into the country, havin'—as her mother gave out when a medical inquiry was talked of—a soul above earthly fame,—since then, sir, there has certainly bin no case to come up to Polly's. And at this heighth of our prosperity appears this young man—this gentleman, as I took him for, with his fine airs and speeches. Me and Polly's had up every day for models. Taking from models, I suppose you are aware, is the art, they 'as to study of looking at one person while drawin' another out of their own heads. At least I was led so to judge by the talk of the young gentlemen,

when the one as had been last drarin' us was out of the room, and when they always agreed as there was no likeness either in the case of myself or Polly. The modellin' took pretty well for some time, and when it began to fail in regard to myself, I must own to bein' to blame. I don't deny as I got tired of it. Sitting so long in one position, in the constant dread of being howled at, as if the person taking of you was in the last agonies, if you move a muscle, is apt to bring on crick in the neck, and nervous twitchin's all over. Then, too, the bein' called an old rascal, and charged with ruining a rising young genius, because self-respect has compelled one to sew up a few of one's rags, was more than I could stand in the cause of hart or haypence, so I give it up. Polly, unfortunately, did not give it up. She was a favourite in other ways than as a model, as she amused them with her chatter and with singing to 'em. They used to meet—shoals of 'em—at one another's lodgings, a purpose to hear her sing. One day young Ambray takes me by storm, coming down upon me with all manner o' names and abuse about Polly, about me letting her be where he had drared her hisself. He used to be took with those fits o' sanctification sometimes ; and it's what I used to hate in him more than anything. So did his friend, I found that out. He'd come all over good at once, and turn a nuisance to everybody till the fit was gone. Of course I was obliged to act by what he said, and forbid Polly going nigh any o' the set agin. Well, we were ruined by it. Polly's ladies crossed to the other side the way as they passed our court. You see the sort of meetings there had bin at Ambray's and the others' lodgings had made the evening parties scarce of young gentlemen; consequently Polly was past being forgiven—her poor name was picked to pieces, and ne'er a bit o' straw or basket stuff could the child get to plat it together agin. I don't say as your friend didn't have a life of it. Bein' the only one of the young men as took the affair to heart, and tried to help us as well as he could, he was of course fixed on as the worst; which at that time I am bound to say he was not, except in respect of having first led her amongst 'em. I never see anything like it in my life. The parish rose agin' him. I couldn't but pity him myself at that time. They tried to find out his father's address, that he might be wrote to ; but, bless you, my lord had kep' it so close, nobody even knew his father was a miller. He never let his own landlady see the address on his letters. They wanted to get money form him to send Polly to a school; and here the poor fellow hadn't paid his rent for I don't know how long. *I* would ha' let him alone with all my heart, then I would. He tried for a week or two to ride over it, and went about as proud and bright as ever; but one day he had to give in—they drove him to a fever. We heard from his landlady as he was very comfortable, two old maiden la.lies, with parish interests, having took upon themselves to take their knitting every day and sit beside his bed, and talk to him the whole afternoon, in hopes to bring him to a better mind. Altogether, what with peculiar cooking—as cooking often *is* peculiar when rent is backward—and what with the over-excitement of too much female society and an unusual rush of organs on the street, the poor young man was made *so* comfortable that it was said he wasn't likely ever to leave his bed again in this life. •Having but just heard this, judge o' my astonishment when one morning my door opens and I hear a quick, unsteady step come in, and something breathing short and fast, then feel the table shake, and hear Polly cry out, and then hear a voice saying to her, ' My child, we are not likely to make each other happy, God knows; but that these fools may see how good I think you, I will give you as honest a name as ever was, and put an end to their blabbing and make your life as peaceful as I can.' I had just presence of mind enough to go up and tell Traps, a friend o' mine in the bird line, who came down and spoke up to Mr. George, not only giving the consent of the family, meanin' me, as was too much shook by surprise to give it myself, but likewise made hisself a comfort to the young man in telling him how everything was to be managed for the wedding to take place as it might be the day after to-morrow. Traps was rather pressing in his offers to 'go home with him, and never leave him till the day, and he would have done so but that, as he told me, young Ambray give him such a look as he certainly *could* not and *did* not like. No sooner was he out of the house than Traps says to me, ' I hope all may turn out well, Bardsley,' which caused a quarrel, being that sort of observation which, when things *are* to all appearances turning out uncommon well, is lowering to the spirits. It was repeated by Traps more than once through that day and the next. Young Ambray came in for a few minutes on that next day to arrange the time we were to meet and other matters. Traps again was pressing in his offers to

attend him home, and again remarked upon his look as not liking it at all."

Bardsley ceased speaking and sat still a moment, after which he turned with sudden vehemence to Michael, crying,—

" Well! what more do you want? Am I to go into *that* day for you? No. *You* may fancy it yourself as *he* must 'a done; though he never see it, it must 'a reached him somehow; he couldn't live begone where he might without a-picturing of it to hisself—the church—the crowds in it—the waiting—the riot when the time was past and he had never come—Polly, like a corpse, carried home by Traps—the crowd howling."

Pausing again, the old man's face grew fierce, as if his ears still heard the tumult of that morning confusing him with useless anger and distress. Michael looked at him with pity. Several times he had been near interrupting him by some question that he longed to put, but remembering that it might show the old man his previous ignorance of these events in George's life, had refrained in time.

" Was there," he ventured to ask Bardsley gently some moments after he had ceased speaking, " was there any idea afloat at all among you of what caused him to change at the last ?"

" There was some talk," answered Bardsley sullenly, " of a letter from a young lady in the country that his landlady had give him that morning."

" And you never saw him again till——"

" Till you saved my life from him—no, I didn't."

Michael walked slowly to and fro between Bardsley and the sea for a minute or two, then stopped before him. He was thinking why should he not let Bardsley tell the story to George's father after all? Was there anything unforgivable in it to him? As the worst thing in it had apparently been done from devotion to Nora, could the miller hear it without much pity and full forgiveness? Then Michael remembered the question would immediately arise, why had *he* taken upon himself to shelter George? He stood imagining the look, the surprise, the questioning, the suspicion of Ambray, on learning for the first time that Michael Swift, the servant who had come to him as an utter stranger, had known his son. He anticipated all the questions that would be on the miller's lips—why had he concealed from them that he had known him; and then,—*where had he seen George last !*

That thought would have decided Michael, even if it had not been followed by the recollection that the story of the last night on which Bardsley had seen George would necessarily be told by him to the miller so far as Bardsley knew it, and that then the rest would be demanded of himself—how breathlessly he could well imagine.

So Michael told himself that while he still guarded that secret which was between him and the dead, this burden he had taken upon himself yesterday must be borne.

The question now was, how should he satisfy Bardsley sufficiently to keep him from again applying to the miller or endeavouring to discover George?

"Well, Bardsley, you have kept as near the truth as could be expected of *you*," he said, "and I promise you as much shall be done for you as can be, if you leave it to me and trouble George Ambray's father no more."

"I shall see young Ambray himself somehow," declared Bardsley. "He's a-coming into money, and he shall be made to pay for this, first thing."

"You will do nothing of the kind," answered Michael. "You will not see him or get anything from him but what you get through me. You can tell by my having let my master think it was me you meant had ruined you, as you called it, how determined I am in this."

Michael then sat down near him, and again explained to him the uselessness of appealing to Ambray, who had at present no means whatever of helping him. He hinted that George being obliged, for reasons he could not go into now, to keep out of the way, had empowered Michael to act for him in all his affairs as he thought best.

"And if," said Michael, "you pledge your word to come here no more, and to try and lead your grand-daughter into a better way of life, I will take the responsibility, on George Ambray's account, of giving you the means of doing so."

"Hark!" said Bardsley, raising his finger. "Talk o' angels—here she comes."

Michael looked both ways along the beach, but saw no one. Listening, however, he heard Polly's voice behind the cliff, and was not surprised that the artists should have been amused by her singing, which reminded him alternately of rough street-vendors and the sweetest wild birds, London Saturday nights and dewy mornings in the country.

"She's a-singing," explained Bardsley, "so as I shall hear and holler out to let her know where I am. She's a sweet little pipe of her own, ain't she? Hush! keep still, and

let's see if she don't find me out without me moving."

By this time Polly came in sight, with an empty basket on her head. She had ceased singing for a moment, but as she came along towards them she began again, putting her little brown hand to the side of her mouth, that the breeze might not blow her voice from the beach, and prevent its being heard by her grandfather, whom she was seeking. Michael was amused by her little song, as she gave the last line of each verse like a regular street cry:—

"All up and down old London town
In many a court and alley,
All day I cry 'Come buy, O buy
My lilies of the valley!

' Here's wilets too, all wet with doo,
Fair ladies, for your tilets;
All up the street they smells so sweet,
O who will buy my wilets?

" Here take this lot for half a grot,
I'se got so drenched and chilly,
And never selled, for all I've yelled,
A blessed daffodilly!

" I'll ketch it so when home I go
With ne'er another fard'n;
I'd ryther die than have to cry
Sweet flow'r-roots for yer gard'n!"

Polly, by the time her song was finished, had gone past them some yards; and the expression of proud glee with which Bardsley waited in his certainty as to her soon perceiving him was dying from his face when she stood still and half turned in troubled, tender bewilderment.

Bardsley heard her; his smile expanded again, and he laid one finger on his lips and held another up warningly to Michael. The next instant Polly's basket was sent flying, and she sprang towards the old man with a peal of laughter.

"Ah, hah! you old Turk! You was going to cheat me, was you?" she cried, coming down on the beach beside him with a by no means graceful flop. "Here's a pretty hunt I've had for you. And who's this you're a-talkin' to?"

"This is a friend o' Mr. George Ambray's, Polly," answered Bardsley seriously.

Polly became suddenly decorous, and drooping her face against her grandfather, and fingering his buttons as in old days, inquired in a low shy voice—

"It ain't Mr. Brown, daddy, is it, as drared me, standing on a cheer on one toe, with the tambourine?"

"No, Polly, it ain't," replied her grandfather.

"Is it the gentleman as I was a angel with wings on for?" asked Polly dubiously.

"No, nor him neither, Polly."

"Is it him," asked Polly, "as took me with

the doves on my shoulder? Oh, how they scratched!"

"No, guess again," said Bardsley, laughing. Michael had also laughed a little, at which Polly flushed and sprang lightly up, and, standing before him in a charming attitude of recognition, said, shaking her head, and smiling and sighing at once, with the joy and pain of old memories—

"Ah! I remember now! You took me finding Moses in Mrs. Green's back-parlour!"

"No, no," laughed Michael gently, "still wrong, Polly, all wrong."

Polly sat down by her grandfather, after which she said quietly—

"I know him, daddy; he was in the mill last night."

"Right at last," answered Bardsley.

Michael then talked over with him the several ways by which the old man proposed to employ himself and Polly under the advantages now offered. Michael urged another endeavour to get Polly taken back into the blind school, but at the mention of it she so drooped that he had not the heart to go on talking about what might after all prove unmanageable.

Page 71.

Bardsley dwelt with regret on the pity it was Polly's blindness prevented her from enjoying the advantages she might have had as the pupil of Traps's in the bird-painting— a prospect which he appeared unable to think of without emotion.

Nothing was settled when Michael left them, after making an appointment for the next day. He would gladly have got them off to London at once, and so avoid the danger of another meeting with Ambray, but this he could not do till he wrote to his father for money.

When he had walked some little distance along the beach in the direction of the town, Polly came running after him, begging saucily for a sixpence.

As Michael gave it to her he laid his hand on her shoulder, and looking at her eyes glittering at the coin, though they could not see it, said—

"You never saw George Ambray, Polly? You never had your sight when you knew him?"

Polly shook her head. Michael saw that a change had come over her when his name was mentioned. Her laughing lips became set, her eyelids fell like some dead things, and her eyeballs rolled under them in pain.

Michael was sorry for what he had done; but as he *had* spoken and the change *had* come, it was a sad pleasure to him to talk of George again.

" Then you remember nothing about him but his voice, Polly?" he asked softly. " You do not know what he was like ?"

Polly's shoulder rose under his hand ; her set lips parted and let out a long shuddering breath, on which faintly and tenderly were borne the words—

" *I* knowed what he was like."

" How, my poor girl, when you never saw him ?"

The shoulder rose again, the long breath came again, murmuring softly and with faint triumph—

" But I ketched him all by ear."

" And you cared for him, Polly, so very, very much ?"

At this question the tragic little face only grew paler, remaining motionless as marble.

" Are you very angry with him, Polly, then, for using you so ill ?"

The pain all passed out of her face, which was raised to Michael with the smile of one who, having been reminded of many sorrows, is suddenly spoken to of a cherished blessing.

" He never used me ill," said Polly, with quiet, deep exultation. " That's only what *they* think. He know'd what was best. I never thought he used me ill not coming. I hope he's know'd all along as I never did."

" And yet, Polly, they say you fainted in the church."

" I was frightened for him," answered Polly. " They made such a row. I thought they'd hurt him—kill him."

She shuddered, and Michael took his hand quickly from her shoulder, and looked upon the stones with eyes full of bitter gloom.

Then he wished her good-bye abruptly, and left her.

Polly stood for some time in a sort of sorrowful trance, when she suddenly became aware of her sixpence. With a happy little cry, she tossed it up and caught it, and ran towards Bardsley.

" I say ! " called Polly, " what'll yer have for dinner? I'm a-going to toss—heads, bacon ; tails, herrin's."

" What is it you're a tossing with, Polly ?" asked Bardsley, turning round greedily.

On Polly's putting the sixpence in his hand, he smiled.

" A couple o' penny loaves and one saveloy, Polly, must be the bill o' fare to-day," he said, putting it in his pocket; "for the other threepence I intend to use in purchasin' paper, envelope, and stamp. Ink we can borrer."

" Whatever for, daddy?" asked Polly, hungry and disappointed.

" To get our scholarly young friend at the Barge to write to Traps to-night for us, Polly," he answered, buttoning up his coat with unusual energy, " events havin' occurred as I require the light of Traps's calm judgment on."

CHAPTER XXV.

IT had been one of the mournfullest days to the old couple at the High Mills.

Nora had blamed Ambray for destroying, in his violence and folly, the arrangement to which she had had such difficulty in bringing Mrs. Grist to consent.

When the miller asked her if she would have him keep such a character as Bardsley had described Michael's, and as Michael had accepted as his, Nora declared that the man should at least have had time and opportunity allowed him to speak in his own defence—that his truthfulness was in his favour. He would not, she reasoned, have accepted, as he had done, the charges made against him if they were really as heavy as Ambray thought them ; and if he had not hoped to clear himself sufficiently for his master still to retain him. She spoke of the honest indignation she had seen in his face and manner from the moment she had come into the cottage ; and altogether caused Ambray to regard his own conduct in so bad a light, that he, being one of those persons who no sooner see an unfavourable reflection of themselves than they are seized by a desire to smash the looking-glass, soon ordered her to go with very little more ceremony than he had shown Michael.

Mrs. Ambray, who had taken no part in the quarrel, but in alternately pulling Ambray's tall figure back into his chair from which he kept rising angrily, and in patting and stroking Nora's hands, was thankful when her niece had gone and she had but one temper to manage.

To soothe this one she tried a thousand arts, even descending to a little abuse of Michael ; at which Ambray told her to hold her tongue, declaring that however bad the man might be, he had behaved well enough to her. Three or four hours she was on her feet attending to his comforts, his cough mixture, which he had made over again half-a-dozen times, his chest plaister, his rheumatic ankle and shoulder, and the innumerable requirements of a selfish man sick in heart and body; for all of which attention, when she at last sat down, aching in every limb, she was rewarded by seeing him drop his grey head in his hands, and hearing him moan into them—

"My God! what have I done to be left alone in the world like this?"

His wife, stung for his sake as well as her own, looked upon him with inexpressible pity and tenderness.

"It's hard for you that you should feel that, John," she said; "God knows what I should do if *I* did."

Ambray was not so intellectually swinish as to be quite ignorant of the worth of the pearls of affection that were cast so lavishly before him by the most leal old heart that ever beat; but in perceiving them and their value he was only troubled at times by a vague sense of waste, as one might be in using some precious material for a purpose for which the commonest would do as well. He needed in Esther but a nurse and servant —a supplier of common physical wants; his heart was closed obstinately to all affection, hope, or comfort from any source but one; and as from that nothing came, his spirit starved and soured, so that he, in his turn, had nothing to give. A beggar in vain himself, others must needs beg vainly of him. Thus he excused himself to himself for his hardness, and when he saw his wife suffer at it, blamed the cause of his own suffering—George.

Since a morning in George's second summer when Ambray had watched him from the mill, using both his baby hands and setting his dimpled feet against a ridge to give him strength to tug a scarlet poppy from the corn, his affection for the child and the ambition the act suggested that he should reap a long life's harvest from his grandfather's land, had become a passion. At first this had met with but little hope to nourish it, but in time his brother's early death and the prospect of George's marriage with Nora had so strengthened it, that it overcame every other feeling; life itself was but a slave to it.

Thus when Ambray on the day following Michael's departure sat reflecting how this hope, this idol, had been injured by his soreness of temper,—which had first driven away the man whose presence had enabled them to subsist through this weary waiting, and next had hurt and offended George's be-

trothed herself, it was no wonder that his heart should be sick and full of despair.

His harsh treatment of Michael had been wrung from him by simple and bitter jealousy at God's having given one man such a son, while he who had staked his all upon his child—who had not retained or wished to retain one hope apart from him—was thus deserted, neglected, defied. Often he had felt inclined to lift his hand and strike Michael when he saw his dark eyes gleaming tenderly over one of old Swift's short, cold, ill-spelt letters.

For this reason he was but sulkily and dully pleased when at noon a fish-boy brought him a letter from Michael, asking forgiveness for his rough departure and permission to return, and telling him how he was arranging to assist those who had been injured, though not, Michael assured him, so greatly as Bardsley would have had him to believe.

Mrs. Ambray dared not remain in the room for fear her husband should see the relief and thankfulness in her face when, after having asked him what he should do about the letter, he had replied —

"Nothing—and if he comes—he comes."

So when, after dark, the door opened, and Michael looked hesitatingly in, his great shoulders drawn up, his head bowed, his pardon-begging eyes dazed by the candlelight—a picture of profound and humble contrition, he was not forbidden to enter and seat himself in his old corner.

The next morning, when Mrs. Ambray saw the sails sweeping lazily round in a languid sweet sea-breeze, and Michael white from head to foot, standing on the little terrace and looking across the Buckholt fields, she was obliged to hide behind the bee-hives, that she might have a thankful cry without being scolded for it.

Ambray did not speak to Michael for several days. Life evidently was not to go on at the High Mills even as smoothly as it had done in the earlier part of the summer.

Michael's father wrote one day to tell him his money was all gone, and on another to tell him that an old blind man had been worrying them with mysterious demands in Michael's name. At this critical time Michael dared not cease sending the small sum Bardsley had received from him since his and Polly's return to London. To obtain this money now he was obliged to beg Ambray to allow him to work some hours daily for Mrs. Grist, explaining to him his necessity for doing so. Ambray did not refuse his consent, but was rather glad to

"LISTENING CLOSE TO THE WINDOW, HIS HAND BEHIND HIS EAR."

Page 81.

have this thing to taunt Michael with, so that his life—what with overwork, unkindness constant and galling, and the weight of three other persons' troubles—was no easy burden to him. He generally bore these taunts about Polly in silence and gentleness, but once or twice he had been unable to keep himself from turning upon Ambray with an indignant and passionate burst of laughter, which, though abruptly and sternly stopped, none the le s had filled the old man with subdued fury.

Dissension seemed to ripen in the valley with the corn that harvest. Ma'r S'one brought rumours of wars from the farm, where it seemed Mrs. Grist was encouraging an unwelcome wooer of Nora's, to her niece's distress and Ambray's rage. There seemed no fear so strong in him as that of Nora breaking her engagement with George. If he heard of any of her friends from the Bay going to see her, he would never rest until he had learnt all he could about them; and Nora seldom had a letter but he would hear of it, and demand of her the writer's name, and sometimes the contents of the letter also.

Michael knew that Nora tried hard to keep patience and peace in her heart through all this, but he often saw her leave the miller's cottage with flushed cheeks and weary eyes, and walk home with a slow and springless step.

He noticed, too, that she began to catch some of the feverish, fresh expectancy that had possessed Ambray of late, and that seemed increasing upon him so that almost every sound made him start and tremble.

One night Michael heard him say to his wife in suppressed excitement—

"Esther, that boy's coming—I feel it—I feel he might come in at any moment."

The next day he told Nora the same thing, and her eyes filled as she looked at him solemnly and answered—

"How strange! I have felt so too."

The only times of rest Michael knew in those days, so full of restlessness and fever, were the evenings when he stole down the white village road, over which the shadows of the thatched cottages lay so softly and still, and leant upon the gate at Buckholt Farm. For it was at these times Nora's voice came out to complete the sweetness of the summer night, of the lake-like fields of heavy harvest dew, the star-jewelled mill-sails—still and moving—and the unseen sea, giving the valley breath with which to tell its odours.

Generally Michael would see Ma'r S'one listening close to the window, his hand behind his ear, his wondering little eyes fixed on his young mistress as she sang, with all her soul in her face—like a modern St. Cecilia trying to draw down the angel of peace.

Michael loved best to steal away before she rose, because sometimes her sigh, or her look into the night, haunted him too long with its sweet patience and wonder, its foreboding or hope. Neither did he care to hear the invariable and solemn exclamation of Ma'r S'one, as his smock disappeared round the house :—

"The Lord furgive Ma'rs Garge!"

The harvest came.

One morning as they sat at breakfast the first band of reapers went by the window.

Ambray started up, and, going to the door, looked after them with eyes half frenzied.

"My God!" he cried, "is that it? Must I see this year's sheaves hugging each other over all my father's land without knowing if I shall ever hold my boy again? Oh, if he is not coming, let the harvest rot !"

He stretched his long arms out through the open door, and lifted up his face with a mingling of malediction and prayer fearful to see.

Michael rose, got past him, and went into the mill.

The whole morning he sat at one of the little windows without moving, watching the cottage-door and Ambray, who frequently came out of it, and walked a few yards in the sun, looking now with a quieter gloom at the reapers at their work.

At last, suddenly, and quite before he was aware of his approach, Ambray felt Michael's hand touching his arm.

"Master," he said, breathing as if he had just run from some great distance, instead of Ambray's having seen him sitting quietly in the mill but a minute since. "May I speak to you ?"

"Why, what is the matter with you ?" asked Ambray with puzzled sternness, stepping back as he looked at him, and noticed that Michael was paler than he ever saw living man look, and that his eyes were at once more resolute and more full of agony than any eyes his own had yet encountered.

There was but one object concerning which Ambray could feel hope or fear—one source to which he could imagine such anguish as he saw here must belong.

"George !" he almost shouted, laying his hands on Michael's shoulders, and looking upon him as if he would devour his news out of his soul before his lips could speak it. "Is it about George ?"

6

"Let me come and tell you," answered Michael. "Let me tell you in the mill."

Half leaning on him, half supporting him to make him move faster, Ambray went with him into the mill.

They stood by the long deal shaft exactly as they stood there when Michael first came, and where he had looked up and nodded as the miller said, "I have a son in London," and had felt that movement to be the greatest crime of which he had in all his life been guilty.

Ambray laid his hand upon the shaft now as he had done that day.

Michael also took hold of it to keep himself from falling.

As their eyes met again Michael saw that Ambray had had time to reason with himself—to think that the news which looked so terrible in Michael's eyes need not necessarily be about his son.

Then, without an instant's pause, the words came with a dull monotony—like a bitter lesson learnt by heart and soul—

"I saved an old man's life from a young man who would have killed him—if I—had not used violence to the young man, who was strong—very strong. I used violence—I killed him—no one knows I did it—no one but you—his—his——"

Michael's voice failed him; he saw that the miller drew himself back, erect and strong—that the hope which had risen in his eyes was determined to die hard.

Michael clung to the shaft like the last wretch left upon a wreck to the swaying mast, and cried—

"Have mercy upon me, master!"

"Unlucky wretch!" murmured Ambray, bewildered, "what have I to do with mercy? You have really done this thing you say you have? You have killed a man? _You?_"

At this moment, the bell attached to the mill-door rang; a flood of light fell on their faces; a girl had come for a small measure of barley-meal.

Michael looked at her, and heard her demand, with a dull, vague wonder; a horror such as, if the dead could feel, they might know at seeing some one waiting a customary service from their hands.

He did not move except to take one hand from the shaft, and stand erect beside it.

Ambray with a strong step went and took a measure and filled it, and poured the barley into the girl's apron; Michael staring at him with suspended breath; appalled by the sight of his calmness, which showed how little of his task was yet done.

He saw that hope, like some hurt, wild creature was stung to fresh strength in him by the shock it had received, and was prepared to defend its fierce, faint life to the last.

When the girl had gone and Ambray had closed the door upon her, he turned to Michael with this look of assurance and defiance in his eyes, and Michael cried out in a voice scarcely louder than a breath, but audible and pain-burdened as the breath about to pass away for ever—

"You must understand me! I must make you understand me! This young man——"

His voice died, and they looked at each other in utter silence.

It seemed that minutes passed in this way before Michael again clung to the shaft as he had done before, and cried—

"Have mercy upon me — it was your son!"

Suddenly, before he well knew how Ambray had approached or taken hold of him, Michael was half running with feet like lead—half being dragged along—past the field of fallen corn towards the cottage.

The next moment he was standing before Mrs. Ambray and Nora, and a voice such as he had never heard, but by which all fears of the past seemed uttered afresh, was shouting over him—

"What have you told me? Repeat it here—before this woman that bore him, and this girl—repeat it!"

PART VII.

N ORA had been sitting at Mrs. Ambray's feet reading to her, until heat, weariness, and the music of a rich, soft voice had sent the old woman into a gentle sleep. She had dreamt of George, and her dreams, coming out of sounds so pleasant, were themselves joyful, making her have a sense of the desired presence living and moving in the house, filling its master with gladness, and herself with peace. Nora, when she saw the old arms tremble, and the sweet old mouth move as with a sense of smiles, and with whispers of the well-loved name, knew how it was with her. She allowed herself to fall under the same spell, to imagine—not the moment of George Ambray's coming, when the hope and fear so long at war within her must, at her first look in his face, close in a last conflict, and receive, one of them, its death-blow; not this moment, too full of acute joy or pain to be imagined in any quiet mood such as the afternoon encouraged, but the peace that would come afterwards. It was of this she dreamed; the deep, sweet lull when the excitement of the prodigal's return, with its feasting and tears and passion, its rejoicing and shame should be past, the wonder over, beholders wearied and gone, the house left with no voucher for its joy but the dear pardoned one himself, scarcely daring to show the l ve and gratitude in his chastened eyes, or to let it speak in his broken and seldom-litted voice. Of this and the vying of forgiven and forgivers in humility of bearing towards each other, of the few words spoken, the long, full silences, the restraint of each heart over itself in its tender

dread of again disturbing by a too loving look or tone the newly-stilled waters in dear eyes, the recognition of this care in one another—making the eyes to swim in spite of it—of these things Nora dreamed, not sleeping, but looking up from her book to the portrait of George, her head on Mrs. Ambray's knee when the footsteps startled her.

She knew Ambray's step instantly, but whose the other with him and why they came in so much haste she asked herself in a sus· pense that would not for many moments have been supportable. Had George come home? What so likely as that he should go to his father at the mill, and that Ambray, unable to express the readiness and fulness of his pardon, had hurried him here to receive theirs first.

It was scarcely two minutes from the time she heard the steps to the appearance of Michael and the miller at the door, yet in that interval the idea of George's return became as a reality to Nora—her suspense, her terror was now all as to what his face would tell her, when it should appear, of his faith or faithlessness towards her.

She had risen and was standing with her hand on Mrs. Ambray's chair—pale, cold— her eyes looking upward, praying she thought, but really doing no more than seeking to bargain with God for her desire, offering—as so many at such moments offer—joy after joy, hope after hope, out of life's unknown store, for the possession of the one thing then and there so coveted.

Then the door was pushed open and the two men burst upon her sight and her ears like a storm, Ambray shouting—

" Repeat it here before this woman that bore him, and this girl—repeat it ! "

Almost in the same instant Nora, looking into the eyes of Michael, remembered the fears with which they had filled her on the morning he had come to her at Stone Crouch. The panic his words had then stilled returned upon her now, and as if no time had passed since then, when the lacework frame had fallen from her hands as she stood demanding the truth of him, as if no summer had intervened to hide the rough rooks' nests in the poplars with its living architecture, or to heap treasure on the wind-swept meadows sloping to the sea. Nora took up her long silenced cry—

" O, what is it ? Tell me. You came to

tell me at Stone Crouch. You have known ever since. I think you have known he is dead. Is that it? Is he dead!"

In looking at her and summoning strength to answer her, Michael for the moment forgot all else—even his master. The pity for her which had become a part of his very nature since he had first seen her in the mill, so overcame him, that he was forced to fall forward and lean with his arms on the table as he answered her in words that seemed dragged up one by one by a superhuman effort.

"It—is—so. The young man is dead!"

Mrs. Ambray, but half awake, was sitting upright in her chair when the words reached her ears.

The face of Nora, the attitude of Michael, left her in no doubt as to the meaning of what she had heard; and she rose to meet not her own misery, which she put aside as a thing that could, and too surely *would* wait, but her husband's, that she knew would take him up in its power as the wind takes a withered leaf.

It so happened that for once Ambray thought of her before himself, not through any unwonted return of affection, but simply because *her* loss, *her* sorrow, did not seem so vast and difficult a thing to realise as his own.

He met her as she came to him, and kissed her with lips cold as ice, murmuring, while keeping his arm round her—

"Poor mother—poor soul! Dead! Her son dead!"

Then, as if the contemplation of her loss lifted his senses to some idea of his own, his arm slipped from her, his eyes looked upward, and he threw his hands up, palms outwards, like one who would push off a descending weight, saying—

"Dead! My son dead!"

"The young man is dead!" repeated Michael, gathering himself up from where he had fallen with his arms on the table, and turning from Nora to Ambray.

At the sound of his voice the miller let fall his arms and looked at him. Michael met his look with eyes in which fear, pity, and pain were almost overcome by a certain patience and resignation, which showed this moment had been looked for and dwelt upon long enough to have rendered its awfulness familiar to him before it came to pass. In spite, however, of this, his suffering was beyond anything he had ever imagined it could be when Ambray turned from looking helplessly into the face of an indomitable and remorseless fate to the instrument that had been used by it to deal him this blow, and the fearful relief, light, and fury that filled his eyes as he remembered that here he was not *so* helpless, made Michael extend his hands in a mute appeal for mercy. Such a look—as that with which a general losing a battle through the treachery of one man might turn his eyes from the spectacle of loss and blood he cannot stay to the traitor in his power—Ambray turned on Michael.

Even Nora, standing, white, transfixed, stunned by the change that had come over life and all the world at Michael's words, was penetrated by fresh fear as she saw this look.

Mrs. Ambray clung to her husband's arm with a sense of the worst having yet to come.

"Mercy!" cried Michael faintly, with extended hands.

"How did my son die?" asked Ambray, shaking off his wife and folding his arms.

"I will tell you—you shall hear all—all," answered Michael, repeating his gesture of entreaty and protestation.

"I will," said Ambray, looking at him with a fearful calmness. "I will hear all. Look you, I will have out of you every word my boy said. I will have you make me see how he died as if it happened here before me."

At this Michael's eyes filled, and he smiled almost with triumph as he cried—

"There was ever gold left by dying man, or deed of millions value, so treasured as the least of his last words has been by me, for the sake of those he went from so untimely and unaware. Sooner would I have forgot to see, or hear, or speak than this. I have said it all as I mean to tell it you now. I have said it on my bed at night, and in the mill, till I have it by heart."

Ambray, with the terrible forethought of a torturer, perceiving that his victim's strength would not endure to the desired end, pointed to a bench in the middle of the room, and said—

"Sit!"

Michael, after stretching up his arm against the wall, frowning and dizzy, as if he were feeling for the regulator in some mill where the sails were flying ready to be wrenched away, and the air was dusty with the raining meal, dragged himself to the bench and sat down.

The others stood near him, and he spoke—sometimes his hands locked in each other, and his head and shoulders stooping low,—his eyes fixed on the floor, sometimes looking up from one to another of his listeners' faces.

Ambray stood close before him, his eye glittering with jealous anger whenever Michael looked, or appeared to be directing what he said towards either of the others. Michael never paused to think, the tale was already made; the very manner in which he began it —speaking of things that they knew—showed that it had been put together long ago, and learnt, as he had said, "by heart," with too much pain to admit of even those alterations which time and certain circumstances seemed to render necessary.

"My father," said Michael, stooping low and looking as if he read what he was saying on the floor between his feet and Ambray's, "has a small corn-shop on the green at Thames Dutton. There are rooms over it which in summer-time we let to such as come to fish or to row on the river."

At this Michael's eyes looked slowly up from amidst them all and rested on some pieces of an old fishing-rod tied carefully together and hung against the wall. Ambray looked in the same direction, and then his eyes and Michael's met, and Michael's fell again.

"On the tenth of last August in the evening I had come home from the mills where I worked, and was standing in the little garden at the side of the shop nailing an apricot to the wall while my little sister held the nails and bits of list for me. My mother was inside calling to us to train a branch nearer to the parlour window. My father sat at the shop door reading his newspaper. He had been reading something aloud to us which had made us laugh. I was laughing very much.—[I have never laughed so since.]"

When Michael said anything which was not in the heart-learnt story, the difference was made plainly apparent by some change of voice or look. Several times it happened that some little fact which helped to colour the incident he might be telling was remembered by him now and mentioned ; but when this was so, it stood out like fresh paint on a dry picture, or a written comment on the margin of a printed page. These manifest additions came generally in short, complete sentences, interrupting the flow of the carefully-considered, formally-worded recital or confession, and almost in every instance throwing a sort of lurid reality upon the moment or thing which it concerned.

"While I was laughing and looking down at my sister, and trying not to let go the nail I was stretching up to hammer in, I saw her turn serious all in a minute and hang down her head as if she was ashamed

of having laughed so loud. This made me look round towards the road, and then I saw a young man—a young man standing still—looking at us. I noticed that he was ill [the weight of the small bag that he carried seemed too much for him, and his eyes frowned with pain as they looked at us]. I did not wonder then why my sister had stopped laughing, for he looked at it was a kind of affront to him to see us so. In another instant we heard him, when we had turned away, speaking to my father about the rooms. He wished to take them for some weeks. He went in and looked at them, and said that he would take them. He told my father that his name was George Grant, that he was an artist ; but my father is nervous about money, he refused to receive this young man unless he paid him some at once. When my father told him this he said it would not be convenient, and went away. As he went along the road I could see that he hardly knew how to drag one foot after the other, and had often to put his hand on the railings of the green to keep himself from falling. He went right on to the bridge and disappeared from our sight. Before long he came back, looking very wild and weary, and it all at once came to my mind that he had nothing to pay the bridge toll with. He lay down at the far end of the green. [Somehow I could not take my eyes off him till they fetched me out to cricket]. I went out to cricket about seven o'clock and this young man lay all the time watching us. [Mostly I thought he looked as if he would be glad for the ground to open and give him a grave as he lay ; but sometimes he would lift up his head and watch us mostly like an old man who has given everything up, and only remembers what he used to do ; but sometimes he would look very different, half scornful like one far a-head of us, and shout out that such a one bowled too high or too low, or cry "bravo!" or growl out heartily at a blunderer.] I don't know how I came to make up my mind to speak to him, but we did somehow at dusk, when we were alone on the green met to talk over what had been said by my father about the rooms, and were as good friends as if we had known each other for months. He came home with me—he had the rooms — allowing me to settle the difference with my father. He stayed with us till——"

It was here that Michael evidently came to some expression in his story which he found it was unwise or impossible to utter, and, failing to find one more fit for his purpose, sat suffering frightfully in the knowledge of how much worse his silence was than the words he had held back would have been.

As he paused, looking down upon the floor, he saw Ambray's feet silently move a little nearer to him.

Michael lifted his hands and eyes in a mute entreaty for patience, and again stooping low, let the blank left by the discarded words pass unfilled, and went on.

"He was the first friend I ever had in my life, and he called *me* friend—God knows why—he had everything to give—I nothing but gratitude—the willing service of my clumsy hands—my few spare hours, my little money—such a liking as almost passed my affection for my father and mother and all belonging me; this I gave him, and the wonder, the honest though worthless praise of all my mind. And for this he gave me his confidence, as much of his time and company as my small leisure could hold; called me friend; made my life a different thing for me from what it had ever been before. I dropped most others of my acquaintance, out of fear he would not care to see his friend with any so humble as they were. To make his painting-room ready for him was my first task in the morning; at night, so long as he would talk I listened, more lost in him than in the best book I ever read. I heard his real name. I heard of all here. His father, that he trusted to make proud of him yet; his mother, that he thought to comfort yet; the lady that he hoped to make himself worthy of, and then give up his claim, to win it back, he said, in some humbler and worthier manner. I heard of all. On the third of December he read out to me how some actor, a young friend of his, was to appear in a new play at the —— theatre, and seemed so grieved he could not go to see him, that he hardly touched his breakfast. I asked at the mills for a holiday, went to London, bought two tickets for the pit, and took them to him, making believe they had been given me at the mills, and we went together and saw his friend. He had a great success, and George was wild to speak to him. He was afraid to go to him behind the scenes because he was sure to meet many people he most wished to shun, for the same reason that he had taken another name for a time. He sent me round with a message to his friend. I was not able to give it—they said the young man was gone. When I came back to the top of the street, where I had left George, I found a crowd there. Before I saw him I heard his voice crying out in a great passion. I could not hear what he said. I pushed my way to where he was, for I was afraid for him—he had drank too much, we both had. I saw him struggling with an old blind man. I saw then that the crowd had nothing to do with them, but were round an oyster stall. George was trying to get away from the old man, who held him with fingers like iron, and the old man was calling out to some one at the stall to help him; but all there were taken up with a dispute, the owner of the stall having charged some one with stealing a knife. At the first instant I saw him, George was using only one hand, and holding the other back as far as he could. Directly I came up the blind man shouted louder—then George's other hand swung round towards him, and I saw a knife in it. I rushed to him calling, 'Hold, George!' But the blind man's last shout had made the crowd hear. We heard a rush of feet towards us. George made a desperate struggle to free himself. The blind man held on to his coat with his teeth as well as his hands. Before I could part them by fair means, George, mad at hearing the crowd coming, would have used his hand with the knife in it if I had not caught it. I caught it, and held it by the wrist. Then with his left hand he clutched the old man's throat. I saw his blind eyes roll and turn upward—his lips grow black; but he held George still: if he had died he would have died holding him. The crowd came running close. George shook him. My eyes were on the blind old face. I thought to see death on it in an instant. I struck at George's hands with the handle of the knife, which I had got from him, then with the blade. Then suddenly the struggle was between ourselves alone."

Michael paused.

"The struggle was between yourselves alone," said Ambray, in a clear voice; "you, Michael Swift, and my son, George Ambray."

Michael looked up at him, then rose, looked on the floor, and up again at the miller.

"I cannot," he said helplessly, "tell what happened in the struggle."

"But you shall," said Ambray, coming a step nearer to him, and speaking in a voice of unnatural quietness and strength.

"I cannot," repeated Michael.

"You shall!"

"I cannot. The next thing I remember, George was lying on the ground, the knife was in him. I tried to draw it out. I could not; my fingers were helpless as the dead, and it was fast in. The roughs were now upon us, calling to one another that it was young Ambray, as if they had been looking for him some time to do him harm. When I made them see how it was with him, one asked who had done it, and I looked round and said 'He is gone,' and at this they took it to be one of themselves who had done it, and made off. I called to one of the stall-men to fetch me a cab. While it was coming, George turned on my arm as I knelt holding him, and cried out, 'Michael! you butcher! you fiend! you have done for me! Take out the knife!'"

While saying this Michael had stood with his hands crossed at the wrists, and hanging before him as if they had chains on them, and spoke in a voice of one rather making confession before a judge, than to those who had been injured by his act.

Ambray had moved further away from him, and stood with his arms folded, his eyes fixed upon him.

Mrs. Ambray had for the time forgotten her husband, and it was George's mother only that Michael felt gazing upon him from her eyes.

Nora, who had for some time been standing at the table just as she stood to receive Michael's answer to her question, had at the last words slipped upon her knees, and, resting her elbows on the table, held her clenched hands under her chin to keep herself from shrieking.

As Michael, having paused for want of voice, turned his eyes about him, and observed the attitude and expression of each, memory and self-possession threatened to fail him; but Ambray seeing this danger in his wild eyes and panting chest, cried in a clear, inexorable voice—

"Go on. My son said, 'Take out the knife.'"

"Yes," returned Michael faintly, almost gratefully; "and I took it out, and his blood rushed on me. When the cab came I lifted him in, telling the man he had been stabbed by the roughs we had quarrelled with. He heard what I said; and when we were alone, and I sat huddled in the bottom of the cab to support him, he moaned out, 'You murderer, I shall not live to contradict you!' The cabman of his own accord stopped at a surgeon's near; but, scarcely in my right mind with fright, I told him the young man wished to be taken home at once. George again had heard me, and burst into tears as his face lay on my shoulder, and said, 'Now I must really die, Michael, if I am to get no help till then.' I said, 'No, no!' and kept

breathing on his hands and forehead to warm them, but they got cold as stone. All the latter part of the journey I thought he was dying, or dead, he was so still; but as we passed the light at the bridge toll-gate, I saw his eyes looking at me. When we stopped at our house my father came with a light and cried out at the sight of me lifting George from the cab. I said to him, 'Help me, father, Grant has been stabbed by some blackguards we quarrelled with outside the theatre.' I carried him up to his room. The knife had gone into his side here, below the heart. My father sent one of my brothers for a doctor. When he came, my father and mother assisted him—for I stood just inside the door unable to move. All this time George did not speak, but only moaned whenever they touched him. At last the doctor stood by the bed, with his hat in his hand, and said, 'Good night, my lad, I have done all that I can for you.' George said, 'Good night, sir,' and held out his hand. And I thought 'Now will be my ruin.' But he did not speak of me, but asked—with a—with a smile—' Doctor, will it be one hour, or not so long?' And then the doctor said, 'My lad, it may be three or four.' 'Three or four,' George said, then asked my father, 'Where is Michael?' I went to him, and he asked the others to leave us. When they had gone he said, 'Michael, come, don't be afraid. I can hold my tongue for three hours, and after that who is to know?' I fell down by the bed, and cried out, 'Don't, George, don't—if this is to be—if you are to die, I shall give myself up. They shall hang me.' He touched me with his hand, weak and light as a feather, and said, ' Do not trouble me now, Michael. I cannot have my father—or my mother—or—her—at my death-bed; let me have my friend, and don't let him be troubled.' For half an hour we were very still, holding hands. In about this time George gave a sigh, and said, 'I ought to rouse myself; there are some things I must tell you. I have been thinking I was telling you, and all the time never opening my mouth. I am feeling very strange; I scarcely think it will be three hours, Michael.' Then he told me the things he wished to tell me. Some day they may be told by me again, but not now."

"You will keep back nothing my son said that night," commanded Ambray, who was now listening with his back turned upon Michael.

Michael remained silent a moment. At last he said—

"When I told you that every word of his should be repeated, I had forgotten that these things I speak of could not be told, as I promised him that I would keep them from you. Will you wish me to break my word to him?"

As Ambray did not answer, Michael went on, as if he had his consent to leave the matters of which he had spoken untold.

"Soon after this George seemed to fall asleep. It was near three in the morning, and I think he slept for half an hour. He woke, clutching at the counterpane, and calling, 'Michael, Michael! wake, wake!' I said, 'In heaven's name, George, do you think that *I* could sleep?' Then he said, 'Up, up, lift me up.' I raised him, and he clung to me, whispering, 'It is no use, Michael, I must go home.' His cheeks were wet, his forehead was all in lines, but his mouth smiled. I said, 'Home, George?' not understanding, and he said, 'I must go there now in my mind, I mean, instead of looking from here for help. If there is a forgiving God, it is there only I can find Him—where I was born—where I left Him—where I lost Him. Why did I come away? Ah, to get back! Michael, Michael, to get back!'"

Ambray's folded arms loosened and fell, like a band suddenly snapped, by the motion of his chest.

"He lay—George lay—with his head on my shoulder," Michael went on, "and his voice close at my ear. 'Now, now,' he said, 'I will think of it, I will remember it, while my life—is going from me; my life—does that mean my soul, Michael? is this what they call the spirit—this strength, that is tearing itself up from every part of me like a tree with roots and fibres not loosed by age, but cruelly wrenched while it has strongest hold?' And I said, 'And by my hand, George, by my hand.' 'Hush!' he whispered; 'let me remember, and perhaps this life—this soul, is it?—may go to the place I am remembering, seeing——'"

By this time Nora had risen and come close to Michael, up at whose face she gazed almost breathlessly.

Ambray stood—still with his back to them—looking out through the open door upon those scenes towards which Michael showed George's last thoughts had struggled.

"For some little time," continued Michael, "he lay with his arms over my shoulders, trembling very much, and making sudden starts. 'George,' I said to him, 'is the pain so great?' (of his wound I meant), and he said, 'Yes, it is a pain to me to see it all so faintly. Ah, have I loved it so little to have so forgotten! Yes, hold me higher. I begin to see the shapes of the fields; the mist goes; grand, grand downs! A very world of them, Michael!' and then, trembling more still, he said, 'And ah, those farm clusters, Michael! Clumsy, sweet—sweet rustic bouquets of ricks—and houses—and homes dotting the dear horizon and the valley's slopes and deeps—shall I *never* see them any more—never, never smell their bleaching hay or wood-fires in the breeze? *my* breeze that turns the mill. It is very dark. God! let me find the way—home—father—father, father!'

"George!" cried Ambray, stretching out his arms and lifting his face to the scenes last pictured without brush or pencil by the dying painter, "O let him find me! O let the wandering spirit come!"

At this cry Michael paused and struggled with himself; then went on, speaking more quickly like one feeling his endurance to be near an end. .

"When George had said—what I have said—he shook and clung so, that I knew that the end must be coming. At last he let me lay him down, and was still—he was very still. In a minute I saw his lips move. I hoped he might be praying, for he had not, I think, prayed yet. But when I had sate for some time hoping this, he moaned out as if he had but just found voice after trying for it long, 'Michael, do you hear me?' I said, 'God help me, no, George, I have not heard you. What is it, dear lad?' Then he looked at me, and put his hand on mine and said, 'You will not let them want, my father and mother, so that they will cry out against me for my neglect, my cruelty?' I went on my knees at his bed, and my answer was, 'George Ambray, to-night as I have sat beside you I have sworn to God to go to the High Mills and be your father's servant if it be possible to make him take me, and under cover of this service be a son to him so far as he may let me.' 'You will!' George said smiling, and with faint eyes running over. 'You will go to the old people and work for them.' 'Ay, like a slave,' I said, 'and guard them like a dog, grateful to God if He will let me give my life to them for yours that I have lost for them so early.' The comfort of this promise, for it did comfort him much, reached him just in time. His face changed so much and so suddenly, that I turned stiff as I knelt watching. Then I saw the wish to speak torturing him, and bent down and strained my very soul to hear. I heard at last, 'My father!' and I nodded and said,

'Comfort, George, he shall hear from me some day how he was with you at this last. And the lady,' I said, 'the lady whose life is this night ruined, shall I tell *her* this too?' He looked at me; I thought a great trouble came in his eyes. I waited, looking as well as listening for the answer. Fresh pain seized him; it was his last; in it he turned to me with a look that seemed to mean 'I *would* speak of other things, but I have but time for the one nearest to my heart,' and so looking cried out once more, 'My father!' And his head fell, his teeth locked—it was over."

"His first word—and—his last!" murmured Ambray, looking upward in tenderest exultation; suddenly he seemed to remember Nora, and the pain she might be suffering at George's apparent neglect of her in his last hours, for he went to her and touched her shoulder, saying—

"Forgive him—dear child—poor child—he loved you—yes, yes—he loved you—but father and son—father and child—there is no tie—O there can be no tie like it!—none —none."

A touch came on Michael's hand. It was Mrs. Ambray's—cold and trembling.

"Was it without one prayer?" she asked; "without one word of prayer?"

"Prayer!" cried Ambray, turning upon them before Michael could answer. "And why should *he* have prayed? Does the babe on its mother's breast cry for its mother? Does the bird nested in the corn cry out for food? Do you suppose God was not glad enough to take back such work of His, and that George did not know it? Go on."

"I said—I said that it was over," pleaded Michael.

"Over!" cried Ambray, turning upon him fiercely; "why the breath has scarcely left his lips—I mean—I will know all the rest—but perhaps you hurried him warm into his grave—my slaughtered lamb! Did you so? —butcher! Where is he buried? Was there no inquest?"

"There was an inquest," answered Michael, "the verdict, *manslaughter against a person or persons unknown*. He was buried in the churchyard at Thames Dutton, on the eighth of December. I sat in his room all the five days and four nights. On the night before they came to nail his coffin down, I was half mad to think he was so soon to be shut from sight and none belonging to him to see him before it was so. His face was wonderful, most beautiful. That it should be closed up without any eye more dear to him than mine to look on it, or any lips to

set a parting kiss on it, unmanned me more than all the rest. 'I asked myself is there *no* honour I can do him at this last hour? None? Then I thought of my little sister I had offended him about so often by keeping her out of his sight; a little lass of fifteen she was—fair as a lily, and as weak and simple; and I was over proud and careful of her, and often made George angry by sending her away from us when she would come to look at his pictures; I am very sorry—but—she is my only sister. I went up and brought her down, amazed, out of her sleep. There was a tall white flower upon the staircase window—I don't know the name of it, but it is common; we always have one there in the winter. Not a week before, George had seen my sister looking at it, half opened, and had said to me, 'Why Michael, soon you will have to tell me which is which," and I had been vexed and sent her to her work. I remembered this as I brought her down past the flower that night, and I told her to gather it and bring it with her. While she was doing so I saw out in the moonlight the two men coming across the green to nail his coffin. So I made her hurry and lay her flower beside him—the long stalk at his side, and the large blossom on his shoulder—and I made her kiss him for each of the three I was cheating of this last sight of him. Then the quiet knock came at the street door, and I took the child in my arms and carried her fainting to her mother, and my father came down with me to see—to see it done, and it was done."

Ambray had gone and stood before the portrait of George that hung over the mantelpiece, and was looking up at it with folded arms and eyes full of ecstatic light and tears, to keep which from falling he held his rugged brows dragged up.

When he had been so for some time after Michael had ceased speaking, he suddenly threw up his clasped hands towards the picture, crying in a low, thick voice—

"A flower to honour *you!* What flower ever opened upon earth fit for such close fellowship with such a face? Oh beautiful! Oh cruelly used! George, George!"

Helplessly as a child might sit and watch the up-curled wave from which it cannot run —darkening and foaming in suspended force before its break and rush—the three watched Ambray in the silence that followed this cry, at once so scornful and so tender.

When at last the face was lifted from the hands wherein it had fallen, and turned towards them, its expression was one of simple recollection and horror.

"Why, Esther!" he exclaimed. "Nora! God help our miserable, helpless law! Do you know I verily believe this man will escape hanging."

As in his passionate declaration of this fear he flung his hands towards where Michael sat stooping as if he had been half crushed by a weight and could not straighten himself, Nora turned quickly in shuddering remonstrance, as Michael had seen her do when the life of a worm or fly was threatened. She said nothing; but the turning of her head, the quick breath, the shudder, told him all that he dared yet ask of God concerning her—whether he was a guilty, despicable wretch in her eyes, or only a most unfortunate man.

This thing, slight as it was, sent a thrill of warmth, of life, through his chilled and stunned senses, and he was able to lift up his head and look with gentleness at Ambray as he stood before him.

"I came to work it out, master; I could do no more," he pleaded.

"Hold your tongue," said Ambray, white and shrill with fury; "call the insult of living

Page 83.

in my presence and grinding my corn—work—and old as I am I—I will take the law in my own hands."

"Oh, John, John!" cried Mrs. Ambray, coming between them; "have you not both enough to suffer without talking of *more* punishment—more misery?"

"I will," cried Ambray, "if they will not punish him, or if he tries to slip the law, I'll take it in my own hands. No punishment! Why I'd rather appear before that boy's grandfather and uncles with a halter round my own neck than have to tell them that his murderer lives—goes free. But who talks of it? Here, Esther, you must go—go to two or three people that I will tell you of; and Nora go to General Milwood's—I must have advice and help. And yet—friends! friends! I dread 'em! I've a good mind to have him up to London—myself—and hear what the law can do—myself. I will. That's what I'll do. To-morrow is Tuesday. There'll be Dynely's cart going to the Bay. But what is this man to be done with all night? Can no one advise me, or help me? What shall I do with him?"

"HE OPENED THE DOOR. AMBRAY WAS SITTING RIGHT BEFORE IT."

Page 93.

" Ambray ! Ambray !" cried Michael, rising and turning upon him with eyes big with pity, reproach, and sorrowful scorn. " Do you think all your lawing, even if it brought death itself, is more to me compared with your grief than a sparrow's peck to a man upon the rack? I did not wish to shun the *law*; it was not the fear of that kept me from stopping at the first surgeon's with that poor lad—if all had come out at once I should have had evidence enough on my side to make my punishment a mere nothing. I am certain of it—certain. But if all the law could do, supposing the utmost had been done, would it have paid you for his loss, would it have given you bread, and one to serve you in your need and loneliness, and kept you from cursing the man who had brought all this upon you? If the law could have comforted you by having me, it should have had me ; for it was this was my great dread and turned me coward—this that has come upon me after all. Well, if the law can comfort you now, let it, let it! But to talk as if no prison were strong enough to hold one night a man for whom all the world, all life is a prison, till you set him free by your forgiveness, is a mockery, an insult even I will not bear. Ha, master! how am I speaking? I beg your pardon—I do—forgive me! but, indeed, you do not know. You do not know me, or you would feel that to imprison me, to bind me to you any faster than I am bound already, is like tying a hair round hands fettered with iron. Let me go. I will be in the mill when you want me."

The miller made no movement to detain him, but when he had reached the gate at the end of the little garden, Michael knew the tall figure was in the door-way looking after him and watching him up the mill-field.

CHAPTER XXVII.

TILL he had seen Nora crossing the Buckholt fields, Michael never moved from the window from which he had watched Ambray all the long August morning.

By this time the sun was setting; all the colours of the downs were turning soft and sad under the shadows. As Nora went home with her back to the west, her shadow lay before her half across the field ; and Michael watched its weary sway and the weary form following it till the little pane of glass through which he looked seemed to thicken and darken, and he could see it no more.

He got up and went to the window that looked down on the strip of road where he could see the team.

A large trim brewer's dray was standing before it.

Michael no sooner caught sight of it than he took his cap, but forgetting to put it on, ran out of the mill and across the field to Ambray's cottage.

He opened the door. Ambray was sitting right before it.

" Gillied's dray is here —at the Team," he said. " I cannot rest any more than you ; why should we wait till morning ?"

Ambray half rose, but his wife coming between them, placed her hands tremblingly on his shoulder and pushed him back in his chair.

" No, no," she whispered with her lips on his burning forehead. " In the morning Nora will bring us money. You have no money now. What can you do without ? Wait till the morning."

Then turning quickly towards Michael, she drew him out, whispering angrily—

" Why did you come? I had but just quieted him. He has been like a madman. Go," she said, sinking her voice still lower, drawing him further out, and pressing his arm with her shaking hands—" go in the dray yourself. Get from him, and save us from further misery ! Go !"

Michael went from the cottage straight to the Team, but only to stand staring at the dray till it drove off, when he again returned to the mill.

He groped about in the dusk over such little tasks of labour and forethought as the absence of himself and Ambray, and the coming of a stranger, seemed to render necessary.

It was not so much a sense of duty which made him do this, as it was an instinct that impelled him to guard himself from surrendering thus early in the night to the frightful sense of injustice, misery, and despair that was gaining fresh strength in him every moment.

The night came on hot and dark.

He was passing one of the windows on the shooting-floor when he saw a light in the mill-field.

The instant that Michael looked, the light showed him a figure a few yards away from it, which he recognised as Ma'r S'one's.

Seeing this, he fixed his whole attention on the light, and saw the gleam of a white hand, then of a face, then he felt rather than heard a step ; while a name trembled on his lips.

It was Nora carrying a lantern under her shawl.

She came to the mill-door and stood listening.

PART VIII

CHAPTER XXVI.

WHEN Michael saw Nora he shrank back into a corner of the dusky little room. He stood like a stone figure carved there when the wall was made; his head and shoulders bent so as to fit under the sloping ceiling; his brows drawn up; his nostrils wide; his lips kept apart by thick-coming breaths; his eyes turned to the opening in the floor with inexpressible dread.

His torture was to begin afresh he felt. Nora, unable to believe in or endure the idea he had given of George's faint regard for her, had come to demand more of him : to implore him by all he had lost to her to tell her if there had really been no message, no last word forgotten in Ambray's terrifying presence, and which he could now remember and repeat to her. The thought of this stricken widowed heart coming to plead to him against the double widowhood his history of George's last days suggested in hinting at the death of George's love before his own death, filled Michael with such alarm and pain, he had not the power to move when Nora knocked, or to answer when she opened the mill door and called his name,—

" Michael Swift."

He pressed back more tightly, straining his lowered head and shoulders against ceiling and wall as if he meant to lift and throw them off like some movable burthen.

" Ma'rs Michael !" cried Ma'r S'one.

Michael heard them come up as far as the grinding-floor, and stand still there.

" He is not here, Ma'r S'one," said Nora under her breath. " He has gone."

" 'Cline our 'erts ! he's aarf !" answered Ma'r S'one lower down the mill.

The dots of light from the lantern holes moved from where they had been resting on the wall, by which was the square opening leading to the steps.

No sooner did Michael grow conscious that his visitors were giving up their search for him and going away, than the idea of being left alone to the long night, the bitter morning, the strange journey, the terrible companion, became suddenly so insupportable he could not keep his agony from bursting from him.

" Ma'r S'one !" he cried in a kind of frenzy, " Ma'r S'one !"

After a short pause, a voice from below answered tremblingly, and as if remonstrating against some influence that would hold it silent—

" 'Cline our 'erts to keep this la' ! Hollo ! Ma'rs Michael ! where be ? "

By this time Michael was repentant of his cowardice, his cry. The dots of light came back upon the wall ; they danced higher, passed to the ceiling, the dusk lightened.

First appeared the intricate embroidery of the back of Ma'r S'one's smock collar—then his head, its silver hair flat with the sweat of a harvest day's labour; then a timorous hand grasping the rope balustrade, an enormous boot, hob-nailed, clay-coloured, and a mere thread of a gaitered leg attached, a struggle, a little panting and creaking, and Ma'r S'one was landed on the shooting-floor.

Nora, better used to the mill-steps, rose up to Michael's view, with her lantern in her hand and her light about her, gently, softly, as mist from the hollows at harvest—a vision as wraith-like and tender as the unexpected image of the moon in dark waters, to eyes too full of tears to look upward for the moon herself.

Michael, who had been unable to look anywhere yet but down deeper and deeper into his great sorrow, finding suddenly this light and loveliness in its black depth, felt his soul hushed, awed, and for the moment mysteriously comforted. It was now that he felt for the first time with strange joy and almost with terror that the sweetness of her presence to him was a fact that was to remain unchanged by all that had happened this day, and that being unchanged was too truly unchangeable. He at once suffered over this feeling and gloried in it. He gloried in it as one unassailable treasure that neither Nora, nor Ambray, nor law could take from him, let all do their worst. He suffered over it because of the thought that it would be useless to him as known but unreachable wealth to a starving man.

Nora did not approach any nearer than sufficed for her to set her lantern down, and then lifted her eyes and saw Michael looking like some half-human bat; for from the corner where he stood the walls with their crossed and recrossed laths spread round him like dark, sinewy wings, of which his figure, with its bowed head, and arms laid back, seemed the centre.

He strained back closer as she raised her eyes to his, catching her breath, and shuddering at the sight of him. She saw the misery in his eyes, but had no leisure from her own sorrow to give it notice or thought This sorrow—Michael's own gift—looking up at him from eyes so surrendered to it that it and their beauty seemed one strange light, so overcame him that the large drops fell from his own, making black spots in the flour dust on the floor.

"Why have you not gone?" asked Nora.

She spoke in a low voice, and sighed afterwards, as one watching by the dead speaks low and then sighs, remembering how indifferent alike to silence and sound are the ears they guard.

Her voice was awful to Michael, bringing him suddenly into the secret chamber of her sorrow, and to the re-opened coffin where the young athlete lay, still challenging his last conqueror, matching the strength of his dead beauty and youth against the worms.

"Why have you not gone?" repeated Nora. This time she spoke wearily and reproachfully, as if wondering how he could retain her from a vigil so sad and sacred as her soul must keep that night.

"Gone!" echoed Michael, looking down on the black drops on the floor, and not knowing what he answered.

"Yes," said Nora, with a yet more weary impatience; "I am surprised your are still here. You must know that it is better for you to be away out of his reach. You must know we shall have enough to bear. Go—pray go!"

"Go!" Michael again repeated after her.

"Yes; do you not understand? We wish you out of his way. There is danger for both of you while he knows where you are. We all feel you had better go. Now do you understand?"

"Yes, yes," answered Michael, clutching the rafters on either side of him, and pressing with his stooping shoulders and head against the walls and ceiling till all the slight mill-top shook, and Ma'r S'one looked round, murmuring, "'Cline our 'erts!" "I understand. It is expected I shall go—run away—escape—hide myself."

"Certainly it is," answered Nora.

"Like a murderer," said Michael with excessive gentleness, but such anguish, that Nora, for the first time since she had been in the mill, had her attention drawn to him for his own sake. Stepping up to the floor, she saw his face fully, and its misery.

Michael perceived this, and was near falling upon his knees and letting out all the longing of his soul for a little pity, but then he also saw that she no sooner had given him and his fearful plight this brief attention than her own sorrow, growing jealous, seized all her soul back again to itself, and its object; and the impatient wringing of the hands, with which she turned away from him, he interpreted into the complaint, "O why,—why should I be troubled with this man's misery—have I not enough to bear—is it not unnatural that I should have to think of him —to pity him? Why does he not go out of the path of those he has bereaved so awfully?"

This double change in her was watched by Michael with a wistfulness as patient and meek as it was intense.

At the last change he came from where he had stood, and taking up the lantern placed it in Ma'r S'one's hesitating hands.

"Hold it high now, Ma'r S'one," he said; "and low when you are out—so—so when you pass the corner of the ten acre, and this way as you cross Stone-Slip—be careful there."

Then turning to Nora, he laid one hand on the wall, and extended the other toward the steps, with that gentle eloquence of gesture so un-English, and perhaps peculiar to himself.

"If it would be any real good to you, my going," he said, "I would go; but I know it would not; he would never rest till—till the thing was brought before the world. Why not let it be? Do not trouble—I will be my master's keeper, as well as his prisoner. He shall come to no harm while he is doing this against me—and then——"

Nora looked up at him, stung by what she thought this wretched man's folly, into something like curiosity, and repeating impatiently, "And then?"

This look—the first that had ever come upon him from her—not questioning of others,

but directed at himself, and at his fate solely
—for the moment made Michael unable to
speak. He lowered his eyes, that she might
not see their great gratitude, and withdrew
the cause of it in shuddering self-reproach.

"And then," he said, as soon as he could
speak (strong self-control pressing on him
made his voice as sweetly and truly modulated
as the sound of some instrument at the touch
of fingers full at once of tenderness and
power); "then, when all is over, and he feels
he has got justice—when he has had the law
on me—he will be easier to manage—more
satisfied and quiet. But do not trouble, he
will get no hurt on my account, either from
me or for me—unless I really did as you say
—escape from him now—*that* would madden
him."

A sense of conviction came to Nora, but
she repelled it.

"This must not be," she said, looking up
at him with eyes full of helpless distress.
"As *he*—as George forgave you "—a mourn-
ful authority stole into her voice in saying
this—" you shall not suffer the same as if he
had not done so. You must know that.
You must know his wish is sacred to us.
For his sake, then," she added, more coldly
and imperiously, "we wish you to go before
more harm is done, before his name and
life——"

She ceased, turning away her face; then,
again fronting Michael, said firmly—

"And his *death* shall be brought in such a
way before the world. You must question
no more what your duty is. You must go.
Surely you will not—you dare not—refuse to
do so, when you know we—*I* wish it—
require it."

"You would be blamed," said Michael
gently. "I would do what you wish, but
that what I must do for your—your good,
your peace, your best chance of peace, is
different from that. No. It must be gone
through with; it is better it should be gone
through with. I must stay. My master
must find me here in the morning."

"I must send others to reason with you;
I cannot," said Nora, drawing her shawl
closer, and laying her hand on the rope
balustrade.

Ma'r S'one, ever since Michael gave him
the lantern, had been painfully absorbed in
trying to remember and to practise the
lesson he had received as to its use, start-
ling Nora and Michael, and making his own
small eyes blink, by darting the light about in
all directions.

When Nora began to descend the steps,

he followed, holding the lantern so as to
cast the light well behind him, and turning a
look of almost frenzied anxiety on Michael
to see if he was acting according to his orders.
Michael quietly took it from him and went
down with it, giving it back into his eager
but nervous hands at the mill door.

Nora turned here suddenly and looked at
Michael.

He knew at once the thing he so dreaded
was coming.

"Michael Swift," she said, "you have
acted rather strangely with regard to myself
once or twice. I should not have noticed it
—*now* I must. I must ask you to tell me
truly, as you would have your God deal
mercifully with you in this great trouble that
is on you, if you have been tempted to keep
back some other message of George Ambray's than those you have given ?"

Michael looked into Nora's searching eyes
with a profound and lowly sympathy. It
was evident to her that as he looked at her
his thoughts went deeper into the grief that
prompted the questioner than the question
itself.

"Oh, Miss Ambray!" he said at last, his
voice and eyes full of reverence and pity.
"George could not understand you. Your
letters, your beautiful letters—forgive me,
but they were lost upon him. He knew that
they were beautiful; he said so to me often
as he read them; but——"

"To *you!*" cried Nora in haughty and
sharp pain.

"But," continued Michael, not startled
from his train of thought, "he read those
wise and beautiful, most beautiful passages of
comfort, as if—as if it was from a book; he
read them, not—not taking them as—as a
man perishing of thirst takes water—as sweet
astonishing answers to those questions that
trouble and disappointment makes one ask
oneself without any hope of having them
answered. George was a boy; he had not
come to want these things you gave him. He
suffered; but as yet a little money that
would make him welcome among his
friends was what gave him most comfort, was
what made him as happy as could be. A five-
pound note in a letter was more to him than
wise, beautiful words. He could not help it,
any more than a child; it was so; it was his
nature. He would say to me, 'Why, Michael,
there's not a man in England gets such letters
as I do. Bless her! I'll put this by and read
it to-morrow; we mustn't lose a minute of ·
this tide,' and there, upon his mantel-piece,
the letter would be left, an evening, a day,

sometimes two or three days, and I—I, who had been so wonderstruck, so lost and dumb in hearing him read the beginning as to make him look at me and say, 'Ah, poor old Michael, *you* don't understand this sort of thing'—I would have to see it there, to touch it in sorting his things, to hold it in my hand, open. Oh, it was then I knew for the first time I was a patient man."

"What of his letters?" asked Nora, hiding her sting under a look of angry suspicion. "Were all destroyed!"

"Destroyed!" repeated Michael. shrinking a little from the advance of the wandering ray of Ma'r S'one's lantern. "Yes, yes, his letters were destroyed."

"I asked you," said Nora sternly, "were *all* his letters destroyed?"

If Michael had not known Ma'r S'one to be the most harmless creature in existence, he would certainly have strongly suspected him of "malice aforethought" at this moment, for his lantern light rested steadily on his face.

"A few—I think a few were—were not destroyed," he answered.

"Were these which were saved mine?" asked Nora.

"There might—yes, there might be some of yours, certainly. I could not say—not positively—to the contrary."

"Michael Swift, if *you* have these letters, give them to me."

"In the morning then," answered Michael, scarcely to be heard. "I will give them in the morning."

"Have you them *here?*"

"In the morning," cried Michael imploringly. "I will give them in the morning."

"*Have* you them here?"

"Yes, they are here."

"Then give them to me instantly."

Ambray, in one of the fits of magnanimity common to most tyrants, had given up the huge deal desk in the corner of the ground-floor to Michael's exclusive use. To this Michael now went, and in a moment returned from it with a packet in his two hands, looking down at it as he came.

"Why!" exclaimed Nora the instant she saw them, "these *are* my letters—these are all my letters."

"Yes, these are *all* your letters."

He did not immediately give into her outstretched hand the packet, but held it, looking down at it, his chin on his breast.

"I have but two other books in the world," he said gently; "my Bible and my Shakspere. And this," he added, giving the packet into her hand with a smile, that seemed half

light half water in his eyes, "*this* was the key to both. I never understood them till *this* taught me how. Take it, take it; the night's work is complete!"

"You are a strange and most unfortunate man," said Nora, turning towards the door. "I can say no more; others must reason with you about this perversity."

She went out sighing, with a sense of a sorrow that she could not look into because of her own sorrow. And Ma'r S'one, a ter turning to Michael and crying with tremulous sympathy, but in a whisper, for fear of offending Nora, "Oh, Ma'rs Michael, Lord ha' marcy 'pon us, and 'cline our 'erts to keep this la!" tottered after her, casting the light of his lantern brightly back into the mill.

"Ay, George, it is complete," cried Michael, looking up into the black, hot, starless night. "It is complete!"

CHAPTER XXIX.

Though Michael found himself acting as if he had resolved upon the course which he was taking, he had not really done so. He was not sure the morning would find him as he had told Nora it should—still in Ambray's power. A strong instinct that it would do so had moved him to say what he had said to her; but when she was gone he considered her words and Mrs. Ambray's as to his flight, and fell into a state of tormenting and hopeless indecision.

Meanwhile he had a fearful sense of Time marching away stealthily and silently his only defences—the night and early morning hours.

Sleepless, and sick with fatigue and want of food, which he had not tasted since the bread fell from his hand when the reapers had passed at breakfast time, he sat and listened to the sharp rasping cry of the corn-crake and the chirping of the crickets, the only musicians awake to chant their shrill and jubilant harvest song. Sometimes—but very seldom—a low rich murmur went through and through the corn as if these noisy creatures had disturbed the earth's slumber, and made her heart sigh under its rich burthen and whisper "hush!" and the whisper spread from field to field all over the dark undulations of the valley—the wheat uttered it mellowly, the barley rustled with it more than the wheat, the rye whispered it more airily than all. The long fields bore it to the sea, the sea turned the small low hush into a mighty one.

Michael, whose sorrow could not be

"hushed," sat at the open mill-door, taking from the night that additional and profound dreariness which is so often found in the insensibility of outward things to human suffering. In natures submissive and gentle like his, thought goes on still wonderingly and inquiringly under the greatest sorrow, the mind lifts itself and looks with patience and awe on the new and dark world into which it is cast, and sees so much sooner than the passion-blinded mourner the small rifts in the clouds where stars may come, or the light on the horizon from which the day may break. The first stars in the rifts that Michael's patient eyes beheld were the thoughts of his home, and of having at last some sympathy from those who he felt could but learn all he had suffered and was yet to suffer with amazement and pity. More than this Michael did not expect from his family when the truth should be made known to them; but the thought of this pity in the dear faces gave him of itself much comfort, having been denied all sympathy so long. It seemed to him that no sentence which could be passed on him could be so very hard when accompanied by his father's indignant protestations, his mother's silent, clinging embrace, his brothers' black, helpless, but sympathetic looks, and his little sister's tears and caresses. These were the stars in the rifts; but the sun might rise—there might be the deep, glad comfort of hearing that Nora herself was turning merciful towards him as her grief grew less bitter and absorbing. She had friends and money at her command, who could tell what she might not do towards lessening his punishment? and what so sweet as liberty coming by a gift from her hand?

So sat this meek Daniel all the night, guarding himself with humble and gentle hopes, against the lions of disappointment, injustice, terror, and despair, that crouched around him in the darkness.

The morning came, not yet with any sound of human life and work, but that first dewy glory of the day so seldom seen except by the eyes that wake to suffering or lonely toil.

Michael's spirit, which had known communion with so many of these hours, gazed up even on this daybreak with the shrinking tenderness of a child at the aggrieved eyes of a beautiful mother teaching him with tears that pain must be given him for his good.

This warm and lovely morning, like a mother indeed, took Michael from the black nurse night; and with the fresh songs of her bright lips, and the warmth and light of her smile, that awakened the rest of the world, soothed *him* to the sleep he so much needed.

The morning came—the working morning, with the ring of the anvil, the creaking of cottage gates and draw-wells, and the chopping and breaking of faggots.

When Michael opened his eyes, the first thing they saw was a face at the window, looking in upon him with an expression which brought all the truth at once to his mind. The face belonged to a labourer of Mrs. Grist's; he had seen it at the Team on the first day of his arrival at the High Mills, and now the sight of it instantly brought to his recollection the kind of terror he had had in looking on the assembled faces that day, and in wondering what judges their owners would prove if his strange case should ever come before them. They had stared at him then with no more regard for what he thought than if he had been a dog. This morning, when face after face closed up the window as the signal was passed that Michael was awake, there was the same expression, accompanied with one of blank unhesitating abhorrence.

He rose, and for the first time since his confession felt a passion for escape, for release from the torture preparing for him. At this movement, and at his wild glance round, figures filled up the door, and he knew he no longer had any choice as to keeping his promise to his master.

He sat down again, only wondering now what the time was, how long it would be before half-past nine, when Dynely, the carrier, would drive up his tilted cart to the Team.

. CHAPTER XXX.

MANY a morn'ng had Michael watched the loading and the slow laborious setting forth of this one and only public conveyance to and from Lamberhurst and the Bay. He had heard of it before he came to the High Mills, George had made him laugh with his description of its progress and adventures on the few occasions when necessity had obliged him to make use of it. Little had he thought to hear the words "Dynely's cart," which had always been uttered with a smile by George, used by his father at such a moment, and with such meaning, as he had done last night.

Was it nine yet? he wondered, or had he even more than half an hour to sit here with these eyes upon him! He forgot, as people under great mental suffering do forget, that half his sickness and deathly fear was caused by want of food and common physical exhaustion. He thought all his suffering was caused by the horror of his position, and so was all the more alarmed for himself and his fortitude during the days that were to come.

With a breath of relief he looked up when he heard a stir amongst his gaolers, and one of them announced, in a low excited voice, " Here be Armbray ! "

From the lethargic excitement, mutterings, and nudgings that ensued, Michael understood that there was something even more noticeable than the approach of his master being watched, and presently saw that the old man was not alone.

He had obtained an order for Michael's arrest, and two men to take charge of him to London.

Mrs. Ambray came behind them with some breakfast for the pris ner; which it was reported all over Lamberhurst, with righteous horror, he thanked her for, and ate and drank "like a Christian."

Ambray, as he approached his servant, and delivered him up to the men he ha l brought, neither looked nor avoided looking at Michael's face, raised towards him with a wistful curiosity, in which there was no reproach, no consciousness of self at all.

Mrs. Ambray stood watching Michael eat the food she had brought with no more feeling for him on her white, absorbed, and pain-drawn face than if he had been a dog that she was feeding.

Michael, as he looked at her and saw this, thought the bread he was eating must choke him. They had been such friends—once or twice she had said to him " my son," giving him, all unconsciously, a foretaste of the greatest joy and triumph he ever wished to know in this life—the triumph of being called " my son " by Ambray when all should be known, the heavy penalty paid, the pardon earned and rendered.

As for Ambray, it was easy to see he only now lived and breathed in his purpose of punishing his son's destroyer—of " having the law upon him."

" It will cheat me ; it will give me as little as it dares, I know," he had said to his wife ; " it always does. But what I can have out of it I will, and then—then I'll leave him to God." And with what prayers for divine vengeance he would do this, his voice and thickening veins across his brow avowed.

" Leave him to God now, John," Mrs. Ambray had implored. " You hear what

they all say, how little his punishment can be except from his own conscience. Oh, stay and comfort your poor dear heart—and me. I do think you forget I am that lad's, that precious angel's mother, I really do ! "

Ambray turned upon her impatiently, opening his mouth to ask her how she supposed he could have endured her existence near him so long if it had not been for his remembrance of this fact ; but seeing her pathetic old eyes caught the sense of his words before they were uttered, he was satisfied, and shut his mouth again without speaking.

In answer to another appeal from his wife and niece together, he had cried out, trembling all over at the very idea of the inaction they advised :

" Why, why, one would think you were mad ! What in the world could I do if I did not prosecute this man ? Sit here, walk out, lie down at night, live on this land that was my father's, hearing—as I should—no sheep bleat but what would mind me of our last lamb of the fold crying out to me in death ! Seeing with my failing sight nothing but him," and Ambray had started, and seemed actually looking on the vision that he called up, and trembling as if in the very presence he imagined—" but him, my pale boy, bled to death, white, beckoning me with his flower, as white ! O Esther ! O Nora ! You have cost me this ! Say no more, oppose me no more ! "

So Michael, and his two new acquaintances, and Ambray, met the astonished carrier at the Team, and were made room for in the tilted cart, among the parcels, baskets, and two women, each with a brood of small sun-bonnets and infantine smocks. From amidst these Michael's eye soon drew a little friend to sit upon his knee and be a shield for his stooping face against the glances of such wayfarers as might chance to know him.

CHAPTER XXXI.

SITTING cramped under the tilt of Dynely's cart Michael, from behind his little golden-haired shield, lifted his eyes to take their last look at the High Mills.

Though now quite still, while all their kindred, standing few and far between on the faint horizon, kept up a dreamy motion, the High Mills looked instinct with life that morning, not unlike, Michael thought, two vigorous gigantic grasshoppers braced ready for a leap.

How different all was from what it had been

that March day when he first came into the village! He had thought his new world wonderful enough then—and indeed its beauty had been great—but at that time it was like some lovely beggar maiden sparely clad and fed, her green gown patched with russet, her sweet breath fitful and uncertain, now wild, now soft. Since then, like a rich prince, had come the summer, and married her; arraying her in golden harvest robes, and lavishing upon her all the glories of his kingdom.

Through a slit in the tilt Michael's great eyes, worn and sad, but moist with good-will and liking, took this last look; and he bore the picture with him, and often saw it afterwards in prison.

Yes, in the exercise-yard at morning, beyond the cropped heads and listless figures, in all their uniform and insignia of vice and sorrow, beyond the little band of the defeated soldiers of sin, bent on their monotonous and inglorious march, beyond the white walls that grow close, and become as a film upon the eyeball, and press in upon the very soul, beyond or through all this would rise that fair, green world.

In all its August glory it would come before him; the woods spreading up the hill-side in great dark masses; no foliage, no separate form, nor any variety of colour apparent; but only the dull, soft, velvety undulating ground; the swelling corn-fields, and those farm clusters for the soft russet tints of which George Ambray's eyes had yearned in death; the little thatched cottages, each with its stack of faggots near it, almost as big as itself, reminding one of a white straw-hatted master and black naked serf; the emerald meadows speckled with sheep; and over all such glorious abundance and warmth of colour, such fervour and excess of it in spots and on things where no human artist would dream of expending his skill. Round all rose the soft line of hills against the sky, like a new wave of earth just up-gathered, faint-tinted, humid, as if light shone through them.

On these and over all were the mills, looking scarcely like fixtures at all, but newly alighted, busy-winged creatures, incidental to the time of year, to the season of the corn.

Michael did not think of bearing it away to be his prison picture as he looked at it from the tilted cart; he thought of the harvest, of the contrast it was to *his* harvest which he was reaping from that little grain of

hope he had sown here, and looked for through all the summer, and which had come up such a bitter tare.

The possession of that hope had been the only thing which had seemed to render life supportable since George's death; and now he was obliged to own, as he glanced at Ambray, that it had been an unnatural one; that all his struggle had been against the laws of nature.

So all now was over. The stain must be left upon the mill-stone; heaven would send him no such wind as should enable him to grind it out. George's old father and mother must be left childless and servantless; and he who would have been their son and their servant bear in his soul for ever the reproach and bitterness of their thoughts of him—of their loneliness.

CHAPTER XXXII

MICHAEL had no fear about his trial; indeed he looked forward to it with that kind of melancholy satisfaction with which a neglected member of a family will sometimes regard the idea of a long illness because of its bringing him for a time the constant remembrance and attention of those for whose sympathy he yearns.

It was the only comfort now left to him, that thought of the return to those primitive, simple, unvarnished affections, whose strength, it seemed to him, must outlive all changes. For a little while his bruised, stunned heart, might give itself up to the exquisite comfort of keen sympathy, of passionate solicitation, from the dear hearts too unsophisticated and rough for feigning. All through that hot and dreary drive among the parcels, smocks, and sun-bonnets, this quiet prisoner beguiled the time with imaginary looks, acts, and conversations of the large family in the tiny house at Thames Dutton when all should be known there. The thought that his father could feel anything but horror and sympathy at knowing all he had suffered at the time of Grant's death, never occurred to trouble him. He only pictured him and his mother trembling for his life, while his brothers would disperse in twos and talk of him, and sweet little Cicely would cry by herself till some of them found and comforted her. Dear old home! dear old times! thought Michael; there would be but the few, few years in prison—there *could* not be many—and then all would come back again —the solid honest life, with its solid, honest pleasures, and the High Mills and their story become but as a dream.

CHAPTER XXXIII.

THE sails of the High Mills hung motionless for seven weeks.

In that time Michael Swift, apart from h's trial for the death of George Ambray, experienced a trial of a kind which few perhaps are called upon to undergo, and which ends in either giving the person so tried great and peculiar advantages over the rest of his fellow-creatures, or in utterly ruining him. The result of this second trial of Michael's, was not known to himself or to any one on earth at the time when he received his sentence for the manslaughter of George Ambray and was taken to prison. All he knew himself yet was, that his loosening hold on hope had been beaten off, as it were, finger by finger.

It was not that his case had been dealt with hardly. While caring very little *how* it went, Michael could not help feeling all through it a certain dull surprise at the leniency with which his great error was regarded by the world. It seemed to him that if he had heard his father read all this that went on from day to day so wearily as old Swift used to read out such cases, with the vague idea that no law proceedings could be *quite* legal without his judgment being passed upon them—it seemed to Michael that if he had heard his own case so read, he would have thought the prisoner ought to consider himself peculiarly fortunate in his trial. The truth was that Michael at the end of all, when he heard he was only to be imprisoned for a year, even suffered a shock at the knowledge that he would be so soon in possession of the liberty for which there seemed no use in all the world.

In *this* darkness no stars in the rifts gleamed for his wild and wandering gaze. At the time when he had lifted his eyes trustingly and gratefully to look for them in the time of his great need they had all fled. He found himself denied all sympathy in his own flesh and blood. By some strange freak of his weak intellect, ever supported by his strong obstinacy, old Joseph Swift was led into condemning his son as something a few degrees better than a murderer; and, being despotic ruler over all judgments in his own house, forced the whole family to regard him in the same light, to their great wretchedness.

Michael's spirit was so stunned and sickened within him when this state of things revealed itself, that he scarcely knew or cared

what was going on around him in the court where he stood so many hours, listening like one in a dream.

The only thing he had any interest in was the grateful and loving obstinacy of Polly Bardsley, in her refusal to give evidence against the man who had saved her grandfather's life.

Her sweet weary face turning from her questioners, her pretty flaxen hair having to be incessantly thrust back into her bonnet by her red little hands, and her petulant "*I* dun know," in answer to all questions, haunted Michael throughout the year of his imprisonment. He often wondered to what end her rebellion against Bardsley had brought her; for Polly was only one day in court, the morning after this she had disappeared from her home, and the evidence which Bardsley and "Traps" were giving against Michael was stopped through the blind beggar's distress, and his departure in search of her.

How often Michael wondered, months afterwards, if they had met; or if the two still wandered apart through the miserable winter days, in their great darkness, like two lost familiar spirits seeking each other after death!

Joseph Swift, in his new character of martyr, which his view of Michael's calamity obliged him to assume, was so over-conscientious at the trial as to make himself thoroughly unpopular.

Michael pitied him. He knew the old man had the true Spartan spirit in him, though it was only to be the slave of a wrong idea. After the first surprise Michael showed no pain at anything he said. Sometimes when he went out of his way to mention a thing that did his son harm, the sad eyes would turn and look at him in dull, callous wonder. The secrets which George Ambray had confided to him at his death, and which Michael had refused to tell George's father, were now revealed to the world, and proved only fresh revelations of sin and error.

Ambray heard them, and heard also the whole truth of Bardsley's story, with increased hatred towards Michael. Yet it was not he who had brought these things against George, but the evidence marshalled against him by Ambray himself which had laid open the truth; they came to light indeed so simply that Michael was amazed, and could half fancy the spirit of his friend was present, refusing to let him any longer bear the burthen of his sins.

The most striking feature of the trial was

the contrast in the position of the two fathers.

With obstinate martyrdom in his rosy little face, blue eye, and sleek silver hair, stood Joseph Swift—one of the many silly ensigns that make themselves a nuisance on life's battle-field by persisting in clutching the wrong colours to the death. Conscious rectitude, and high-minded indifference as to results, made him feel himself a hero, too great to be ever appreciated on earth; though all the time his foolish old heart ached at the sight of Michael standing so patient, reproachless, vaguely wondering.

How different the old miller looked! No blameless and clear conscience lent such light to his hollow eye, and firmness to his tall shaking form. Trembling constantly, now leaping up, now sinking prostrate, at one moment brightening and listening in passionate hope when the evidence against the prisoner seemed growing serious, at the next bent double, grinding one clenched hand in the palm of the other, he would mutter, " My boy! my boy! May he get justice in heaven, for he never will here!"

But infinitely worse than the loss of the vengeance for which he thirsted was the ill fame that rose, obscuring the brightness of his idol, and that in so doing showed Michael's character more and more honest and spotless in all but the one stain. It nearly maddened Ambray to think that he was there defending his son with such passionate vehemence, and a not too great regard for truth, yet proving him less worthy at every step, while "that absurd old Swift," with all his severity, only brought more light to shine on Michael's good life. It was bitter, too, beyond expression, for him to feel that his own faith in Michael had become stronger than any one's; that even whenever a suspicion of dishonesty or meanness of any kind rested on Michael for a moment in the course of the trial, Ambray had always a hateful confidence in its being instantly removed, or at least unmerited.

Once when Joseph Swift *did* seem about to bring something serious against Michael, when, with stern heroism in his eye, and his blue-and-white spotted handkerchief mopping away at his bald crown, he confessed that his son had two months before his departure for the High Mills committed forgery on him—his own father—Ambray's heart beat high. The next instant he fell back as if a cannon-ball had struck him—the crime proved George's, though the shame and blame had been borne by Michael, according to his last

vows to his friend. This came out through Michael's sister.

Another theme for morbid jealous thought that Ambray took with him from this trial was the recollection of Michael's manner towards his father—his sincere pity for the needless pain he was giving himself—his gentle answers when the revelations of Swift's domestic tyranny elicited comments of surprise, or caused such questions to be put to Michael as —" What? Do you mean to say that when you were earning that sum weekly your father only allowed you this? What was his reason?"

Michael, instead of explaining that in all things but good living Swift was the greatest miser on earth, would only turn his head and answer, looking with gentle respect at the excited little man, " *My father is peculiar.*" This answer was given to the same sort of question so many times by Michael in his sad self-absorption that it became famous in the court.

Mrs. Ambray, down at the High Mills, read it in the papers, and showed it to Nora with tears in her eyes, asking if it was not like the honest simple soul—if she could not hear him saying it?

When all was over, and the sentence passed, Ambray threw up his arms, and with fearful looks and words called for a Higher judgment on the prisoner, and fell down in a fit.

Michael's face was turned towards him, and appeared at most without expression except for a strained look in the eyes.

Most people who saw him thought his heart had hardened—that he had grown careless—but a lawyer who happened to know a little of a law higher than that he professed, remarked as the prisoner left the court—

"That man will come out of prison an angel or a devil."

CHAPTER XXXIV.

" WELL, Ma'r S'one, so t'hopp'n begins o' Toosday. Think the weather'll bear out?"

Ma'r S'one, whose back formed one of a row of backs visible through the long latticed window of the Team, first lowered with difficulty and rested on his knee the pint pewter mug, from which he had been drinking for the sake of "peace and quiet," then, after trembling with diffidence at the honour of being addressed instead of any of his neighbours, and after glancing timidly on either side of him to see if any one had taken offence at it or would like to answer in his stead, looked up and replied, with studied cheerfulness—

"Yees, we begin hopp'n o' Toosday, Ma'rs Dynely. Missis be dunned her hirin'—a pretty middlin' fair lot—she's got this year—not quite so rough as laarst. As fur weather, Ma'rs Dynely, there be rain somewheres, and we must hope the Arlmighty ull be over wi' it 'fore Toosday—but 'cline our 'erts."

"I arlwis say as a wet hopp'n's onlucky," remarked a neighbour of Ma'r S'one's in a slate-grey smock, and with as sombre a countenance.

Ma'r S'one looked as much impressed as possible, murmuring in a very low voice lest any one else should object to the remark—

"Sure!"

"Why, rain don't do t'hops no heert as I've heerd tell on," observed another of the window row, smiling with one eye and but one side of his mouth, as his pipe was in it, and wagging his head at the end of Dynely's whip as if he saw there more support to his argument than he cared to let out all at once. "Not as I've ever heard tell on, it didn't."

"Sure!" said Ma'r S'one again, as deferentially as he had done to the other speaker.

"What say yourself, Ma'r S'one?" asked Dynely, placing himself opposite the door that he might watch the tilted cart and large white horse given to backing, by which he was drawing upon himself the indignation of the several dogs waiting for their master outside the Team, and the gentler comments of the hens dozing under the holly hedge; "what say—yourself—Ma'r S'one?"

Ma'r S'one, thus appealed to, looked as startled and bewildered as a little boy at the bottom of the class suddenly asked a question which those at the top cannot answer.

At last he got up, and taking his long fork and seeking forgiveness in every eye for his presumption, answered—

"Well, Ma'rs Dynely, I don't want fur to goo an' fly in nobody's face, I don't—but 'cernin' the hops and the rain, 'cernin' them I caan't, I really caan't say as it doos 'em any good. No, Ma'rs Dynely, I caan't; and if the Lord ull be over wi' it 'fore Toosday—not as I'd interfere—'cline our 'erts! No."

"Doos t'hops no heert, a little rain don't," persisted the smoker at the window, still keeping his eye on Dynely's whip in its changed position, and still smiling as if he said, "You may move my argument about, but I can find it."

"Well," remarked another of the row in the window with the tone of one about to start an entirely new idea, "what I say is—

myself I doos—is as th' rain farls th' haardest on the pickers."

"That bees it, sir," averred Ma'r S'one, shaking his head sadly; "it farls haardest on the pickers and the measurer" (Ma'r S'one himself was Mrs. Grist's measurer). "See th' old people it gives the rheumatis—the rain does—and put 'em out, and they can't pick so quick. And the young folks they comes to look out for to get married, and the rain spiles the bunnets and arl that, and they don't pick so quick; and then when comes measuring time, the measure bean't what they s'pected, and they arl farls on me, old and young they doos, and it's 'Look how that old Ma'r S'one's been cheatin',' and tells me I'm gett'n too old to do the measurin' 'tarl fair, and did ort to give it up—and if I giv.s a shake more, just for peace and quiet, there's missis ready to rail out: 'Ma'r S'one, Ma'r S'one, be this a charity hop-garden, as you bees squeezin' down the measures like that?'"

Ma'r S'one's difficult position during the hop-picking season was considered over in silence.

Conversation was slow at this hour of the afternoon, when the September sun was blazing on the heads and backs at the Team window, and the hens kept up an intermittent comfortable grumble under the hedge of the garden across the road, while the cat, like a jungle tiger, sprang about among the lettuce and herb beds to eye them from different points of view, making a rustling in the crisp vegetables as she tore off in frenzied anxiety to escape temptation.

Sometimes an observation would be made or a question put by one of the lethargic loungers in the little bar-room, and not replied to till some cart-wheels, to which all had listened, had been waited for, and had passed, and their sound died away.

"Poor old Ambray's had a time ave it since this end o' laarst year," remarked the carrier, "when I brought him home in my caart after lawin' that Michael Swift."

A lumbering sound was heard along the Tidhurst road, and listened to until it turned into the lane at the church fields towards the large hop-gardens.

"Ye es," said some one full ten minutes after the last remark had been made. "They say—I dun know who was a saying—were it you, Ma'r S'one?—somebody was a sayin' they bin pooty nigh starvin' this laarst month."

Ma'r S'one only sighed out his favourite entreaty, and shook his head sadly.

"Old Armbray won't have nothin' to do

with Miss Nara, or she wouldn't let 'em want—not she," said the carrier.

" Be this true, Ma'r S'one?" inquired Ma'r S'one's next neighbour, " 'bout old Ambray and Esther a-goin' hoppin' down at your missis's."

" Yees," answered Ma'r S'one, turning up the end of his fork and shaking his head as he stared at it with watery eyes. " It be true

'nough; they come to arst her to let 'em arn a little this hoppin'."

The Tuesday was as fine a September day as ever dawned upon the moving poles—sun-bonnets and brown hands busy at earliest light.

An hour later the tall old couple came leaning on each other to take their place and task in the busy garden.

Page 95.

Both their hands shook as they first touched the hops.

Esther meekly gathered hers, but Ambray's hand fell as if it had been burnt, and he lifted his face and looked up through the lovely garlands in an ecstasy of bitterness.

CHAPTER XXXV.

FEW changes but those brought by the

seasons had come to Lamberhurst during the year of Michael Swift's imprisonment.

It is true Ma'r S'one had, this hop-picking time, to be content with side views only of the weather when he came out to open the oast-house doors in the morning, his back being now so much bent as to render any other view impossible. But while such glimpses showed him fair skies, he was infinitely thankful, and ready to endure the grumbling of the pickers with surprising patience.

Perhaps, too, the grey-walled church had a few more of those tiny dents with which it was covered, as if through Time having let so many of his baby years cut their teeth on it.

As for the High Mills themselves, they reflected, as mills will do, the fortunes of their master. The white one wanted but a background of snowy clouds to render its soiled chalky hue positively ghastly. The black mill had changed its state of slow decay to one of such rapid ruin, that poor Ambray could half suspect it of making suicidal attacks on itself in the night; or of being the victim of some furious Quixote, for whose tracks across the barley the miller looked with half suspicious eyes, as he came forth yawning wearily in the face of the rising sun.

All the year he had worked harder than he had ever done in his life. After the prostration that had made his days all like one long dark dream for weeks after Michael's trial, there had come with returning strength a passionate desire to hide his feebleness and his broken heart from the world which he considered to have used him so cruelly. It should see, he told himself, whether or not his boy's mother had need to depend on the "unpunished" murderer for her daily bread. It should see that *he* at least was not crushed to the earth with shame at the fall of his idol. He would show it that he gloried still in his son's memory—that no revelations had yet, nor ever could, lessen his love for him or lay low his pride.

In the winter evenings he had sat with the Bible that had belonged to his great-grandfather open before him—not seeking in it any comfort, but only gazing at the beloved name —the last of the long list on each of the two pages recording births and deaths; and dreaming of the time when scornful eyes should see the sabbath sun shine in upon that name on the church wall just over where its owner used to bend or lift in prayer or song his careless comely face.

The "nest egg" of the store for this cherished purpose was taken from the first money that came into his hand after the trial, and was hidden in the mill where none but himself could find it. It would not do to tell Esther. He might fall ill, and she would at need take it for his comfort.

He had in truth almost ceased talking to her about George; he thought her grief was too soon lost in care for himself; and he

was imbittered against her for this, though he took all her care as his due. Yet there were times when he would almost exult in the thought that he *only*—the father to whom George had cried out at his death—he *only* loved him still beyond all things. He was eager to cherish his own joyless life that the young man's name might not yet die out of the world, when "for when I am in the grave," he said, "who will speak well of him? The mother who bore him forgets him; the woman who was nearly his wife is already comforted and again happy; his friends who led him astray—of them, who hears anything? —while as for *me*, my very food and drink is still to me as his funeral cake and wine—I drink to him, I eat to him, I get up in the morning and force my limbs and pains into my clothes, and work and win my daily bread that his only mourner may remain yet a little longer in the world, in case that out of heaven, or worse still, out of hell, my boy should look back and see himself forgotten —so soon—*so* soon.'

Therefore, the great mill-sails laboured round for George, lying a stranger in the churchyard at Thames Dutton, as they had laboured round for him when he sat a little flaxen-headed child clapping his hands at them; the difference being that then a broad ruddy face would often come to the mill-window and look down with fondly concealed love and pride, while *now* a white face would come there and look up with eyes on whose bitter waters the same love and pride, all wounded as they were, rode boldly still, like two defiant war-maimed ships upon a troubled sea.

People thought all the first half of the year how well the old man bore himself in his bereavement, how steadily he worked, how little he complained of his ailments to what he used to do. But in time a change came over him. Instead of rising in the morning immediately he woke, and seizing on his clothes with trembling, resolute fingers, he would sit up and stare at the light, then fall back on his pillow, letting the cold, sluggish tears creep from his unwincing eyes. The *comfort* which his own devotion to his son's memory had given him was beginning to leave him, though the devotion itself did not change. The idea of living and working on purpose to honour George's name was one which time robbed of its tenderness and tangibility. Recollection began to fail; the beloved image grew faint, so faint; the eyes of his soul ached with straining to see it; it was dying from him—he was being left alone;

he had been almost content to live for the sake of a shade—a spectre—*that* he thought at least would be with him always; and now *that* was vanishing; the very echo of the voice he had so loved was growing silent—the faint sweetness of the fallen rose was leaving the dead leaves, passionately as he tried to retain it. He could scarcely now remember things about his son which Esther had thought it impossible for him to forget; and whenever he discovered this to be the case he suffered frightfully. He showed unwonted gratitude when his wife recalled to his memory things about George concerning which he was confused in this manner—

"Thank you, Esther," he would say, laying his shaking hand on hers; "thank you —yes, you're right. Oh! I remember now; don't let me forget that again, Esther; don't, for God's sake, let me forget it again."

Finding as he did the grave's victory growing greater every day—hearing as he did only a deeper silence each time his soul listened and knocked at those doors of awful mystery that had closed on all he loved—he sat down and contemplated the black, sunless world aghast and helpless like a child left in the dark.

He could not work; but for his wife's toil both might have starved. He was furious at the thought of help from Nora, whom he charged with utter falsity and fickleness because she did not die, or continue to wear mourning for George. Neither would he knowingly receive anything beyond what he considered his due from Mrs. Grist, who had refused to help him in the prosecution of Michael.

He did not mind the thought of starving himself—as for his wife he did not think about her. Sometimes when his breath left him in a fit of coughing, he hoped it might never come back again. If his foot slipped on the mill-steps he regretted he had not fallen and been killed. He wooed death, and found it, as its wooers generally do, the bitterest of coquettes.

The only star that ever shone for him in all the blackness of life was a lurid and baleful one enough. It was the thought of Michael, of some possible revenge, and the darker his life grew the more this attracted and charmed him; though it was so far off as to cause him to gnash his teeth and moan at it, like a madman through the bars of his cage at the unreachable object for which he wishes.

The goodness that had attached itself to Michael's name at the trial was now the chief theme of Ambray's thoughts—memory in losing its grasp of George became strong in its hold on Michael—not one good trait in his character was forgotten, or ever failed in being thought over to feed and nourish the hatred which was now as strong a passion as the old man's grief.

He mentioned his name to no one. None guessed the thoughts with which he beguiled the long hours as he sat in the house before his fireless grate, or out in the sun under the motionless mills.

Old Esther, looking up from her work at him, would shed many a tear for the faithful servant he had lost. Once, when Ambray sat with his long face framed in his bony fingers staring at the still sails with their coverings wrapt about them in shroud-like fashion, his wife said to him with tears—

"Ah, John, what would you give to see 'em going round again, and hear that Michael clamping up and down the stairs with his great gruff voice singing his '*Heigh, Will! and ho, Will! whistle for a breeze!*'—or his great easy figure lolling there in the doorway?"

Ambray dropped his hands from his face and gazed up at her as she stood beside him. It was clear he realised the picture vividly. Then he got up and walked round the mill several times, looking up at it often, and was unusually excited all the rest of the day.

It was just before the hop season that Esther one morning, while waiting upon her husband, suddenly fell down, and lay at his feet, supporting herself on her elbow, and gasping faintly.

"Why, what's the matter now?" asked Ambray, recoiling, with the bandage that she had been binding round his rheumatic arm hanging half off; "What's the matter with the woman now?"

"O dear!" moaned Esther faintly. "I'm afraid, John, I've gone too low."

"Too low!" repeated Ambray. "Yes, I should think you had. I want to know what you've gone so low for?"

"O dear! I'm afraid, John—don't worrit yourself—but I'm afraid it's for want of food."

"For want of food!" echoed the miller, putting his hand to his forehead and looking down at her in feeble perplexity. "Why, how's that, Esther? You're dreaming, woman. If it was *that*—*I* should be bad too. *I'm* not hungry. *I've* had enough."

Esther smiled as her elbow gave way, and her cheek touched the brick floor.

"Yes, dear," she said, "that's it. You've

had it *all* these two days. God bless you!"

It was this little scene that had led to M'ar S'one's good heart being pained by the sight of the old couple coming to ask his mistress to allow them to join in the hop-picking.

CHAPTER XXXVI.

MRS. GRIST'S hop-picking lasted just a fortnight.

During this season nearly all Southdown-shire seems to abandon itself to a kind of hop idolatry. The small village shops are mostly open only for an hour early in the morning, and then closed till dusk, and any chance customers seeking admittance are told from some upper window or neighbouring door that its owner "bees gone a-hoppin'," the informant being generally a cripple, or too aged a person to go a-hopping likewise.

As early as five o'clock in the morning one may see on the high parts of the roads, or hear in the misty hollows, the family parties proceeding in their carts with dangling kettles and sleepy children to the different hop gardens. Scarcely a child is to be met without hops in its hat or a paper of the worms they call "hop-dogs" in its hands. The cottage chimneys are smokeless all day, the hardy monthly roses—Southdownshire's autumn glory—vivid scentless scarlet and sweet pink—open and beat themselves to death unnoticed on the latticed windows and still doors. While one looks and wonders at the stillness and desertion, the very sparrows on the thatch-edge seem trying to explain its cause, to express in dumb show the fact that the inmates are "gone a-hopping."

Most of the gardens seem strangely out of the way and secluded, but whether through the trees having begun to thin, or whether the eye at this season naturally looks for them, the oast houses certainly have a prominence and importance in the landscape they never had before throughout the year. Perhaps the faint odours of the hops themselves issuing from these is after all the true reason of this. Whatever it may be, there they are, consequential, and looking like an old woman shawled and bonneted for some important mission.

The last day of Mrs. Grist's hopping was as fine as the first; but some heavy rain intervening, had given what Ambray called a "sharp edge" to his cough, and he had much difficulty in keeping to his task through the day.

In the afternoon, when the pickers divided into little tea parties, he and Esther sat alone, just outside the poles, to eat their bread and drink their bottle of cold tea that they might be refreshed for the last two hours of picking.

On one side of them the incessant gossip went on, at the other a little stream of water trickled cheerily down the hill.

Ambray sat staring into this water as he ate, his face averted from the poles. Esther's eyes were fixed on him, though she inclined her ear a little to catch the bit of news and the gossip which while she had life must needs have interest for her.

Ambray had noticed this, and was letting contempt for woman's frivolity and weakness swell the bitterness that already filled his soul without being conscious that he was himself listening, the difference being that *his* ears received the men's remarks only, while Esther's heard but the shriller voices of her own sex.

If both had remembered and repeated what they listened to, as they paused after their meal, before getting up, they would have given each a totally different account from the other.

Esther's would have been this,—

"I waant a frock fur little Ann; be woilit fash'nerbul, think you?"

"Well, *I* bees goin' to have brown meriny for *my* two gals."

"Bees you! well you do s'prise me. But now I waants somethin' downright oncommon fur 'ur. Set up, miss, and leave aarf throwin' th'y 'op dogs in my tea, will you! See she's a goo'n to school next week, and there's sich mischief as never wur if a child fin's itself worse dressed than the others, so I waant fur 'ur to have somethin' reel fash'nerbul an' good—like what none o' the rest—they Moon's child'n and arl them caant get. I thart a nice woilit—"

"I'm s'prised now as you fancies wilit. Your 'usband's sister's got one."

"Noo!"

"She bees."

"Who telled you?"

"Jane—she wur pickin' down at Leweses, side o' old Mary Vidler."

"O my 'ert! I *bees* glad you telled me, naasty mischief-maakin' thing; I bees sick of her naame! My 'usband's just been over theer, and caant tark o' nothing else. Noo I won't have a woilit if I know it."

"Movver, I *waants* a wilit. You said I'd hev a wilit if you picked a bin."

"Then you won't hev it, miss. You put that theer doll's 'ead in that tea-pot agin!

Likely I'll pick a bin or aarf a bin wi' *you* to mind. She's ben arl set on woilit 'cause she see Miss Armbrey in one yest'y."

"Not down at her aunt's, sure? I wur telled she wouldn't speak to her agin."

"Who telled you that?"

"Orrey Moon heered it up at Stone Crouch, pickin' side o' Betsy's brother."

At the time Esther took sad heed of this, Ambray was listening unconsciously to the talk of the husbands in the same group.

"So old G'ist's baught that farm o' Ray's. Know wut she's gev fo' it?"

"Noo—nat more'ns worth, *I* lay."

"Don't think much o' the land up that end myself. Be she go'n to plough that theer holler, or fence it aurf?"

"I caant tell you. Ma'r S'one, be your missis go'n to fence aurf that holler up at thet field or to plough it?"

"She hevn't quite made up her mind yet, Missis hevn't—not 'bout that holler."

"She art to plough it, Ma'r S'one."

"It 'ud be good fur her to plough it, sir; I 'grees to that; it's the best corn as grows in th' holler—so 'tis, sure."

"Nonsense, Ma'r S'one; you persuade her to fence it aarf."

"Or it ud be very handy, fenced aarf; so 'twould sir, sure."

"I was told corn never didn't, nor never wouldn't grow, not in theer holler."

"Who telled you that?"

"Why I wur pickin' side o' Tom laarst week, and he said your faather-in-la said so."

"Waugh! My faather-in-la! Old idjut! Lot *he* knows, 'cept to set the wemmen jawin' at ye. 'Cause he's a gaardener, and potters 'bout his bit o' ground arl day, there's my wife at me everlastin' 'bout our bit; it's 'faather has paarsley arl the year round,' or 'faather' this, or 'faather' that. Ugh! *he* said so, did he? Then arl the more fur that I say, G'ist's a fool if she don't plough that holler."

Doubtless, if the hearing had been reversed—if Esther had listened to the gruff gutteral tones and Ambray to the shrill ones—both would have found the logic they heard defective. As it was, it of course appeared perfectly natural. But what faraway, unreal things these that the pickers talked of seemed to both! They sat outside the garden and all its worldly interests like two children who in the great game of life had been quarrelled with and ordered to stop playing. Lonely and sad and inexpressibly weary, they waited to be taken by the hand from the road whose dust *was* dust to them, never again to be made into playthings and imaginary viands; the mud-pies which had cost so much labour in making were irrevocably mud again; they had dropped them from their hands, and now watched their companions still making them with dull and dreamy interest, half envious, half pitying.

The sweet-voiced water in the ravine beside them, though incomprehensible in what it uttered as the talk of grown people to infants, seemed to have a meaning, a comfort, a reliableness deeper than the human voices on the other side of them. So had that of the little air-sailor, the skylark, letting itself up and down in its hammock of song: so had the wind, creeping through the woods like music through a ball-room, and setting the autumnal brocades of gold and green and brown all richly rustling.

Nature's face was sweet as her voice at that hour: the aged eyes looked up into the golden clearness, and closed in pain. Her smile fell upon them, but was not for them. It was as if it had cast them off before death was ready to take them. They seemed waiting in some intermediate stage in which the miseries of both had access to their souls.

Ambray beheld in the lovely scene before them the house where he was born, whose doors and stairs the hopes and dreams of his wakefulness and his slumber had never ceased to haunt. These had not been selfish dreams —they had sprung from all the better part of his nature, and he knew this, and mused over their destruction, and upon the God whom he charged with destroying them, with a doubt and sarcasm of spirit that appalled himself even while he could not put it from him. If his life and losses were part of a divine plan, what a cruel plan it was that these things should be necessary! How could it benefit God for Him first to fill those windows with the sweet vision of George's children, and then to wash it out with George's blood, so that now those windows, glittering in the sun, had as tragic a look to him as beloved eyes whose joy had suddenly been turned into horror?

He withdrew his gaze from them shudderingly, and looked down upon the running water.

He heard the voice of her who had usurped his place in his father's house and lands speaking in vulgar dictatorial tones to the hop-pickers in that very garden where she, a shoeless, ragged tramp, had pleased his brother's easily attracted eye. Was *this*, too, part of the divine plan men talked of, for grey hairs to be thus abased to the earth while still the earth refused to cover them?

Mrs. Grist approached, her silk dress rustling harshly against the hop-poles.

Ambray set up his shoulders and lowered his head.

" Well, John Ambray, how are *you* getting on? M'ar S'one tells me you're doing wonderful. How are you, Esther? you don't look over well ; but, la! we can't expect to be young always—can we? I'm thankful for arl of us as we've had a fine finish-up day. I shall pay up o' Friday. Good evening, I must go and find M'ar S'one."

She went rustling away, leaving Ambray's head lower than ever on his shoulders, and his lips parted in a bitter smile as he looked into the water.

Most of the pickers were rising and resuming their tasks. A little group, nearest the miller and his wife, began a wild, rhapsodical Methodist hymn. An old woman cried out to Esther through the poles :

" Come, Esther, you arlwis used to beat us arl. Sing a bit, woman, it'ull do ye good."

Esther, who had been looking wistfully towards the singers, at this turned her sorrowful old face proudly away.

Her husband, still bending over the rivulet, had heard the invitation and interpreted the bitterness of her silence. He held his hand out to her, without looking up, and as she took it, closed his shaking fingers over hers, saying or almost groaning,—

" *By the waters of Babylon we sat down and wept.*"

At this the cup, so full already, overflowed. Esther dashed her apron up to her eyes, and for the next few minutes Ambray's bony fingers covered all his face.

CHAPTER XXXVII.

THE whole of Mrs. Grist's hops were safely picked before sunset, and Ambray and Esther went home while the light was still golden and warm along the road.

At those who passed them by, guessing what their earnings would come to, according to Ma'r S'one's measuring, and talking of the ways in which they should be spent, the haggard old eyes looked as they might have done at creatures of another world.

To the aged poor of Southdownshire these last days of hop-picking are mostly sad enough in the retrospection that they compel. The young voices around them declaring they will not be content without the greatest prize

that a hop-picker can win, reminds them how they also made the same boast, how year by year both hope and realisation have dwindled, till at last they are glad to earn a warm garment to cover them, a little tobacco or snuff to deaden the sharp reality of the long winter hours, a penny or two to win the services of grandchildren strong and careless, or the smile of great-grandchildren, helpless and as yet innocent of worldly hopes as themselves.

The memory of their own youth and its hopes stole over Ambray and Esther with the faint narcotic odours of the drying hops from the oast houses, and made their feeble steps and breathing more feeble still, as, leaning on each other, they toiled up towards the High Mills.

The white lane was hot and wearisome at this hour, and the south wind did nothing but blow the dust, which flew into the eyes of the old miller and his wife, and encircled their stooping forms so as to cause Ambray to smile bitterly, and mutter, as Esther murmured at it on his account,

" Why should it stand on ceremony with what will so soon belong to it? It comes for *us*, as we won't go to *it*."

This dust and the heat, the quick cloud of gnats before their eyes, and the steepness of the road made them oblivious of a sound and light which otherwise must have much sooner attracted their attention. As it was they had passed the spot where Michael first saw the white tip of the mill-sail flash up against the sky before Esther happened to raise her eyes. When she did so, she started back crying,

" Oh, my heart! John, the mill's going !"

The miller strained his eyes passionately through dust, gnats, and sun ; then caught his wife's arm with both hands, and looked into her face.

" Esther," he said, in a quick whisper, " has she done it at last? Has she taken them from us? Has she put some one in it, Esther?"

" No, no ; nonsense," answered Mrs. Ambray, trying to keep herself from shaking, " it's those boys again, John. Of course it is."

" Rascals !" ejaculated the miller, with a strange mixture of relief and anger. " Yes, of course it must be them. I'll teach 'em—but —but, Esther, they've set it right for the wind ; those rascals never got it just right like that. Oh! if she has, Esther !"

" It's the boys, John, it's the boys," said Esther reassuringly. " They'll make off as soon as they see us. Let's hurry up ; don't stand here frightening yourself like this. Come."

They pressed on together, each supporting arm trying to conceal its trembling from the other.

Ambray stood still as they reached the mill-field.

He had no voice, but as he turned to Esther shaking his head and moving his lips she understood him to say—

"It's not the boys. She has done it. She has put some one in."

After this he strode on before her towards the mill, and did not stop till he stood close under it. He paused before the half-open door listening without making any movement to enter. Then he walked round looking up at all the windows.

As he again met Esther at the door he said with the calmness of utter despair—

"If she's let it—if she's put any one into it, I shall burn it, Esther. I shall burn it to the ground."

He had not finished speaking before Esther's hand caught his and held it against her heart, and looking at her face, he saw it raised towards the mill with colour coming on its white cheeks, tears brimming and softening the eyes, hope parting the thin lips.

"John," said she, "as I'm a living woman I think——"

"What! what!" gasped Ambray, shaking her arm and turning his back on the mill that he might keep off a sound, a sense he was beginning faintly to perceive. "What, Esther, what?"

"Yes!" cried Esther joyfully, pushing past him and standing by the mill-door with both hands caught back almost to her shoulders, and her head bent and inclined to one side in the eagerness with which she listened. "Yes, yes! It is! It is!" she cried, bringing her hands one over the other on her side.

"What, woman, what?"

"It's Michael Swift's voice and step as sure as my old heart's a-beating!"

The miller crept up to her and stood between her and the open door, listening and fixing his eyes on her face as if looking for it to assist by its expression his feebler senses.

Standing thus they both heard the run of unmistakable feet down one of the upper ladders, and the deep honest roll of an unmistakable voice rising and sinking with the noise of the stone and sails,—

> "Heigh, Will! and ho, Will!
> Whistle for a breeze.
> Run, Will, turn the mill,
> Set it to the seas."

The little bell up over the grindstone tinkled, it was answered by a shout half cheery, half grumbling, just such as Michael used to answer it with to Ambray's grim amusement in the old days, then the feet went clamping up higher and higher, and when the voice was next heard it came from the tiny square window of the shooting floor.

Ambray let out his suspended breath, crept a few steps further away from the mill, then looked up at this window pressing both hands on his throat as if to hold in his cough, which was shaking him. Mrs. Ambray followed and stood at his side, holding up her finger and leaning forwards to watch his face with such a smile on her own as had not lit its wan features for many years.

The great shadow of the sails swept round at their feet as the voice rolled out with the immemorial mill tune, to which every miller has his own words, imitating in alternate lines the peculiar "thump-thump" of the sails and their soft prolonged rush.

> "Day breaks, the breeze wakes,
> Bless it every mouth!
> Run, Will, turn the mill,
> Set it to the south."

Mrs. Ambray in her excitement had moved her hand tremblingly in time to the song. Ambray seeing this had seized her wrist, and held it down with a grasp like iron.

Then they heard the steps and the voice lower in the mill—the noise of the door opening on the little terrace. Ambray's breath came quicker; his pressure against his own throat and on Esther's hand tightened.

The well-known figure stood in the little doorway in an attitude so familiar to the eyes watching it, that it seemed as if all must be a dream since the day it stood there last.

How many times the miller and his wife had seen it looking exactly as it did now, leaning against one side the door in an utter abandonment to rest and ease, the back of the hand laid across the forehead, pushing off the cap, the black eyes looking right away over Buckholt fields, never wincing as the tips of the sails flashed round before them, but gazing on dreamily while the same mysterious words which nobody could ever understand came rolling out, as they did now :—

> "Hi, Will! say why, Will,
> You, when she comes forth,
> Find, Will, the wind, Will,
> Al-ways in the north."

Ambray, looking round at the aspect of the land, and smelling the hops in the breeze, remembered that the story of his son's death was no dream. Michael had never been here so late in the year. It was all true enough. He and Esther had picked Mrs. Grist's hops —this was the last day—they had come home

—had seen the sails moving—this man was Michael Swift ; Michael Swift had come back to the High Mills.

He watched him shut the little door, and listened to his feet coming lower till he heard the sound of his step half smothered by the dust on the ground-floor.

Ambray turned his eyes to the half-open door. As he did so it was pushed quite open. Michael's eyes met his.

At that moment Mrs. Ambray ran to Michael and clutched at his shoulder, looking in his face and shaking her head in speechless emotion.

Ambray seemed surprised at this, for he gave a sigh of horror, and retreated a few steps while watching them intently.

Michael looked at him, scarcely heeding Mrs. Ambray's clinging hands and eloquent face.

He was very pale ; his face looked smaller, his eyes larger, Ambray thought, his clothes hung upon him loosely.

"My son," said Mrs. Ambray, "do you mock us, my son? Where are you bound for, and why do you come here, setting the old mill going, and making us remember what you were to us? How have you the heart to do this, Michael Swift?"

Ambray, with his eyes still upon Michael, seemed so lost in curiosity as to what his answer would be, he forgot to keep any control over his face.

Michael, still apparently ignoring Mrs. Ambray's presence, spoke to him in the manner and voice of one making the simplest matter-of-fact statement, though his eyes were full of suffering and his lips white.

"My time is up," he said. "You have had the law upon me. I have come again. Why not? Your son bought you my services, *he* gives them to you—not I. You need them. They are yours. There is nothing to pay for them, not even forgiveness if you still choose to hold it back."

Ambray looked at him still, weighing every word.

His first thought when he understood all Michael had said was how he should conceal his own increasing excitement. It was almost more than he could bear, the idea of having this unlooked-for change in his life—of having constantly before his eyes—in his service, in his power—the only object of interest the world contained for him.

He looked at Michael, wishing he could speak the words necessary to decide his staying. He trembled lest in his inability to do this he might lose him.

"By all that's good in this wicked world," sobbed Mrs. Ambray, "the Lord will repay you, Michael. He surely will. When were you out of prison? How long have you been in the mill? What have you had? Near starving, I dare say. Come—come home."

For once in her life Esther, in her delight and enthusiasm over Michael, showed a defiant disregard of Ambray, never looking at him as she tried to draw Michael homewards.

But Michael gently broke from her, and went nearer to the old man.

"What do you say, master?" he asked. "You have had the law upon me as you wished. *That* is over. I have come to go on keeping my promise to George. Do you forbid me?"

At these words the miller approached a step nearer, his white face became more excited, and he shook his head with peculiar emphasis.

Michael's heart failed him.

"You do *not* forbid me then," he asked, "to come here and work for you again?"

Ambray shook his head even more emphatically, then turned and signed to Esther for her arm, and began to hasten homewards.

Michael stood for a moment, rendered motionless and cold as death by the deep and terrifying mystery of Ambray's expression. Seeing, however, that Esther looked back for him affectionately and anxiously, he roused himself and followed.

CHAPTER XXXVIII.

THE old life began again.

For a whole week Ambray was absorbed by his efforts to realise Michael's presence. When Michael was in the mill he scarcely removed his eyes from it, when Michael sat in George's old place in the chimney corner, where Mrs. Ambray always insisted on placing him, he never looked towards the miller but he encountered the fixed, furtive gaze of that terrible eye.

When Ambray had really learnt to regard his return as a certainty, he gave himself up to long fits of morbid reflection as to how—weak and helpless as he was—the work of punishment might be begun.

He had no desire to fire the mill when he saw Michael's light there in the night. He could sit near Michael with knives on the table between them without the slightest wish to take one up for any terrible purpose ; he could sit with his loaded gun in his hands, watching for the mill rats hours together, and let Michael pass and repass him securely a hundred times. It was not his life he had any wish to strike at. He knew that a life such as his was a complete and a good thing—a triumph—end when and how it might. What he *did* desire with all the strength that remained to him was to see that spirit—in whose brightness and good odour George's had shown so vile and dull before the world—defiled, brought low, maimed, annihilated.

His having returned to the High Mills now—showing that his patience and devotion had triumphed over prison miseries—was in itself a new theme for hatred and wrath to Ambray, glad as he was of the return, which had come to be his first recollection at morning, his last thought at night.

A new thing, too, which he noticed in Michael since his imprisonment, moved in him at once his whole heart's interest, commendation, and intensest bitterness. This was the simple and strong manner in which Michael kept his mind and heart free from the sad influences of the past. He evidently,

Page 106.

the miller thought, regarded his error as a thing already atoned for—forgiven by God. Life, so dark to *him* by reason of so much of its light being shut away under one little lid, was still full of promise and sunshine for Michael, whose hand had caused this shutting away. He never now saw the dark eyes turn sick and confused when they encountered his look, as they had done so often in those days when George's fate was his own fearful secret; their look still was gentle enough, but fearless as the light. Without desisting from his hard work, Michael enjoyed life as much as he could in a place where he was still regarded as little better than a murderer. Not that the inhabitants of Lamberhurst were particularly unjust or hard-hearted, but because a village idea—like a village fever—having once become settled is not easily removed.

When Michael had to pass groups of distrustful and disliking faces, he did so with a half amused, half pitying look in his much-worn but still glad great eyes. When little children, taking the cue from their elders, lay down and kicked and screamed after he had tossed them in the air, or threatened to send them up with the sails, instead of being hurt in his good heart, he laughed till the old miller would come hobbling out to glare at him.

It was in search of some means of smiting down this bright hopefulness, independence, and courage that Ambray brooded through the shortening autumn days and lengthening autumn nights.

The year wore on.

The dead bind was picked from the hoppole, and lay in little black heaps at regular distances between the pole stacks. The berries and the robins' breasts brightened to vivid scarlet in the hedges which lay across the country now—long streaks of warm, rich colour. In the woods, too, the red stood thick, like blood settled at the surface in aged cheeks. The silver hoar-frost came, only visible a moment or two at morning, then snatched away like a forgotten garment of the night. The white hoar-frosts came, lingering hours later, striving with the sun till nearly noon for possession of each rustling leaf and tender blade of grass.

These changes were watched by the old miller with a bitterness indescribable. Would the winter come, he asked himself, and chain him to his bed—as it usually did—while this fearful thirst in his soul was still unsatisfied? If this went on much longer, *would* the mill be safe from fire, the knife lie harmless on the table, or the gun in his hands?

But the day did come at last when the coveted power was given him.

Michael, through a kindly act in a corner of the village where fever was raging, fell ill himself, and lay for five weeks in the old black mill which Ma'r S'one, who was his only nurse, had made habitable for him.

When he came out and resumed his work, he was much changed: his cheerfulness was gone, and he was quick to take offence, and peevish as a child.

Ambray now quietly exulted. Michael fell completely into his power. No swineherd was ever treated with more contumely. Every little duty that fell to his hand was embittered by puerile opposition and abuse; every step he took, every word he uttered, was laid wait for by the same furtive, sleepless tyranny.

The healthful mind was brought so low, it retained now but one idea, which only became the more firmly rooted as the work of ruin went on. This idea was that duty compelled him to stay where he was; then as he grew weaker, it was no longer only duty, but fate also. He felt he had it not in his power to go.

8

He was now reduced to such weakness of body and mind, that when he saw Ambray thrust his letters from home unopened into the fire, he could only stare through his swimming eyes and gnaw his lip in helpless sickness of soul. The miller prevented him also in all his feeble efforts at writing to his family, and delighted in the idea of their looking vainly for his letters as Michael had so long allowed him to look vainly for George's.

Mrs. Ambray did all she could to comfort Michael in these innumerable mortifications and sufferings, but the state of him by whom they were rendered filled her with such terror and anguish, that her whole time was occupied in watching and serving him, and in fruitless endeavours to induce his spirit to let go its fierce grip of this harmless and helpless creature. But it seemed as if nothing save death *could* ever loosen it.

Michael's sufferings deepened with the winter. Ambray kept all his clothes from him but one thin summer mill-suit, in which he went about shivering so that his teeth chattered, and he became an object of pity and commiseration to all the village. The boys only, with that innate cruelty which makes human nature so terrifying a mystery, found untiring amusement in adding to his torture; and Michael had come to such a pass as to weep like a child when they placed things in his way by which he received painful falls, or when they injured the machinery of the mill, or threw stones at the windows.

Ambray seemed to have received a new lease of life from this excitement. It kept him from his usual winter prostration. He had now no other thought than going on with this work of retribution as long as he might. He foresaw that it must be brought to an end some day. Already people were interfering. Two or three clergymen whom Ambray had known and respected in his better days, General Milwood, who had fought with his father at Waterloo, and even Mrs. Grist herself, "for the credit of the family," had been up to the High Mills to remonstrate with the feeble but bitter tyrant there.

At last Nora came. She had been abroad with Miss Milwood, and had but lately come back and heard of Michael's return, his illness, and Ambray's treatment of him.

It was on a cold afternoon that she came, when the sails went harshly round in the east wind, and Michael stood leaning at the mill-door with closed eyes, and breathing on his icy fingers.

Ambray sat at home, cowering over the

fire, and put up his shoulders and let his chin fall as he heard her horse's feet coming.

In another moment she stood before him, declaring her pity for Michael, and calling upon her uncle to put an end to these shameful stories, that met her wherever she went.

As she ceased speaking, Ambray looked up at her and his face softened. Bitterly as he spoke of her in her absence, he could never see her without a certain tenderness and the sense of a different and gentler grief, that fell upon his own hard sorrow like soft rain on frozen ground. He never looked at her but his regret that George should have lost her came upon him as a fresh thing. It did so now, and the thin, white old face smiled at her and wept, forgetting her appeal.

"He has not even heard," she sighed, looking away impatiently.

"Yes, Nora," said the miller, "I hear you; and I *see* you—fresh roses, bright eyes, gay, cold heart!"

"Gay!" echoed Nora, taking off her gloves and warming her hands at the fire: "What I have to bear from Aunt Jane, and what I have to bear from you, keeps my heart very gay, certainly! But if you hear me, uncle, will you think of what I have said? Will you send this man away if you cannot overcome your feelings against him? He will not go, they tell me, unless you *do* send him. *Will* you do so, and stop *this* trouble and disgrace—this wickedness?"

"My child," answered Ambray, taking her hands as she held them to the fire, and looking down at them tenderly—"do *you* dare to judge *me*. *Let the faithful judge the faithful.* Go—the world has many lovers for Nora—but—no son for *me!* Remember this, Nora, and do not judge me."

"This man would be a son to you if you would let him," said Nora. "Why, what a miracle of patience he is, if what I've heard is true! It seems to me he is either an idiot or—he is grand!"

"Go," muttered the miller, dropping her hands, and shrinking down again, as if he had received a blow. "Leave me, Nora, you do no good—you do harm—leave me alone."

"I will!" answered Nora, indignantly; "and I will persuade Michael Swift to leave you. I will go to the mill myself, and try to shew him his folly in being faithful to *you*. *Let the faithful serve the faithful.*"

She went out, and the miller hearing the door close after her, roused himself and looked round.

When he had made sure she was gone, he muttered, stooping low and gazing into the fire,

"He is either an idiot or—he is grand."

He drew back from the fire suddenly, saying, with quiet decision:

"He is not an idiot."

He stood up—holding one trembling hand clenched tightly in the other—

"Is he then—grand?"

At this moment, as Esther came in, he met her, and seizing her arms cried—

"What am I doing, Esther? what am I doing? Making a young Job of him? A martyr! To draw *her* eyes upon him! Is *this* my revenge? He's taken the boy's life —his good name—his mother's love "—he cried, shaking her savagely—"and now—now could it be possible! No, I am mad to think it—mad! Yet, Esther! You should —oh! you should have seen her eyes when she flashed 'em upon me and said, '*or —he is grand!*' She has gone to the mill to speak to him. I will follow her—give me my hat—I will follow her."

CHAPTER XXXIX.

Nora, on her way homeward, rode round by the mill, and stopped at the door. It was partly open, and she rode close up to it and knocked with her whip, and called Michael by name.

Almost directly the door was opened wide; but the ground-floor of the mill being somewhat dark, Nora did not recognise the person who had opened it.

"Is Michael Swift here?" she asked leaning a little forward.

The person appeared deaf, for he did not answer her.

"Michael Swift," repeated Nora, in a louder voice—"is he here?"

"I knew a *man* by that name once," answered a voice that sent a chill through her blood. "*Now, I* bear it."

He stood a little more in the light—she saw him plainly. All the pathos of the wasted strength, the patient misery, the baffled but still heroic strength of purpose, came over her at once out of those great hollow eyes, and she had to turn her face hastily away.

When she spoke, all her decision and vehemence were gone. She was surprised at the timidity and trembling of her voice.

"Why do you stay here?" she said.

"To grind it out."

"It *is* ground out."

"I thank God that I hear you say it."

"Be content, then, and go."

"I cannot do that; I must wait till I hear *him* say it too."

"You will never do that. He would never say it, never think it, unless his whole nature changed, and he is too old to change."

"Yes," answered Michael, in a low voice, full of patient despair, "I think so, too. He is too old to change."

"Then why wait here?"

"I must wait—I must serve him while he lives—or while *I* live."

Nora was silent. She could not think what possessed her that she had suddenly lost all power to oppose him. The old mill seemed to have assumed the dignity of a castle; the wasted, half-imbecile wretch she had heard so much of was causing her to hold down her head meekly before the doorway where he stood.

"Then you will stay?" she said at last, almost humbly.

"Yes."

"Can I not assist you in any way?—you will take no money. Is there nothing by which we may make your life less hard?"

"Thank you—God bless you—no; nothing more."

"More! why I have given you *nothing*, done nothing for you."

"May I tell you about a picture George had at our house?"

"What about it?"

"It was the picture of a ship."

"Yes," said Nora, hearing that his voice trembled.

"Yes; it was the ship of some great man, I cannot tell you who; but he had had some great victory, and those that he had taken captives were being lashed as they were in the galley, with their muscles straining ready to snap, and their eyes starting, and hands bleeding, while up above on the deck the conqueror feasted among ladies crowned with flowers. There was one lady, with her face so turned that her eyes fell on the face of one of the straining galley-slaves; but she did not know where she looked; but *he* did, and you could see he half forgot his slavery, his toil and pain under her look."

"Well?"

"This is all the picture—but—but I wished to tell you of it that I might ask you to think how, if the galley slave forgot his pain under *this* look quite cold and heedless, how he would have felt if he had seen the eyes run over with such—such pity, such sweetness, kindness, gentle pain, and—what! Tears too? Oh! go back then, *my* lady, go back to your feasting and music and merry-making,

let the muscles crack, the blood pour down, the galley slave is happy. He can work until he drops under the lash!"

He ran into the mill, and Nora rode home half blind.

CHAPTER XL.

IT was a month after Nora's visit that one morning Michael, on his way to the mill, heard the bell tolling.

Mrs. Grist had died suddenly in the night.

Michael did not think the news would greatly affect his master, as he knew him to be far more reluctant to accept help from Nora than from his sister-in-law. He was therefore much surprised when on returning to the miller's cottage at noon Mrs. Ambray met him outside the gate with gestures of caution and distress.

"Don't go near him just now, Michael," she whispered; "he would fly at you, he has only just heard."

"What?" asked Michael. "That she's dead?"

"Oh! my son, don't you know what has happened since, Michael? My poor John has come into his own—we are rich, Michael."

"My God!" cried out Michael, letting his face fall to her shoulder with a great sob. "Then I am free—I can go home!"

"You *are* free, you *can* go home, if you will when I have told you all.—Come here."

She drew him to the side of the parlour window and pointed for him to look in at it cautiously.

Michael did so, and saw a sight he never forgot. It was only the old miller sitting at a table by himself, laughing to himself, but it was the most terrible sight Michael had ever looked upon.

"How long has this been?" he asked, dragging Mrs. Ambray away.

Then she told him how long she had kept her fearful secret—some three weeks now—and throwing herself at his feet implored him by all his long patience, by her affection for him, by his heavy responsibility as George's destroyer, to stay with his master still, and help her to conceal his infirmity from the world, lest they should drag him to the madhouse.

Michael gave his promise.

CHAPTER XLI.

MRS. GRIST had taken leave of her farms, hop-gardens, mills, church-tithes, and all her other good things of this world some four months, when, one morning, two pale convalescents, a young man, and an old man, were led out of doors to sit in the May sunshine.

The young man was on the green at Thames Dutton, the old man outside Buckholt farmhouse in Lamberhurst.

The black mill was now a strange sight indeed, having been laid open to its centre by fire.

The invalid at Thames Dutton had his arm in a sling; the one at Buckholt held his Bible open at the list of family names with hands that were covered with burns.

The injuries of both and those of the black mill had but one story.

"What *can* he be thinking of, Ma'r S'one, so many hours?" said Mrs. Ambray, as they both stood watching the old miller, who sat in the sunshine with his eyes fixed on the ground. "The doctor told me again this morning, that as he had been right ever since the shock that brought him to his right mind, he is almost certain to keep right with quiet, and comforts such as, thank God, he has in plenty. But what *can* he think about so long *I* can't imagine."

Neither could Ma'r S'one, had he been presumptuous enough to try.

"What's Tom put Michael right in the sun for like that?" demanded old Swift angrily. "Go and wheel him a little into the shade, Henry."

"There now, you've put him just where the wind catches him. Here, I'll go myself."

"How you fidget over Michael," said Mrs. Swift, as old Joseph returned from poking Michael's head about, jerking his bad arm, and making him thoroughly uneasy—"and I'm sure he's coming round wonderful."

"*Is* he, Maria?" returned Swift, something unusual twinkling in his excitable little blue eyes. "You should have seen him and heard him in church last Sunday, when he was singing out 'Lord, now let'st,'—I couldn't stand it, Maria. I collared him and pushed him down in his seat. I felt as if he was a-singing himself off."

"What fancies you do get in your poor head, Joseph! Well, I hope you'll keep such thoughts off *next* Sunday, or we shan't have a very lively party, and most of 'em coming from such a distance, and plenty of trouble of their own."

The great family dinner coming on the following Sunday was looked forward to by the hollow-eyed invalid with much soreness of heart. All his married brothers, with their wives and children, would be there, trying to look kindly on the one great failure and disappointment of the family—himself.

When the day came and the cloth was laid, and the little parlour was crammed with nephews and nieces and sisters-in-law whom poor Michael had never seen till then, whom it buzzed with all kinds of family interests, great and little, from Tom's chances of entering into partnership with his master to the propensity of Mary's baby for being fretful on Sundays, Michael felt himself like a great useless hulk in the midst of a gay regatta.

His brothers spoke to him kindly enough, but very little, and he did not blame them. What was there to talk about to a failure, a wreck like him? They were a little ashamed of him too, he saw, before their smart wives; even little Cicely had placed herself and her friend with a rose in his button-hole as far from her favourite brother as possible for fear some prison sign might yet be detected on him.

Here he was back in the midst of all, yet never had he felt more isolated from them.

Their small hopes stung his great despair, their small joys made the depths of his great sorrow apparent to him. What was his life to turn to? A place in the little churchyard where George had been so early sent by him seemed to Michael the likeliest and most-to-be-desired change from this present dreary helplessness and apathy.

In the middle of dinner, there was a knock at the street door.

"That's your sister, Joseph," said Mrs. Swift. "Catch *her* waiting for an invitation when anything's going on."

Old Swift commanded his youngest son to go down and open the door to his aunt, and bring her up to dinner.

"But that's not Deborah's step," said he, listening as he heard his son returning with other footsteps after him.

Knives and forks were suspended, curly heads rapped, and babies hushed, that the footsteps might be listened to, and receive due attention.

The sudden silence made Michael look round him with apathetic wonder. Then he, too, heard the footsteps on the stairs.

He no sooner did so than he rose from his chair with white lips and dilated eyes, staring towards the door.

Another instant, and his brother had come into the room, followed by the gaunt figure and long beetle-browed face so fearfully familiar to him.

Ambray was here in his father's house, and

Ma'r S'one was behind him. He was not dreaming : these two were really here !

"Give me some dinner, Swift," said Ambray, seating himself in the chair the son who opened the door to him had left vacant. "I am hungry, so is Ma'r S'one. Come, you two little girls, sit in one chair, and let Ma'r S'one have this."

It seemed to Michael that Ambray certainly had, on entering the room, glanced quickly at him and away again, though he could scarcely believe this now, so entirely did the old man appear to ignore his presence.

Swift, completely taken by surprise, placed loaded plates before his unexpected guests, and continued to remain lost in wonder and speechless amazement, vainly looking for explanation from Michael, who was even more amazed than himself.

Michael knew almost without glancing towards him that Ambray's plate remained untouched, while the grey haggard eye swept every face at table.

"You are rich in sons, Swift," he said. "I know them by their likeness to each other. And a very fair-looking likeness it is ; but handsome is that handsome does, young men, remember that !"

"'Cline our——"

"Hold your tongue, Ma'r S'one," said his master ; "the saying doesn't concern *you*. But, Swift," he continued, turning still more away from Michael, and taking his hand from the table that its trembling might not be noticed, "you had another son once ; how is it I don't see *him* here ? "

"They're all here that ever I had," answered Swift, sharpening his knife. "I never lost any, nor none ever came to any harm, except—ah, except poor Michael; but as a rule, *my* children they've all been brought up as they should be ; there's been no artists or geneses, or anything but what's respectable and honest ever known in the family, and I don't care who hears me say it."

"*That* son *is* here, then?" inquired Ambray, still averting his gaze from where Michael sat.

Swift laid down his knife and fork, and stared. Then to avoid more mistakes about the matter touched the miller with one hand,

while he pointed straight at Michael with the other.

"There's Michael, poor fellow, if it's him you mean."

The miller, not without an effort, turned his eyes for the first time fully upon Michael.

Michael, unable longer to remain quiet, rose, and came to the back of Ambray's chair.

Ambray turned, but instead of looking up at him, bent his head, and fixed his eyes upon the floor.

"And this is Michael Swift," he said in a voice that held all ears attentive. "Yes ; I know him now. I know him by the only wages I ever gave him, that silver in his beard. I know him. You said I could never change Michael—you and Nora, I heard you. I was too old to change, you said. I believed that you were right. I felt that you were. But now, Michael, *now*, you must let age, with one foot in the grave, turn back and give youth the lie."

He laid his arms on the back of the chair and looked up. Michael looked down at him with wild incredulous eyes.

"I have heard all, Michael. I have heard how you stayed by the man who had made a Job of you, how you stayed by him and guarded him in his madness from any chains but your own honest arms. You have a strange look, Michael. Is it too late? I do not forget what house this is, whose last breath was spent here ; yet remembering this, I ask you before I name him, to take his place. Is it too late?"

"Master, is it ground out ? "

"It is, Michael. It is, *my son*."

"And so is his life with it," cried Swift, passionately rising, as Michael lay at the miller's feet like a felled tree.

Joseph Swift proved wrong, for Michael Ambray—the miller made him take his name —was soon as strong and as ready to enjoy to the full the sunshine of life as ever Michael Swift had been.

After two years he married a poor governess, named Nora Ambray.

Ma'r S'one was present at the wedding, and startled every one by crying out with great solemnity after young Ambray had made his vows to Nora—

"'Cline our 'erts to keep this la l"

The End.

NEW AND ATTRACTIVE BOOKS.

Blanche Gilroy.

A Girl's Story. By MARGARET HOSMER, author of "The Morrisons," "Ten Years of a Lifetime," etc. 12mo. Fine cloth. $1.50.

"The characters are drawn with much distinctness and vigor, and the story sweeps on to its end amidst a rushing whirl of cross-purposes with decoying fascination."—*Boston Advertiser.*

Why Did He Not Die?

Or, The Child from the Ebräergang. From the German of AD. VON VOLCKHAUSEN. By MRS. A. L. WISTER, translator of "Old Mam'selle's Secret," "Gold Elsie," etc. 12mo. Fine cloth. $1.75.

"Mrs. Wister's admirable translations are among the books that everybody reads. Few recently-published novels have received more general perusal and approval than ' Only a Girl;' and ' Why Did He Not Die?' possesses in at least an equal degree all the elements of popularity. From the beginning to the end the interest never flags, and the characters and scenes are drawn with great warmth and power."—*N. Y. Herald.*

Tom Pippin's Wedding.

A Novel. By the author of "The Fight at Dame Europa's School." 16mo. Extra cloth, $1.25. Paper cover, 75 cts.

"We must confess that its perusal has caused us more genuine amusement than we have derived from any fiction, not professedly comic, for many a long day. . . . Without doubt this is, if not the most remarkable, certainly the most original, novel of the day."—*London Bookseller.*

The Quiet Miss Godolphin.

By RUTH GARRETT; and A CHANCE CHILD. By EDWARD GARRETT. Joint authors of "Occupations of a Retired Life" and "White as Snow." Illustrated. 16mo. Fine cloth, 75 cts. Paper cover, 50 cts.

These charming stories are marked by a most faithful delineation of character, and by a happy insight into the feelings and prejudices of human nature.

Wear and Tear;

Or, Hints for the Overworked. By S. WEIR MITCHELL, M.D., Member of the National Academy of Sciences, etc. 16mo. Fine cloth. 50 cts.

This tract, which originally appeared in *Lippincott's Magazine,* aroused much attention at the time of its publication, and elicited the praise of the ablest judges. In its present enlarged form it meets an important and growing want. The accurate and popular manner in which it discusses one of the most important topics of the times, and the clearness with which it provides proper and ready means for avoiding waste of mental and physical strength, commend it to the patronage of the whole mass of the people.

Travels of a Doctor.

A Book of Travels of a Doctor of Physic. Containing his Observations made in Certain Portions of the Two Continents. 12mo. Extra cloth, ornamented sides. $2.

"One of the most enjoyable books of travel we have ever read."—*Philada. Evening Bulletin.*